VAGABOND

HEARTSTRINGS

Rere Vermin

Rere Vermin

ISBN: 978-1-964365-68-8

Table of Contents

About the Author

Rere Vermin is a debut writer with a keen eye for life, art, and nature. His experiences as a nurse, self-employed music seller, and traveler have all contributed to this debut.

"I never set out to be weird. It was always other people who called me weird."

Frank Zappa

CHAPTER 1
A VAGABOND HEART 1

His mother had the house back in Ottolenghi mode, perfectly normal down to the last thread, and the sweet air of fresh bread in the kitchen. Matthijs dragged himself into the living room, shoes still wet from the drizzle outside. Geertruida sat at the table with her sudoku, pencil always blunt, cheeks always drawn tight around that determined mouth, as if she couldn't quite let go of the bones beneath.

"Were you planning to shower?" she asked, exactly as he'd expected—no good morning, no warm cup of coffee.

"Maybe. If I can think of a reason," he said. His voice rasped like wet sandpaper.

She didn't even look up. "You went to bed late again. You live like a student."

Student, he thought. As if anyone in Amsterdam ever had their morning cracked open by existential guilt.

"Luckily, I'm not a student," he said, and dropped into the chair opposite her. His coat was still dripping onto the floor, little puddles forming between the Persian rug patterns. Matthijs ran his hand along the crumb-covered edge of the table and wondered if he could handle a banana today.

Geertruida pushed the sudoku to the right, flicked the newspaper toward him with two fingers. "You've got mail," she said. It was an envelope with his name written in the kind of handwriting only lawyers still used.

"Leave it," he said. "Probably another letter about alimony."

"You can't keep ignoring it," she said.

He picked at the edge of the envelope. It felt as if his whole life was pressed between those fibers — every petty incident, every misstep that had ever mattered.

Matthijs stared.

The coffee sat ridiculously far away, on the other side of the kitchen, a half-marathon sprint through the neon whiteness of his mother's ideas about hygiene. Matthijs launched himself toward the counter, grabbed the pot with yesterday's scum on top, and threw the black sludge back like medicine. The taste was harsh, bitter as guilt, with a hint of cardboard. His upper lip trembled from the stuff. He felt

Geertruida's gaze, a cold wind on his neck, even though she supposedly kept her face turned to that puzzle.

She always acted as if he were still a child. Ha, as if children smoked like chimneys and addressed their mother informally in her own house. Yet he didn't bother to argue. It was easier to let her win, to let her small wars claim their victories, just like every young woman who entered his life once thought he could still be saved. When the children used to show up at home after the divorce, he had admired Geertruida for her steel nerves, the way she kept their house a citadel of discipline. Now it no longer mattered: her only project was him.

He grabbed a banana and snapped it open with a popping sound. The inside was slippery, soft as old fingers. "And... how's the bridge club?" he asked without conviction, biting off a piece.

She didn't answer directly but raised her eyebrows, a muscle twitch that conveyed both mockery and disdain. "I don't play bridge anymore. Only people with quicksand for brains keep playing bridge after seventy." As if she secretly hoped he'd take the comment as an opening to dismantle her, to expose whatever twisted beneath that calm surface. But he didn't feel like it.

The conversation felt like seaweed around his ankles.

Matthijs read the envelope, not the contents, and knew exactly what kind of letter it was. Another reminder that there were children who didn't know him beyond a birthday card or a half-hearted Zoom call. On the other side of the world, a giant kid in a worn-out Star Wars T-shirt, or a girl playing frisbee with the little dog he'd bought to placate her mother. All those memories didn't fit inside his head, so he simply ignored them.

He drifted back toward his phone. His fingers tapped out their own mating dance on the screen: Tinder, Bumble, Hinge, back to Tinder. Girls with piano-key teeth and boyish shoulders, girls with poetry in their bios and surprisingly little makeup. The algorithms stared back at him: You don't even know anymore, older man. How about someone your own age?

He scrolled past a woman, tanned and ash-blonde. Chantal. Cheerful lines around her eyes, confident. Profile text: 'Straightforward, no nonsense, dance like nobody's watching, mother of two and done with men who overanalyze everything to death.' Slightly too many exclamation marks, Matthijs thought, but better than 'ambitious and spontaneous' or 'fitgirl.' He swiped right.

Match. Instantly. Two seconds later. As if she'd been waiting all day, except no one ever waited for him, of that he was sure. But Chantal, then. There was something about her that made the morning malaise sink into the bean coffee and groundwater of Dutch autumn. She was… compulsively normal, pleasantly average, the kind of woman who could turn any mishap into a reason to go for Sunday brunch. Perfect. Out of self-preservation, he immediately stalked her on Instagram. Two kids, one already with above-average Dutch teeth; her ex cropped out of the photos; lots of vacations in the kind of hotels where they fold your bedsheets into swans. Chantal smiled in every picture, in a way you couldn't fake unless you were a career professional in pretending to have fun.

He typed the first line, deleted it, typed again. "Hey, Chantal. What brings a serious woman like you to the battlefield of Tinder?" He hated himself before even hitting send, but she replied within a minute. "Hahaha, more of a peacekeeping mission, actually. No drama, no false promises, and no cheesy pickup lines." The bar was immediately set somewhere around knee height. Splendid. She thought fast; he could smell it through the screen. He typed: "A little tension's okay though, right? Some of us live off metaphysical drama." Trying to sound casual, but she shot right back: "Don't overthink. Just look each other in the eyes and see if it clicks."

So, eggs for his money then. A date on Wednesday at De Waterkant, the kind of café that fancied itself "lively" but always smelled of fried shrimp and old jokes. Matthijs read the address five more times, as if afraid he'd misread the message. Then came the dull routine of getting ready: showering (twice, an achievement), a shirt with barely visible stains, cologne that smelled of better days or at least a better man once upon a time. He skipped the barber; that anchor point on his crown wasn't salvageable anyway. In the mirror, he studied his face from every angle. Not bad for fifty-four, if you had a taste for cracked pottery.

He was about to leave when Geertruida stood by the fridge, hip hooked against the door. "You'll be home late?"

"Probably." He didn't look at her. "Don't wait up."

She didn't let it go. "It's another blind date, isn't it?"

"Chantal," he said. "Her name's Chantal. You should try it sometime, finding someone who doesn't do puzzles."

She sniffed, a sound like a vacuum losing pressure. "I just hope you don't both start complaining about your childhoods."

He laughed, and it shot through his nose, breaking the rhythm of his exhale. "That's pretty much the pitch, yeah."

Outside, the drizzle smelled the same as every autumn. A water cannon of wet leaves on paving stones, the air tied tight in blankets of moisture and diesel. He felt vaguely self-conscious in his "best" shirt, as if it glowed beneath the ugliness of his coat. The tram was empty except for a few older people and a boy with a skateboard, the kind of company where no one says a word; the silence does the talking.

De Waterkant already looked half-devoured by the early dark, its windows fogged, the pavement littered with displaced cigarette butts. Chantal stood out as if she carried her own spotlight. She wore something light blue with shiny buttons, her hair not a millimeter out of place. She was already sitting with a glass of white wine, half empty, her wrist loosely curved around the stem. Good gums, he noticed immediately, that smile wasn't just for photos. She reached out her hand (never happened on Tinder before), and he felt a grip that suggested either an athlete or a mother with rules.

"So," she said, "Matthijs." She rolled the name in her mouth the way you test a coin and reject it. "You're not from

Amsterdam, are you? You sound different. Rotterdam? Or abroad?"

He sat down and realized she was watching his movements, like a fitness instructor assessing posture on first impression. "Rotterdam via the rest of the world," he joked, and immediately heard how stupid that sounded. The waitress arrived at once, wearing that look of mild disdain reserved for anyone who ordered wine before Monday. Chantal ordered another glass right away, and for him, a Piña Colada. He felt old doing it, even though he'd decided cocktails were part of his new image. She tapped him on the shoulder as if to whisper something intimate, but just told him which dish was good. She spoke efficiently, not a word wasted. Her voice wrapped up each sentence neatly, the tone of a call-center worker or maybe a former flight attendant. He discovered he had no originality left in him, while she was self-assured.

She wanted to know what kind of work he'd done, so he rolled out his standard story about an ad agency in Tel Aviv: deadlines, clients with absurd demands, the nights he got drunk and photographed the sunrise for a campaign. Chantal listened the way mothers do, head tilted, making sympathetic hums in all the right places, but her hands were busy with the wineglass, making it dance between her fingers, as if her attention preferred to be there instead of with him. He was about to go off on a tangent about how in Israel you could only survive by writing your own laws when her phone buzzed across the table. She opened it with a quick, practiced motion, like a poker dealer, no embarrassment, no explanation. A picture of a child, something about homework. Chantal typed a response and placed the phone neatly back between them. Her gaze stayed on him, checking whether he could keep up.

"Kids of your own?" she asked, casually, like asking if someone's ever been to Sweden.

He hesitated, swallowed. A banal question, impossible answer. "Seven," Matthijs said. He saw her right eyebrow twitch, subtly raised. Chantal paused briefly, glass to her lips, then swallowed without missing a beat. "No way. Really?" That laugh again, just a second too long. No disgust, no cheap joke, just well-received, as if it were about the price of petrol.

Matthijs shrugged, pushing the awkwardness down with another sip. "Made a spreadsheet once to keep track. But after the fourth, you lose count."

"Four different mothers?"

"Five," he corrected. It sounded like a confession, but didn't feel like one. Footnotes in his biography. London, New York, Amsterdam, Tel Aviv, and even once in Den Bosch. Every child is at risk of a different failure.

Chantal giggled, a flash of amusement lighting up her eyes. She tapped her teeth against the glass. "My ex wasn't bad at that either."

Matthijs felt a twinge of relief, or maybe it was just the sugar from the cocktail rushing to his head. "If he hit more than three, you could always apply for a TV show."

Chantal laughed as he'd just told a joke she already knew from her brother. Then she nodded briskly, as if signing a contract: we're both damaged goods, let's not make this complicated. Loud men on the other side of the glass shoved a table into pulp, gesturing wildly, the air thick with aftershave. Chantal gave him a look as if to ask whether he smelled it too, a raised eyebrow, a tiny question mark. For her, it was the elephant in the room; for him, just another noise. Then again, he had his own elephant pen.

Chantal rolled the salt shaker back and forth across the plastic tablecloth. She asked about his work, his hobbies, and she used words like "nice" and "interesting" without irony, which made him softer. She told him about her boys, with the brisk tenderness of someone shaking off a half-frozen pet: the eldest, Ruben, played football at the club where all the dads went to sweat out their mistakes; the youngest, Sari, read everything except what she was supposed to for school. Matthijs nodded and sipped his drink as if it filled him with empathy. They talked about everything Dutch people were supposed to talk about on a first date, streets you wouldn't want to die on, energy prices, and the impossibility of a decent tomato outside Italy. His role was not to explain too much.

A few drinks later, the conversation wobbled but stayed pleasant. Chantal turned out to loathe piano lessons ("a machinery of child abuse, if you ask me") and spent her Saturdays on competitive dancing ("though after COVID it all went a bit limp"). At one point, she rested her elbow on the table and leaned toward him, the scent of citrus and a hint of metal. She spun an anecdote about her ex-husband, how he always forgot breakfast and once brought their child to the wrong school. "It's all funny until it's your own kid," she said, her serious tone softened by the tiny crinkle near her eyes. "And you, Matthijs? Do you keep in touch with those seven of yours?"

He stayed silent too long, tracing the rim of his glass as if the answer might appear there. "Sometimes I Zoom one of them. Send a bit of money. But they're far away... America, Israel, England. They've all got their mothers, you know. I'm not the standard kind of father."

She nodded, slid her glass closer to his, and took a sip without breaking eye contact. "You sound a little regretful, or is that just branding?"

He wanted to laugh, tried, but it came out as a cracked sigh. "Not really." He pursed his lips and looked at her. "Maybe I'm better at making kids than raising them."

She liked that, a flash of white at her lip, eyes curling upward. "Better that than the other way around," she said. "Otherwise, you get all those life coaches who can't make a kid but never shut up about parenting." Then she coughed into her fist, as if to clear the air of seriousness. "At least you're honest. Nobody's standard, if you ask me."

Matthijs hadn't taken her hand, but he had taken the salt shaker. A small sting of wistfulness, the realization that he'd rather stretch out this fragment of a moment than trade it for all the lost years. Still, the old reflex lingered: registering every tiny difference between this date and all the others, every woman before, every path that went wrong. Chantal didn't seem the type to tolerate the silences he usually hid in. She filled them right away, with questions, shared observations, or news about people neither of them knew.

Hours later, a little tipsy, they crossed toward the canal. The water was high. Not literally, their feet were dry, but in his steaming head it already surged. Chantal took his sleeve, talked about the refectory at her high school, how she'd smoked her first cigarette on a canal wall there. No one ever got caught. First-years still offered her mints on the street. Matthijs found himself nodding along to everything, his head buzzing an octave lower with each step. She didn't seem to notice, or maybe swaying was the new normal.

Chantal guided him toward an alley, a shortcut to the tram stop. It smelled sour, as if all the kebab in the city had drained onto the cobblestones with the rain. Matthijs wanted to say he'd had his first kiss there, but his mouth sagged like a broken umbrella. Chantal must have sensed his engine stuttering and gave him a gentle push, pressing him back against the old brick wall. She was still smiling, eyes half-closed, as if someone had just made three traffic lights blink in sync. Her hand found his face, traced his jawline the way you'd test the smoothness of a pear before buying it.

She smelled of expensive perfume and something minty. His breath was probably too rough for a Disney kiss, but she took the risk. Tongues didn't join in tonight; her lips folded over his lower lip and released it slowly. "Not bad for an old rascal," she said, and it sounded like she meant it.

He swallowed, wanted to make a joke about midlife, but the words caught in his throat. Chantal brushed lint from his collar, straightened him, and smiled. She looked at his mouth for a few seconds, as if she'd discovered a new kind of fruit. "Bet you never do second dates?" she asked, soft, quick, almost embarrassed to say it.

Matthijs had to think before answering. Truth was, he didn't do second dates anymore. Or third. Even first dates felt like the aftertaste of a joke told too many times. "Depends," he said, voice flat and a little hoarse. "Sometimes things move faster than that."

She squeezed his hand approvingly, probably felt his knuckles grind beneath her thumb, then let go. The tram screeched around the corner. Chantal said she had the morning shift, so she had to go. She kissed him quickly, gently — her tongue brushing his lower lip like she was sampling a rare olive. Then she turned, stepping almost flirtatiously toward the tram, leaving Matthijs standing under the dripping hood of a lamppost. He felt the trace of her perfume under his nose, the imprint of her hand on his cheek still buzzing like a freshly cut live wire.

"See? Could've been worse," he said softly, to the wet street.

A tram window lit Chantal up like a doll made of plexiglass and blinking neon. She hadn't forgotten him; she waved, briefly, like a waitress adjusting your drink on her way out. Then she drifted away, carriage after carriage, into the damp city. He had to move, too. The street emptied, and the rain dripped like crushed grapes onto the asphalt. He shoved his hands deep into his pockets and hunched his shoulders. Behind him, the tram swayed away, a white line through the grey city, and he thought of those women who paint their toenails at night while the children sleep. What were they doing on the other side of the world when morning began again? Sometimes he thought you shouldn't scatter your children across continents, but then life would reset itself like a flexible harness: you could just as well start over seven times without anything ever really taking root.

His phone buzzed. "Had fun, a bit weird but nice for a change – Chantal," it read, followed by a pesticide spray of emojis. No doubt: within twenty-four hours, a second date would be scheduled, somewhere near the bowling alley, maybe a sneaker shop, and they'd pretend rainbows never existed.

Cycling home felt like drifting on a drunken pontoon. His legs moved without consulting him. The city choked on wet silence. No one laughed. Anyone still greeting strangers was either drunk or mad. Matthijs rode past the grey facades, the humming streetlights, the leaking gutters painting silver streaks on the asphalt. He thought of the salt shaker, of ChatGPT, and of the millions of conversations people had with fakes every day.

His own life was just as generative: throw in a few ingredients, and before you knew it, another variation would appear before you. Mother, woman, child, always in apparent variations, yet always the same story.

The house smelled of warm milk and fabric freshener. The stairs creaked.

At home, Geertruida had cracked the Sudoku and was halving an apple into perfectly equal parts on the counter. The lamps were bright; the air above the stairwell carried the scent of bleach and weak coffee. When he walked in, she didn't look up. "You're late," she said, her voice tight along its edges.

"It wasn't so bad," said Matthijs, his shoes half-untied in the hall. His hands fidgeted in his pockets, searching for half a matchstick, tobacco crumbs. At the edge of his awareness, night clung to morning, day to another day. His collar still felt damp, and under his arms lingered the sour, sweaty trace of nervousness. He drifted toward the kitchen, standing quietly in the doorway.

Geertruida twisted the knife in the fruit as if she had turned the murder of the everyday into an art form. She kept chopping, no need for talking, though plenty hung in the space between them. For a moment, he searched for a way to start a conversation, but his tongue sat lazily in his mouth. Half of him wanted to brag about Chantal — about her cheek, soft as a peach; her laugh, bursting like New Year's fireworks; her sly fingers that had left a trail along his jawline. The other half already felt snowed under, as if there were still checklists to be ticked off before he could float again.

He rummaged through the kitchen cupboard for licorice, as though that might push down the lump in his throat. The unspoken words tumbled over each other, but Geertruida, with the talent of her generation, remained the master of silence.

"Their names?" she asked, seemingly out of nowhere. She meant the children, no need to ask. He rolled the piece of licorice between his thumb and forefinger, finding a kind of reassurance in the candy's firming texture. "Or do you want to hear them all, Mom?"

"You probably don't remember all of them," said Geertruida, her voice suddenly thinner, as though a small crack had opened in it.

He leaned against the counter and shrugged. "Of course I do. Go on, get a pen and paper."

The names followed in a cadence, an old-fashioned litany worth reciting: Eliza, Leah, Samuel, Daisy, Naomi, Bram, Ruby. He was even surprised he didn't have to peek at anything. There were always more than you thought, once you started to count them.

Some of them didn't mean much to him anymore; he only knew Ruby from Sunday morning Zoom calls, the others each caught in their own time zones and moments of glitching connection. He tried to reconstruct their ages now, but somewhere his memory faltered around the twins. His brain always turned the daughters into threads; he pictured them as they once were in Amsterdam, wet-haired after swimming. Maybe that's why they suddenly felt so far away.

Geertruida had sat down. The knife lay flat beside the cutting board, a quiet threat to dough or thumb. "They don't need you, any of them," she said — not as a question.

He nodded, the licorice rolling over his tongue. "Not really, no." He wanted to say something about fathers who never got it right anyway, but that would only make her all the more pointlessly sad. So he said nothing, but bit calmly into the candy, as if he had the whole evening to do it. The silence stung, but he was used to this kind, the sort that got delivered to their house daily, free of charge, with the mail.

Geertruida wiped the cutting board clean, slid the knife into the rack as though the steel still needed to drip out its remains. She walked past him, close enough for him to catch that faint, chemical scent of her fabric softener; that was the smell that had overwritten his childhood, for lack of something more innocent. At the sink, she ran water over her hands. She didn't dry them, just let them stay wet, as if every drop from now on was meant to keep her unstained.

He looked at her fingers, thin lines beneath the skin, nails short and unpainted. Even now, at this late hour. She'd always claimed that women who painted their nails were just camouflaging weakness. He'd never really known what to make of that.

"Chantal," he said. The word struck hard against the tiles. "She was actually nice. Normal. She smelled a little like tonic."

Geertruida stopped what she was doing, turned halfway, leaning against the counter with her hands still wet enough that drops fell onto the blue-checkered cloth around her waist. She didn't come closer, stayed right at the edge of the light, the shadow of her cheekbones cutting diagonally across her face. "Maybe you should make an exception for once," she said, her voice rougher than the countertop. "Just... don't overanalyze everything to pieces for one night."

The old song that mothers used to sing. Sweet, warm, comforting in a way that childlike fingers might have mimicked on wounds. He tried to meet her eyes, but she was already busy with the dishes again, all that resistance folded neatly into small compulsions.

"It's fine like this," she added softly, as if it was meant to hang there unsaid, in the damp neon haze of the kitchen.

Matthijs nodded, not quite a thank you, but his shoulders felt lighter. He walked up the stairs, the banana peel crumpled in his fist like a trophy. Upstairs, it was cold and smelled of plastic plants. His old room, now a museum of congealed disappointment, packed with souvenirs from every life that had once told him: you are temporary. He didn't turn on the light. In the dark, he unlocked his phone and scrolled through his chats, endless finger-swipes across blocks of text from then and now: a mix of subscriptions, newsletters, forgotten flings, old plans that never happened. Not a single real conversation, all fragments. Words like bricks; you couldn't build a house with them.

He saw an unread message from Chantal. A GIF of a cat clawing at a sweater.

"That's what I'm going to do to you tomorrow, just you wait."

She wasn't done with him, not after tonight.

Matthijs let himself fall onto the bed, the duvet still twisted from that morning. His body felt bombed flat by alcohol and anticipation. A strand of hair clung to his cheek, lint from his coat, or maybe a phantom trace of Chantal. He couldn't tell. He lay still, feeling the pulse throb in his temples, the restlessness of a night unwilling to give in to rest. The rain ticked against the windows, softer than he remembered, but enough to remind him the streets outside would keep flowing until morning.

He tried to recall the faces of his children, but got only ripples in time. Sometimes, he wasn't even sure they would recognize him if he showed up one random day at their school gate. Maybe that was for the best.

Sleep came halfway. In the dark, he drifted up and down through his own archives: old birthdays, a glimpse of New York, the smell of wet concrete in an alley where someone once stroked his hair. It lingered, as if none of it had ever really finished. He wasn't a dreamer, yet every night was a kind of scraping against what stayed neatly shelved by day. His mind rotated memories: Chantal's teeth at his shoulder, something about his old Italian teacher whose nails left such deep marks that the sting lasted for days; sometimes a random ex from New York who could never say his name without downing a shot of whiskey first. And somewhere in between, Chantal kept slipping through, the tight knot of her hand around his, the promise of tomorrow pasted onto his brain like a sticker.

The alarm slammed him out of sleep at seven. The first thing he felt was his tongue, paper-dry against his palate. The second: the stupid thrill of a second date, as if his body had never outgrown it. His mother always insisted he should shower. He usually just pretended to. A bath every day is bad for your skin.

He turned on the tap, peed in the tub, and pretended he'd showered.

Barely half an hour passed before his phone started buzzing again, this time with a number from the States. New York or New Jersey; his kickboxing memory had never reached that far. The name appeared right there on the screen, with that eternal plus sign in front, the one that told you it was never a good idea to answer. But he did anyway. Fingers too slow for his brain.

"Matthijs," came the voice, bright as always. No hello, no checking who'd picked up.

"Hey. It's Abigail."

She hit the A with that unmistakable New Yorker snap. In the background, he heard traffic, kids yelling, that kind of white noise Americans seemed to thrive on. Or that she used to thrive on. Her voice was exactly as he remembered: bone-dry, with that faint rasp of too much smoke.

"Hey," he said. A miracle his voice didn't crack.

"Listen, I just got your card. Leah turned six yesterday. You missed the right date by a week. But anyway, she liked the glitter llama."

It all came in one breath. Even apart, Abigail still knew how to bury a conversation under seven layers of no-nonsense.

"Believe it or not, I thought she was turning seven." He tried to make it a joke, but there wasn't much room.

"You remember what she looks like?"

He pictured that half-portrait on the fridge, the rough outlines of her face, a child's version of his own cheekbones, his ginger hair.

"Yeah," he said. "Of course."

He heard Abigail light a cigarette, click, flick, the sharp draw through the filter.

"She's been asking if you're coming to visit. I told her the borders are closed."

She sounded almost bored, as if the problem amused her more than it bothered her.

He tried to imagine it: Leah crouched by a strip of leftover snow on a New York sidewalk, scarf too bright for winter.

"She can always come here," he said, immediately regretting the hollow promise.

You weren't supposed to pack children into suitcases.

"When things calm down," he heard Abigail say, "maybe she'll spend summer with you if you can promise not to freak her out. Or get arrested."

He laughed and felt his body curling in on itself around the conversation.

"No jail, I swear. At least not this month."

"Funny guy," she said. Then came a silence, dull and silver, almost like morning light.

"Coming to America soon," she went on. "She's into time zones now, says if you get on a plane right away, you might make it for breakfast."

She swallowed the last syllables with that weird kind of irony that used to be their shared oxygen.

In his ear echoed the ghosts of before: a Brooklyn apartment, the morning sun over the East River, a bowl of oatmeal with too much sugar. The whole routine of being a father, but only as a role in a play without a director. It wasn't homesickness, Matthijs thought, more like a kind of Vaseline smeared over memory, blurring the sharp edges.

"Maybe I'll stop by," he said, more to the phone than to Abigail herself.

He heard her mouth drop into reluctance, a long silence, then the dry flick of a cigarette being tapped out.

"That'd be something. But don't say it unless you mean it. She remembers when you don't keep your word."

The air on the other end thickened with the faint crackle of exhaled smoke.

"Let me know when you've bought the ticket."

"I will," he said, in the shadow-gray of his childhood bedroom.

"Say hi to Leah for me, yeah?"

"Will do. She loves you. Some days, anyway."

That soft, ironic bend in her voice lingered a moment — then the line went dead.

As always.

He stayed there, the phone bare in his hand.

The rain didn't stop; it tapped like repetitive Morse code somewhere in the plastic window frame.

So they still kept his name alive in America, through anecdotes and birthday cards without stamps.

For a second, he imagined Leah: short, fuzzy hair, her fierce attempts to draw a mailbox on a cardboard box, the childlike fringes of someone who had inherited half his genes.

It hurt, but it stuck.

He tossed the phone into the duvet, rolled over, and stared at the white ceiling.

The ceiling stared back, a pattern of old water stains, gray-yellow veins through lime paint.

He got up, pretending to be in motion.

Down the stairs, the kitchen door creaked, and the fridge growled open.

His mother was already there, nightgown down to her calves, arms crossed.

"So early?" she asked, as if it weren't her daily habit to make carrot soup at six a.m. or reread old emails.

Matthijs fished a tub of quark from the fridge and noticed even the expiration date had passed.

Cheers to the shelf life of dairy; if a person lasted that long, he'd still have spring in his knees.

He scraped along the grainy edge, the sour-milk smell rubbing against his palate.

Each bite tightened the knot in his stomach.

His mother stayed by the counter, turning the rim of a coffee cup between her fingers, sipping without tasting, as if out of duty rather than desire.

She always had that fixed calm, as though nothing was ever allowed to throw her off pattern.

"Is it wet outside?" she asked.

Pointless question, the rain still rattled against every window.

Her eyes stayed on the sink, where the drain burped up sloppy foam.

"It hasn't stopped," he said.

Spoon empty, tub scraped clean.

The chill from the plastic crept into his lips, even his jaw.

"Has Chantal been in touch?" his mother asked, feigning casualness, but her earlobe twitched, that tiny giveaway of tension only a son would notice.

"Texted last night," he said, quark still clinging to his palate. "She wanted a second round."

Geertruida drew her mouth tight in what might have been meant as a smile, but never quite took off.

"Then you'd better learn to shave," she said, tapping her own chin as if something there needed trimming.

He thought she hadn't noticed, but no one, not even a half-forgetting mother, ever missed the scent of perfume on a son who'd always circled femininity.

"I've got a meeting in town," he lied. "Maybe coffee."

He still felt domesticated, as if Chantal had left behind a residual charge.

…left behind in his armpits and between his teeth. His skin was sticky with sleep sweat, but for a moment, he thought: if you just keep ignoring it, no one will notice.

In the hallway mirror, he saw the beard of a Hungarian pro cyclist after a week of the Giro, not bad, really, for someone who always wanted to keep going the wrong way. Shaving had always felt like a kind of penalty, a last attempt to fake control. Still, he picked up the Wilkinson razor, left it waiting on the edge of the sink next to a clearly expired tube of Gillette.

He bought a vending-machine coffee, drank it black from a plastic cup whose rim was just a bit too sharp, and got the idea that today might be one of those days that sticks. Among the faces on the platform, he didn't see Chantal, but maybe she was never there, maybe she only existed as a transitional phenomenon, like heatwaves in September or fog banks at wind force three.

A hazy gray hung over the station square. Matthijs walked on toward the canal, knowing it would be hours before the bowling, the choice for their second date. "Hope you're a strike, haha, I already practiced three times since yesterday," she had texted. He tried to recall the rules of bowling, but all he knew was that you had to wear socks and that the ball should roll against your heel if you wanted to throw it right. Killing time was second nature to him; he avoided the wind under the viaduct and settled on a bench near the marina. Slow water, yellow leaves teasing each other's circles in puddles. His hands found the cigarette pack on their own, as if that was a project of the body, not the mind. Two cigarettes later, he figured he could still send Chantal a joke. Something like how you bowl against your exes: "Always a strike, but you hope for a split." Stupid, but she'd get it.

Right before start time, her message pinged: 'Bit early, ok?' plus a bowling-bear emoji. She never bothered with being cool; her way of entering was to go straight for the center.

In the foyer, she stood by the counter, just taking off her coat, her hair eight degrees looser than yesterday. She ordered a beer for herself and, unexpectedly, a cola for him. "You're driving, right?" she called over the roar of bowling-lane noise. That she remembered he'd left his car after their last date. He laughed, nodded, took the glass, and felt like a kid on a school trip, poor and lost in a circus of smells and neon light. Bowling was even worse than he remembered. The shoes smelled of ammonia and crushed eggs, and even with the thin Wednesday crowd, a cloud of distant school outings and two generations of smoke hung over the lanes.

Chantal had immediately chosen a ball — baby blue, matching her exact weight in kilos. She rolled her fingers over the holes as if checking whether the previous hands were still in there.

Matthijs had nothing to do with bowling. His hands were too big, his thumb wobbled in the holes so that throwing felt like pulling off a wet sock. But she was right, it was a typically Dutch thing to do. On autopilot, he hummed the Star Wars theme playing through the speakers, dutifully waiting for the lane light to turn green. They both dove right in, without silence. Chantal struck in her first turn, arms stretched toward the ceiling as if she had an audience. Then she looked at him with a curious tilt: "And you?" He felt the pressure of the moment and threw the ball with a swing somewhere between hopeless and almost impressive. Not a strike, not a disaster. A few pins fell, a fine score if you didn't care to meet expectations.

Chantal cheered; she couldn't hide her joy, even when it meant nothing. After three frames, she was sure: "You're the disappearing type, aren't you?" she said, nudging him with her shoulder. "Like that ball, cautious at first, but then straight down the gutter." She said it softly, not as an insult, more as a fact now gently laid on the table. She still held the ball, her nail tracing circles around the opening, as if there were more secrets there. Matthijs took a sip of cola, swallowing the sweetness with effort. "Sometimes getting lost is more interesting than arriving," he said — blander than intended. She grinned, folded her hands behind her head, and rocked on her heels, ready for her next turn. The next hour vanished in a pounding rhythm of pins and banter.

Chantal won by a mile, keeping score on a damp napkin that left smudges on her fingers. Every so often, she disappeared to the bathroom; he'd stand by the pinball machine or stare at the tiles above the buffet. Whatever she did in there, he didn't know, but each time she returned, her gaze had shifted slightly, as if some secret now floated between them. After her third break, she sat closer beside him at the scoreboard; their shoulders touched, warm beneath the cold neon. Her hair smelled of something citrusy, or maybe just freshly rained.

"You know," she said quietly, her voice lower than on their first night, "I don't really believe in improving people. Everyone just muddles through." She wiped her damp fingers on the napkin and squeezed it between her knuckles. "But I do think you miss something if you throw everything away while bowling."

He laughed, thinking how little he'd ever managed to hold onto in life. "I'd rather hit the gutter than never throw the ball." Too polished, but better than nothing. His knees tingled restlessly against the table legs, like a football team before kickoff.

Chantal drew her knees up on the bench and looked at him longer than necessary. "Honestly?"

Matthijs nodded, turning the cola glass in small half-circles on the table.

"I think you're not done getting lost yet," she said, eyes aimed nowhere in particular, just across the lane. "Doesn't bother me. But if you do it with me, promise you'll look back now and then, check if the other one's still there." No accusation, no plea, just an agreement, like people used to make at the bus stop.

"Deal," he said, and it felt too big for such a small word.

They finished the last frames in silence. The grind of the wax machines, the music now at night-mode volume, the thud of balls against wood. It must have been around midnight when they stood outside. The air still held the post-rain smell, mixed with taxi exhaust and crumbed coffee from the doorway. Chantal's hair curled where it had gotten wet.

She slid her hand naturally into the crook of his elbow; it felt like an extension of himself, something that had always belonged there.

They walked. Not far, not fast, just to keep moving, letting quiet outweigh closeness. His legs moved automatically. Chantal talked about work, but the details barely landed: jobs, targets, her manager wearing turtlenecks in summer.

The bowling shoes smelled like school sports days: rubber and sweaty linoleum, memories of running through wet grass. Chantal pulled her socks up ("my ankle's a mess, not your fault") and picked a bright green ball, fire-truck type. She aimed, threw, sliced open the pins with such force that he smiled, her own small world thrown hard into place. She turned toward him, eyes bright, expression openly expectant. "You — you must have practiced hard." Her tone was teasing, but her gaze lingered on that awkward patch under his chin, where his shaving had given up.

Matthijs ran his fingers over the ball's ridges, in the sticky silence between words. His arms felt heavier than usual; each movement thickened as if the air here weighed more. His first throw grazed the gutter; a few pins stayed defiantly upright. Chantal laughed, not mockingly, but like you laugh together when something's just off, and that's what makes it right. She tapped his shoulder as he returned, a touch that lingered as a shiver down his arm.

Halfway through the second frame, the air between them started to shift, a duet of words that almost crossed into things you shouldn't say in bowling alleys. Chantal tilted her beer to her lips, drank in one elegant swoop, wiped her mouth with the back of her hand, and studied him, suddenly older than the girl who'd just knocked down every pin.

She asked if he only ever spoke to his kids through screens. Matthijs wanted to lie, but thought, what's the point, under fluorescent lights like these? He told her about Zoom, about birthday cards always a week too early or too late, about days when the Wi-Fi froze, and the faces on screen looked like rubber masks. She tilted her head, not like a therapist, but like someone who couldn't quite place her own losses. He told her about Leah, the daughter in Brooklyn, about the yellow stickers taking over her room, about Abigail moving on as if those eight months had never existed, where he'd been the only one left on earth.

Chantal nodded ("I don't believe that, every woman remembers everything") but let it rest. She didn't pry, rare enough, and shifted to a story about her eldest guessing the right answer on the third try in Mensa Kids or something like that. Her joy was in downplaying things; she never let a moment get heavy. When he was mildly drunk, which he was now, Matthijs always felt life was designed that way: people talking until discomfort dissolved into a joke.

They bowled, the only two adults among streaks of blue light, their voices swallowed by echoes of shrieking teens and the squeaks of air hockey. Chantal was half a head shorter than her attitude suggested, but her presence filled half the neon room with every turn. She pushed herself loudly into the foreground of all that was too banal to lie about: the slim white fingers bending her nails (she hated gel nails, he remembered), the nervous giggle after each strike, as if she made herself clumsy on purpose so he wouldn't feel like the loser.

After an hour, his fingers were so dry it felt like he'd sucked all the moisture out of that filthy bowling ball. "You get used to it," Chantal said, "as you do to exes, cold oatmeal, or phone calls from America."

When she laughed, the skin beneath her eyes creased into fine lines, and despite her make-up-free lashes, there was a deliberate thoughtfulness there. A few turns later, and she had the win so securely in her pocket that he didn't even care how much he lost. The tension lived in smaller things, a look held too long, fingertips brushing on the touchscreen scoreboard, the smell of her hair under the neon, different than outside.

After their third pitcher, a waiter brought them plastic trays of bitterballen with a theatrical hand gesture. "Bon appétit, champions," he said, not a hint of irony. They both looked at him, shared a quick smirk, a flash of connection. Matthijs dipped a bitterbal into mustard until his finger bent from the heat, thinking he'd rather sit with her in this ridiculous melancholy than anywhere else. Inattention was real intimacy. Being together without having to notice.

Chantal ate hers with a knife and fork ("they're too hot," she said, as if it were a legal excuse), her mouth corners white with crust. Matthijs wondered who did that at home, if her kids picked it up, and if her ex sometimes laughed at it.

By the end of the night, when the bitterballen were cold and the pitcher empty, there came that unspoken moment: do you leave, do you go together, do you let the day be what it was? Chantal had no coat, didn't take his arm, but walked exactly two meters closer than a stranger would. They turned the corner by the bowling center, where mist rose, and each streetlight cast a halo over their heads. The air smelled of burnt sugar and water plants. His hand itched to take hers, but he didn't. Better to preserve the wanting than to ruin it with some clumsy gesture of affection.

They took the short route, below, where the canal turned nearly black in the dark, like plastic wrap around a vague dream. Their shadows shrank and stretched with every creaking lamp above them. Matthijs felt damp seeping through his sole, stones stabbing at the edge of his foot, but he didn't care. Here, now, the small pains didn't count. Chantal told him about a grandmother who always slept in knitted socks, even in summer ("especially in summer, otherwise your feet think it's winter"). He laughed with her. His mouth felt stiff and tingly, as if the night had glazed his throat with sugar.

They were quiet crossing the bridge, not awkward, just a digestible silence after all the noise. The city leaked toward night; even the canal water seemed less tense.

She didn't bother making the goodbye harder. By the bike racks, she looked up, not at the sky or stars, but at his face, as if searching for something she'd forgotten to ask. She reached out, half-hesitant. So, he took her hand, out of gratitude more than anything, and felt that her skin was warmer than his. In the flicker of a fluorescent tube, she looked older, her skin with a film of transparency, but still: everything pulsed.

"You turned out better than I expected," she said, and it didn't sound cynical.

He wanted to say something, a joke, a platitude, but his tongue stuck to his palate. So he pressed his lips to her temple, a miniature kiss, safe, almost fatherly. She pulled him closer, reckless as if the street belonged entirely to them. The kiss was better than the first, or maybe the light fell just right, but then there was only her mouth, her warmth, her tongue brushing his teeth. No grand fireworks; just the ordinary magic of confirmation, the sobering realization that this was it, and that it could be beautiful.

"Not bad," she murmured against his mouth. She let go, but didn't step back.

"Neither are you," he mumbled. His hands felt big, clumsy, unsure where to rest. He brushed a strand of hair from her face, too late realizing she might not want that — but she only smiled wider. She noticed his hesitation and took the lead: rested her head briefly against his chest, stayed there, her breath making small clouds in the cold. Her cheek against his shirt button. For a moment, everything stayed like that.

Then she pulled away, pressed the button on her bike lock, switched on the light, a routine inherited from her mother. "I'll text you when I'm home," she said. Her voice wasn't uncertain, more like the plan had already been on the calendar for years. She got on her bike, turned once, nodded a bit too seriously, then slid into the night. The glow of her bike light shimmered raggedly over the asphalt, her silhouette a slow ripple on the canal.

Matthijs stayed there, rubbing his thumb over the patch of skin her hand had warmed. The scent of his aftershave mingled with the citrus of her hair. He decided to walk home; the rain was long gone, and it was refreshing, really, no promise of spectacle, just raw, direct air.

At home, his mother was asleep, or pretending. In the fridge, half a cucumber; on the counter, a post-it: "Was nice to see you laugh. Mom." He read it like a child, over and over, until the letters blurred. UFO-shaped lamp in the corner of the living room, newspapers with half a Sudoku filled in. He thought of the night, of how Chantal's kiss lingered in his pores. He wanted to go back out, hold her twenty more times, until the awkwardness faded into habit.

Morning came sunless but clear enough to mirror his hangover on the windowsill. A dusting of drizzle stuck to the glass, but his head felt empty, sober enough for a text. His fingers still worked, despite the dryness. Chantal hadn't written, or maybe they had both surrendered to the protocol of the silent day after. It suited them, really. Both half-shy, half-proud, waiting to see who'd break first.

Matthijs de Vries looked up at the faint ellipse of his bald spot. That night, he hadn't dreamed. Nor was it a morning full of echoes, no children, no women, no mothers. He made coffee, real coffee this time, for the first time in months, using beans inherited from his eldest son's student years. The smell jolted the house awake. While stirring, he thought of the hot-air balloon ride he'd suggested to Chantal after their second.

It didn't take a week before their third date was set, this time at her place. Chantal lived in a row house at the edge of a new development, everything smelling of fresh construction and wet clay. Even the mailbox felt new, dustless. A tiny front garden with boxwood she trimmed herself every week. The door was ajar, and when he rang the bell, her voice came over the gravel: "You coming in, or do I have to fetch you?"

The hallway was filled with children's drawings and raincoats on hooks. Chantal peeked around the corner, a pink-flowered apron over her clothes. She smiled so wide her cheekbones turned white. Yes, she was nervous, Matthijs could see that, but it suited her. Just human, for once. Their feet tapped the same rhythm on the laminate floor. Soft voices from the living room, the smell of stew and something cake-like, everything humming with that pleasant awkwardness until the kids would burst in.

Inside was no different: gray-blue walls, an Ikea cabinet squeaking at the seam, a dining table covered in felt-tip pens and safe white crackers. Two kids, Ruben with his cocky undercut, Sari with Chantal's lashes, greeted him with the routine of weekend regulars. Chantal introduced him as "my friend," and Matthijs noticed how strange that word tasted in his mouth. None of the kids found it odd.

The afternoon rolled on smoothly, like a Polaroid no one laughed too loudly over. They baked something meant to be pizza, and he let the cheese stick to his fingers; the goo between them was allowed. Ruben talked about school, not because he had to, but because he thought it was cool that an adult actually remembered his name ("that's not a given, you know"). Sari drew the family's old cat in black marker, her head tilted, occasionally checking if someone was watching.

Dinner had the ease of a family, the kind that only feels natural in movies. Here, it just happened. Chantal passed the steaming bowl of pasta across the table, as if on autopilot. Matthijs helped, set bottles down, and poured drinks with clumsy fingers.

At half past ten, they crept upstairs; Ruben was already snoring, Sari lay with her hair over the pillow, and the marker still in her hand. Chantal brushed the softness from her face, slipped back onto the landing, and looked at him with one shoulder raised. "Leave it," she whispered. No explanation, no interview, just the trust to look quietly and let the light shine in its own time.

And at night, when the streets emptied and only the white rustling of rain remained, he didn't fall asleep right away. The air in Chantal's house carried the scent of detergent and herbal tea, and under the duvet, he could hear her breathing beside him. Unlike his previous nights, always alone, always with the bottom already in sight, this felt like a room with substance. The walls were covered in photos. Homemade crafts, tape still visible along the edges. Matthijs lay on his side, trying not to move, not wanting to be the first to break the silence. His body remembered the way she'd laid her leg over his; her skin still cool from the climb upstairs. Her hair slid across his wrist and stayed there, soft, like an anchor. He tried to count her breaths, lost count, and began again. Sometimes his mind slipped back into the old groove, a face full of time zones, ghost images from Brooklyn or Den Bosch, but then she pulled him back with a small tremor of her back against his chest, and he could land again. His hand found hers, their fingers like cutlery in a drawer: awkward, but fitting once you got it right.

In the middle of the night, he woke to the sound of rain hammering harder than ever as if someone had turned up the volume on purpose, just for people who didn't want to sleep. Chantal lay with her back to him, her shoulder blades showing through the T-shirt, soft and sharp at once. In the dark, her neck smelled of honey and a faint sourness, a scent that would stay in his memory for weeks, pointed, more precise than the words she sometimes chewed on. It was always somewhere between becoming serious and not wanting to miss the small sparks. She felt like a raw gift no one bothered to polish. Still awake, he thought, and gently stroked the bare bit of arm that pushed out between sheet and air.

Chantal caught her breath, turned toward him slowly, almost heavily, looked at him with that half-smiling mouth and the undisciplined shadows under her eyes. "You weren't asleep?" she asked, half-lightning from her dream, her voice tighter than by day.

He felt he had to answer. "Awake from the rain," he said. Then: "And from you." Funny how it sounded like a joke but wasn't; she sensed it, ran a finger over his chest. She felt nothing of his thin arms, only the warmth that lingered despite the wet clouds outside. Her leg brushed his calf. That was all she gave.

"A bit awake isn't so bad," she said, crookedly. Her hands dived into his hair, as if she could massage sleep there, and somewhere in that gentle motion she made space for him to stay. Not until morning, not until the alarm or the children, but until the whole house felt like a nest. He thought of how he had always had to sink through nights alone, airy, hard, never enough to remember. Now she simply stayed, a body just big enough to fill everything.

He woke in a garden that smelled of autumn and lemon tea. Chantal still lay against his back, her hair static from the synthetic pillow, her thumb moving idly through his chest hair. He didn't dare turn over, afraid the image would have to be rebuilt in daylight, that this easy closeness would prove a bruise on waking. Sometimes, when she held her breath, it seemed as if she were aware of everything: his heartbeat, the time, or how the night still clung cold to the windowsill.

Morning grew into their room, light wavering along the curtain's edge, and only then did he see how the whole house was filled with children, not real ones, but in crafts and harp-like Sophie the Giraffe figurines, names in marker on mugs. Everything was signed with tape, with crumpled paper strips. The whole attic showed comics of children who were heroes, streets that led to rainbows. Everything pushed against his old idea of normal, that love was something you only earned by doing it wrong. Here it was simply passed along, like a baton in a relay race.

The morning leapt raw and cold into the room, but Chantal stayed in bed another fifteen minutes, always with the same leg curled over his. She didn't say much. Matthijs liked not having to fill the silence. Sometimes, when her eyes were half open, he thought there might be more beneath the surface, a whole sea of things to explore together, but it stayed safely underwater. No rush, that was the point.

The morning burst into the room raw and cold, but Chantal stayed in bed for another fifteen minutes, her leg curled over his, as always. She didn't say much. Matthijs liked not having to fill in the blanks. Sometimes, when her eyes were slightly open, he thought there might be more, a whole sea of things to discover together, but it remained safely below the surface. No rush, that was it. He felt something harden. She felt like a balloon being inflated against her thighs. She took off her pants. She took the dragon in her hand and moistened it with her mouth and tongue. She took it like an ice cream cone on a stick. It disappeared into a cave, where it was pitch black. You couldn't see a thing. You saw a small point of light. Then a dragon appeared, showing its face. It looked more like a dinosaur. A large head with holes for ears. He became fiery and angry. Red with exertion. He worked his way in and out of the cave. The walls began to move. They tightened around this dragon. A juice came out of the wall to extinguish the fire. He hissed, and steam flew through the room. It looked as if it had started snowing. A white substance filled the room. It flew like a rocket through space. Stuck to the walls and floors and disappeared deep into the cave. Sometimes things are just ordinary, without any fanfare. Chantal pulled her T-shirt over her head, her hair falling immediately to the side in a haze that smelled of detergent and something mineral. The silence was not tense, more as if the house had drawn a curtain over their conversation so that no one would have to wake up. The first thing she did was walk to the shower, uncomfortably relaxed, just like yesterday, as if this had always been meant to be.

Chantal s hair falling aside in a haze that smelled of detergent and something mineral. The silence wasn't tense, more as if the house laid a cloth over their voices so no one would wake up. The first thing she did was walk to the shower, awkwardly relaxed, exactly as yesterday, as if it had always been this way.

He heard the tap running, water splashing against tiles, the routine rhythm of her morning shower, as if she were already busy with the next day. After ten minutes, she came out with a towel around her hair, her face a bit sleepy but otherwise unchanged from the night before. She dried him off with her eyes. "Want coffee?" she called, drawing a line of steam on the window with her thumb. She set two mugs on the counter, neatly side by side, as if they had been linked for years. She wore a short bathrobe over that T-shirt, her legs dotted with wet spots on the tiles. She moved without drama, in the cadence of a morning routine, like turning the volume down until the house stood still like a new winter coat. She said nothing about the night. What struck him was the naturalness of sharing — a bottle of oat milk, a bowl of oatmeal she filled for him without asking. He looked at her hands, the red flush around the knuckles from warm water, the thumb with its odd bend from the childhood fracture ("nostalgic, that finger crack," she had told him). Everything was exactly enough, the balance between just right and thoughtless. Chantal made breakfast with the ease of someone who had done it for years. And Matthijs followed her through the house, never out of tune. The light of freshly squeezed orange juice, creaking floorboards, and the click of her spatula on the too-dry pan. She had set aside a plate for him: two slices of bread, some egg, and the strangest jam he had ever seen. "It's called lemon curd," she said at his look. "Try it. It's weird, but good." She scooped a thick yellow blob onto his bread. He tasted it, laughed, and let himself be surprised by how well it fit.

After that, they went with the children to the market. His hand was allowed in Chantal's; Ruben's hand hung in hers as if it had never been otherwise. It was damp-cold outside, the air pricked his fingers, and the asphalt steamed from the manhole covers. They walked in a kind of square, Chantal always just ahead of him. The Saturday market burst like a mosaic of cargo bikes, waffle stands, and children screaming on leashes. Chantal had to touch every second stall, the tulips, the cheese, nuts in a plastic cup, like a ritual to feed the chaos. The children ran off but always stayed within reach, the direction of their voices showing where to look. Matthijs avoided the stalls; his hand stayed in Chantal's, sometimes too long, then jerking loose again, not yet normal, but no longer awkward either.

In the square, Chantal bought a bunch of radishes with the leaves still attached. "You know you can eat the greens too?" she said with that university-tone nonchalance that almost made it sexy. Radish leaves, tossed in salad, those stiff fibers like chewing on a tram ticket. It was the kind of remark that would normally have irritated him endlessly, but he stood there, cold water from the fish stall on his hands, and thought: why not? They joked that in Italy, you fried the stems in oil. Chantal held the shiny radish up by its leaves, a little elegantly, between her fingertips. "You get it, right? About not wasting anything?"

She said it softly so the children wouldn't hear. Meanwhile, Sari was dealing candy bars from a plastic box, and Ruben had gotten a splitter strip for his scooter. The market was a nest of ants.

CHAPTER 2
BUSY IN MANHATTAN

Abigail is steeped in the blue glow of her screen when she snaps her laptop shut and turns toward the kitchen, where Eliza and Leah are staking their breakfast claims with syrupy gestures. Her head still fizzes from the last Zoom call, email notifications blinking somewhere deep in her peripheral vision. Time to see who's choking today on the antics of a nine-year-old and an almost-teenager.

Eliza has smeared Nutella all over her face. Leah is shoving a banana into her backpack, ignoring the napkin her mother offers. Abigail pins a smile to her lips, forces a note of breezy calm.

"Girls, can we try chaos without house rules today? Half of Manhattan hears me yelling at you to catch the bus every morning."

Eliza sticks out her tongue.

"We want lemonade," says Leah, her hand already in the fridge. Of course, Eliza always wants more than the house contains. One more generation like this, and the dental bills alone will rival the U.S. defense budget.

In the background, Slack pings again. She ignores it, focusing instead on the improbably patient rhythm of her daughters: forks, a glass against the counter, soles skidding over tile. Her own mother would have suppressed the chaos in silence and later brewed soup from the memory, but Abigail must wait until Monday evening for a sanctioned breath. Her mother's voice still lives somewhere in her head, knowing, grimly Dutch, mercifully softened by twelve time zones.

Eliza slaps a sock on the table, as if every negotiation might be settled on the spot.

"Mama, when are we going to Dad's?"

She shrugs, guilt tightening its familiar grip around her ribs.

"In a month. You can start thinking about what to pack for the flight. No pets, no friends, and… no Nutella on the new dresses."

Leah kicks at a chair leg. Eliza rolls her eyes in Broadway-worthy despair, letting out a groan so theatrical that Abigail wonders which gene is responsible for that particular flair.

"Papa always makes pancakes. And he lets us stay up late."

Irritated, Abigail brushes her hair from her face and strokes Eliza's head, more to soothe herself than the child. She wants so badly for them to lack nothing: no shortage of roots, or love, or safety. And yet, when she catches her reflection in the laptop screen, she's startled by the woman she sees there, a woman who chats with forty people a day but understands her children's language less and less.

She grabs her coat and waves the girls along. Outside, Manhattan gulps at the cool air; everything moves faster, as if no one has time to let doubt ferment. At the bus stop, Eliza looks at her again.

"You can come with us too," she says, as if she's forgotten who the mother is.

Abigail fakes a cough, pulling out her phone as though an agenda disaster requires immediate rescue. "As soon as I get some time off, sweetheart."

Her voice echoes hollowly off the skyscrapers. Better an echo than silence.

The bus slides around the corner, its sides glowing with siren-pink reflections of the city. Leah climbs the steps, too small for her backpack. Eliza follows without looking back. For a second, Abigail considers waving, but her hand stays in her pocket, curled tight around her keys like an unspoken promise: *your turn will come.*

The morning is suddenly hollow. Sixteen minutes until the first call with Singapore. She walks home, not because she has time to spare, but because she can't bear to dissolve straight back into pixels. Past the deli where bok choy sits outside every Wednesday, past the coffee bar with its unsolicited jazz soundtrack, she breathes the city in like a quick reset.

She thinks of Matthijs—how he's probably in his favorite café right now, sipping coffee that always smells bitterly French, laptop open, lips pursed in that almost-smile that threatens to break at any moment. Even from six thousand kilometres away, he has that uncanny ability to stir up the unrest in her household with a single message: *Your girls won't know what home means, later.*

She thinks: maybe that's the best one can hope for. No homesickness, no roots as anchor lines. Just moving forward—toward the next station, the next digital meeting, the next breakfast.

Her phone buzzes. Abby flicks the screen open: a Slack from the CEO, three calendar invites, and one from her mother—condensed maternal threat wrapped neatly in emojis. She swipes the messages aside, her thumb hovering over the screen as if the operating system itself has momentarily lost its logic.

On the stairwell, a soprano warms up somewhere on the third floor, Italian phrases pouring through an open window. Abigail passes by; the melody resonates inside her skull. She thinks of the last time she lifted her own voice that high—long ago, maybe at Christmas with her daughters, maybe once with Matthijs, at the beach, back when they still believed their drama would stay watertight as long as they shouted over it.

At home, the screen awaits her. Before powering the laptop on, she pours a glass of water, holds it, and feels the cold pulling at her palm. She closes her eyes—just for three beats—and imagines the moment her girls will come home again, as if she could draw them closer with every breath.

She opens her laptop, straightens her smile into the camera, and speaks the first words of her day.

The day folds into a web of calls and spreadsheets, punctuated now and then by the awkward jokes of her junior analyst. Abigail hears herself responding with firm assurance, even when she misses half of what's said—because the other half of her mind is trapped on a forgotten gym bag (Leah's) and an unsigned school form (Eliza's). There's always a shortage: of hours, of hands, of ease. She's learning to live with it—the eternal *no* to spontaneity, the constant postponement of anything that smells like release.

A little after two, her mother calls. Not on WhatsApp—that's *too American*—but a real phone call, direct, as if the ocean between them were just a puddle. Abigail's hand moves instinctively toward "ignore," but her finger hesitates. She answers, and at once hears the gruff, dryly delivered accent.

"So, Abby. Have you forgotten you were ever a child yourself?"

She tries to laugh.

"I never really knew, Mom. I've mostly been a mother—three times over."

"And what are you to yourself, then? Zero times? Do I have to arrange that too?"

Then Ellie falls silent, in that way only mothers can, silence so full of unspoken correction it spans continents.

Abigail twists her mouth, glancing at the screen where statistics multiply endlessly, like parenting mistakes. "Can we talk about the girls later? They miss you."

"Just remember you still have desires of your own," her mother says. "Think of something that isn't a laptop."

She hears herself say *yes*, while her mind says *no*. Then her mother hangs up—no goodbye, no formal ending. Just gone, as if she might appear beside her in the elevator at any moment.

The afternoon clings. Every meeting is ordinary, her face a recurring flash in the webcam, her name threaded through subject lines, her constant availability the only proof of relevance—until, from some obscure corner of the screen, an email appears.

Subject: **HOME.**

She knows immediately who it's from. Matthijs disappears for months and then suddenly reappears with messages that say almost nothing, yet too much. His mother's house, he writes, will soon be up for sale, and maybe the girls would like to come back once more—for pea soup and skating on the canal, "because before you know it, this memory won't exist anymore."

Abigail reads the line three times, seeing the girls in her mind: zipping up their coats, hair in the same messy buns as back then, the smell of damp wool socks in a hallway where the radiator's warmth always carried a faint hiss of steam.

Everyone says children must learn what roots are. But what she wants them to learn is how to *move on*—that sometimes leaving is the highest form of staying whole.

After five minutes, she replies, her tone light, carefully formal, checked for any trace of bite: *Good idea. Let's sort out the details once we know if it's happening.* She forwards it from her private email, imprinting the exchange with professional distance, airy commas, no room for subtext. Immediately after, she blocks all notifications and clears her screen. His message flutters in her inbox like a window suddenly flung open: fresh air rushing in, yes— but also the smell of old carpets and shared secrets once thought safely buried.

The rest of the afternoon, she wavers between satisfaction (*well, that's settled*) and an irrational urge to smash every coffee cup within reach, as if a sudden message from Matthijs had disturbed some delicate karmic balance.

On the spreadsheet inside her head, hypotheses multiply: that he misses her; that he simply enjoys the drama of these sudden bursts of contact; that he can't live without proof of his lingering influence. Nowhere does her heart allow the possibility that he might simply, perhaps, mean well.

Half an hour before the girls are due home, a text arrives from an unfamiliar European number. The timing fits perfectly. She recognizes the pattern.

Coming too? It says. No comma, no capital letter— exactly his way. He always claimed commas killed the flow of conversation, that punctuation was a waste of time for something that would never last longer than the moment itself.

Without thinking, she types: *I've got deadlines until June. But who knows?*

And she knows, even as she hits send, that he'll read the words instantly for what they are: an elegant lie. *Who knows* means *never*. But total honesty would help no one, least of all her daughters, who will soon burst through the door demanding hot chocolate and attention.

Two minutes later, her inbox sighs: **delivery failed.** Undeliverable. The European number doesn't go through.

She laughs out loud. Even an algorithm, it seems, knows when a promise was never meant to be kept.

She tidies her desk, slides papers into drawers, brushes crumbs from the keyboard. The silence builds—New York silence, dense and human. Hundreds of people in her building, each nursing their own losses and little victories, none of them demanding, none of them waiting outside her door with judgment. For a moment, she feels at peace.

When her daughters tumble in, hair damp, cheeks red, carrying the day's competitive noise with them, she leaves her phone on the counter. Eliza makes straight for the kitchen cupboard; Leah collapses against her leg, seeking her hand. Abigail gathers comfort from a bag of mini marshmallows and, for once, adds a little extra to the mugs of chocolate milk.

Maybe—just maybe—not every choice had to be dragged alone toward some lonely terminus. Maybe she could simply stay here, with her daughters and her emails, and maybe their memories didn't have to be prettier or darker than those of other children growing up in two countries at once.

The three of them step over piles of wet coats and shoes strewn across the apartment like a minefield. Leah knocks over her mug and looks up, guilty; the chocolate stain spreads across the counter, touching the edge of a tax form Abigail was supposed to fill out. She doesn't flinch. "Leave it," she says—and hears herself, surprised at how gentle her voice sounds.

Eliza thrusts a phone under her nose, something about a YouTuber using Nutella as a makeup mask. Abigail gives a half-hearted laugh, looking at her daughter through the haze still lingering in her head.

"Let me guess—spread it on your face and skip the skincare budget?"

Eliza grins, chocolate smeared across her mouth, and Leah shouts from the couch that it's true anyway—Nutella's good for stress.

In that instant, Abigail decides it doesn't have to be a battlefield, that this day can simply drain away like a bath of lukewarm milk. She drops down beside Leah, who presses against her, apparently having forgotten their earlier argument about who got to shower first.

"Can I FaceTime Dad later?" Leah asks, slurping up the last of the marshmallows.

Abigail weighs a complex answer but settles on something simple.

"Yes," she says. "Before dinner, preferably."

She looks at her daughters—legs tangled together, the air thick with sugar and damp clothes and everything left unsaid, all the questions only tomorrow can answer.

She reaches for her laptop, catches her reflection: a woman re-examining herself—older than yesterday, perhaps wiser, at least less afraid of her own history. She opens the lid carefully, swipes her work email aside, and types in the search bar: *cheap winter flights Amsterdam.* Just to look, she tells herself, just because she can.

Behind her, the girls' voices rise—a duet of laughter and something that will probably become an argument if she doesn't intervene. Abigail turns, watching this improvisation of joy and disorder, and can't remember why she ever thought she needed to control it. This, she realizes, is home—split between time zones and screens and the warm chaos of a living room full of stains.

Maybe she'll call someone later. Or no one at all. That choice can wait, like the trail of Nutella and the weight of her mother's commentary. She pours herself another mug of cocoa, thinking of Eliza's Nutella-smeared smile over her cup, of Leah's small hand resting wordlessly in hers. Maybe it's enough, right now, simply to hold them before they rush back out into the world with their shoes and their opinions. She brushes a strand of hair from Leah's face, steals a marshmallow, and bites down experimentally: yes, sugar works in any crisis.

"Remember," Eliza says suddenly, "how Grandma in the Netherlands always gave us cake, even when it wasn't our birthday?"

She says it casually, a kitchen-table observation, but Abigail feels her stomach tighten. All those years spent on moving forward, always forward—and now the memories are sneaking back through her children.

"That was Grandma's secret weapon," she says. "Cake as a peace offering. To keep everyone together."

Leah looks up, crumbs on her lips. "Maybe we can send her a photo? Of our breakfast table?" She grabs Abigail's phone without asking and snaps a blurry picture of herself and her sister, both in pajamas, hair wild as if Ellie would have expected anything else.

Later, after sending the girls to their rooms for homework, Abigail sinks onto the couch. Outside, the late sun settles on battered brick. The city hums drowsily. So many screens, so much noise—and now, only this slow, seeping silence. She accidentally taps her phone camera and sees herself: dark circles, a creased shirt, a smile that never quite made it to her eyes.

You were a child once. What are you to yourself now? The echo lingers. She thinks of her mother, her daughters, even Matthijs with his sly late-night texts. Always put others first; their stories are more important. She tries to flip the script: what if she were allowed, now and then, to be the center? To act not in the service of anyone else? But even the thought feels like sabotage to the system her life depends on.

Maybe that's what Ellie meant—that desire doesn't live in spreadsheets or neatly filled-out forms, but in stolen marshmallows and half-written emails that never find their way.

That evening, the girls lie in bed, a sliver of light under the door. Abigail leans against it, heart stuttering with the rhythm of the floorboards. She hears Leah murmuring in her sleep—*mama, mama, don't go*—and it's too much and too little all at once.

She creeps back to the couch, opens her laptop—not for work, but to scroll through old emails from Matthijs. Not for his faux-gallant humor, but to trace what she once felt. To find out if she'd ever been anything more than a functioning inbox. Maybe that had been enough once: to-do lists, hotel bookings, holidays checked off like trophies of shared memory. She scrolls through messages about tooth fairies and swimming lessons, *calls you later,* and *I'll send the report tomorrow.*

Sometimes, slipped between lines, a fragment about her: that he missed her, or thought she was cool, or didn't know where she got all her energy, but that it made him nervous—in a good way.

She rereads her own replies. Always polite. Always ending with a joke. Even across absurd time zones, she managed to produce a version of care without urgency. A mother who served pizza on Monday nights and chaired meetings in Haarlemmermeer on Thursdays, in sneakers.

She exhales deeply, eyes shut tight, picturing her girls somewhere in pajamas, climbing over tables on the other side of the world, what she'd like to remember, what anyone is allowed to keep when every emotion has a meeting to attend.

She clicks through old photos: there they are, Leah and Eliza in a rubber dinghy on the North Sea. Her heart swells—not with nostalgia but with the rage that it can't be that way again, not ever. And yet—and yet—maybe by tomorrow they'll have forgotten it once was different. Maybe that's their gift, their lifeline: the instinct not to linger.

A new Slack thread pops up—team outing suggestions for March: bowling (awful), karaoke (worse), escape rooms (instant panic attack). Someone's made a meme of her with a coffee cup: *She runs on deadlines and denial.* Abby drops her head onto her arm and snorts with laughter. Honestly—who doesn't?

She gets up, walks to the window, and stares down at the city. Manhattan stretches beneath her like a shaken-out tablecloth, white-yellow with streetlights, a grid of millions who, at the end of the day, just want to forget they'll have to rise again. Not a single light is special enough to justify her existence. But if you removed them all, there'd be nothing left.

She stays there for a long time, fingertips against the glass, the warmth inside, and the muffled hum of the city blending into a slow, lulling comfort. She thinks of Ellie's disciplined silences, of her own quiet rebellions against inherited rules, of how every revolution, in the end, has to be self-managed.

Her thoughts are interrupted by a ping—Leah's sent a selfie. Coming home, or running ahead?

Every message from Matthijs had that same pulse, that breathless rhythm—as if he were always sprinting forward, away from old pain—while she had to stop, wait for the traffic of their shared past to clear. She still remembers laughing at his opening lines, even when she knew they were all deflections, humor as dagger and shield. Even in this digital archive, the words still point her back to herself:

Do you laugh when you work, or work because you wouldn't laugh otherwise?

He was always musing, even when the rest of the world had stopped listening.

The flight was delayed, routed through Dublin, and somewhere around the fourth hour, she drifted into a trance between sleeping commuters and overaged people in business. Even here, trapped in the same narrow economy row, her daughters seemed to cover more ground than she ever had. Eliza slumped against her shoulder, mumbling half-formed thoughts about bad Wi-Fi and the scientific value of Nutella. Leah traced names into the condensation on the window: "Mama" above "Papa," then a fading "Leah," as if she could erase her own story before it hardened.

In the night above the Atlantic, somewhere between the rattle of cold air and the hum of the fuselage, Abigail thought of Ellie—her mother—with her unyielding routines, her freezer packed to its moral capacity, her suspicion of anything digital. What would she think of these migrating shadows who refused to anchor themselves anywhere, who wanted only to keep moving from one passage to the next? Would she sniff and say this wasn't a life, drifting through transit zones? Or would she secretly recognize it, the same hunger disguised as discipline, the urge to escape her own reflection before it settled into permanence?

By the time they landed, the Netherlands lay flat and gray as ever. The girls missed the first bridge over the canal; they were staring out the window, looking for something they couldn't name—something that might explain why the air here felt both heavier and thinner at once.

Naturally, Matthijs arrived at Schiphol in the shadow of his own indecision.

As if he were waiting for the children, but really for himself—for that far-reaching glimpse of his girls had never, despite everything, been an act of willing distance.

They looked surprisingly small in the arrivals hall.

So accustomed to the frames of their own selfies that the first embrace felt awkward for at least four seconds. God, how they looked like Abby up close—the corners of their mouths, those squared shoulders inside coats cut three sizes too sharp.

Leah held her passport up like a shield; Eliza scanned the space with that half-faked nonchalance of teenagers pretending not to be impressed. He laughed, patted both their heads at once, and immediately felt both redundant and indispensable.

"So. Ready for pea soup and way too much wet snow?" he tried, jokingly. It landed nowhere.

Each carried a small suitcase packed with unmistakable American logic: hoodies, chargers, no umbrella. Jet lag had reddened their eyes, and the look on their faces was a mix of reproach and victory—they had made it, but under protest.

To Matthijs, that felt familiar—the universe had never quite taken his side. But he could live with less.

Only in the car, on the highway between the airport and Amsterdam, did silence begin to cling to them like a cold, wet cloth around the neck. He tried to gauge whether the jet lag was bad.

Eliza stayed on her screen, and Leah stared out the window.

"You hungry?" he asked, almost afraid of the answer.

They nodded in unison, without urgency.

"We just ate on the plane," Leah said at last, her voice one degree colder than the air outside.

He turned on the radio—nostalgia channel—and immediately got Kinderen voor Kinderen ("I had such an amazing dream…").

They drove in silence through the damp morning, the highway a ribbon of mist and sodium light. Each billboard looked slightly out of focus, as if the country itself had forgotten how to advertise certainty. Leah pressed her nose to the window; Eliza yawned theatrically, filming raindrops as they slid down the glass. The GPS spoke Dutch in a voice so polite it sounded almost ashamed.

Matthijs had borrowed a car too small for the luggage, and the heater breathed faintly of dust and regret. "Almost there," he said, though the sentence seemed to belong to a much longer conversation they'd never quite finished.

When they turned off toward Amsterdam, the fields appeared—flat, soaked, and heartbreakingly literal. Nothing in this country was symbolic; even its nostalgia came with drainage. Abigail felt her body tense at the first sight of waterlogged grass, the narrow ditches cutting the land into obedient rectangles. The girls murmured something about how everything smelled like wet wood and bread. She wanted to laugh, but didn't.

Geertruida s house stood the same as ever: curtains drawn to mid-window, a single geranium stubbornly alive behind the glass. His mother opened the door before they could ring. "You're thin," she said by way of greeting, and kissed each granddaughter twice, as if to erase the years with protocol.

Inside, the heat hit them like a soft reprimand. The radio played low; the kitchen smelled of broth and patience.

Geertruida handed Abigail a towel for the girls' hair, then asked,

"Was the flight long?"

"Long enough," Abigail said. It was the kind of exchange they'd perfected—surface calm layered over a lifetime of small evasions.

When the girls ran upstairs, their voices echoing through the wooden house, Geertruida poured coffee the way she always did: too strong, too hot, and in cups that belonged to no particular era. "You look tired," she said. Abigail smiled without teeth. "I'm between time zones. It'll pass."
His mother nodded, as if fatigue were a character flaw she could still correct with practice.

Later, after dinner, when the girls had fallen asleep in twin beds that smelled faintly of lavender sachets and attic dust, Abigail stepped outside. The night air was colder than she remembered, clear and unromantic. Across the canal, a single window still burned yellow, its reflection rippling over the water like a pulse.

She thought of Manhattan—its sleepless hum, the chrome loneliness of her apartment, the smell of burnt coffee at 6 a.m.—and wondered which version of herself would greet her when she went back. Or if, by some quiet miracle, she wouldn't need to.

From inside, she heard his mother moving dishes, the slow rhythm of a woman who never stopped tidying what couldn't really be cleaned. Leah called her name in her sleep. Eliza mumbled something about skating.

Abigail took a long breath of the cold Dutch air, feeling it settle somewhere between her ribs. Maybe home wasn't a place you returned to but a moment you agreed not to leave.

She closed her eyes, and for the first time in a long while, she didn't imagine an elsewhere. Only the sound of her daughters breathing in the next room, and the soft, stubborn heartbeat of this drenched, familiar country.

It was as if someone were mocking him, those soundtracks from his own childhood pasted into the FM ether. He wondered whether to send Abby an update, whether that would seem too eager. She once told him: *"Not everything needs immediate validation, Matthijs— sometimes absence does the work."*

At his mother's house, everything felt as it always had. The sound of the door closer, the crinkle of plastic bags echoing down the hall.

His mother looked at the girls with a kind of love that expressed itself in direct orders: "Shoes off inside! No stains on the rug." Leah buried herself in her suitcase, hunting for a hoodie. Eliza turned on music that instantly aged the walls—every beat from New York seemed to make the house ten years older. Yes, that's how things went here.

Matthijs lingered in the kitchen. His mother handed out cookies, had everything sliced and ready, breathing heavily between stories.

"Abby should see how those girls are growing," she said, and Matthijs thought: *She sees it. She counts every millimeter as a loss of herself.*

He scanned the counter—three kinds of spread, four cartons of milk, so much redundancy it almost turned into luxury.

He decided he'd make pancakes later, simply because it felt necessary.

That evening, on the couch, Leah asked, "How old were you when you left?" She said it with her nose in a book, as if it didn't concern her.

Matthijs hesitated, felt a kind of nervousness rooting under his skin—not quite regret, more like a missing gene. "Nineteen," he said. "And I didn't come back until I was almost thirty."

Eliza laughed, her echo bouncing lightly through the room.

"So you can just leave, and it doesn't matter?"

He wanted to say *yes*, but his mother looked up, hand still in the chips bag, and her silent judgment felt like a trench.

"It always matters," she said.

Eliza glanced up from her phone; Leah raised an eyebrow. Matthijs thought—maybe it was true that all roads never really led away from this table, from these people, with their discount-brand milk.

They stayed longer than planned. Time slid off them like condensation from double glazing in December. By day, they walked through the park near the old station, where the girls snapped selfies with wilted geese in the background.

The first days broke apart into syrupy little anecdotes.

Leah fell on the ice rink after exactly three meters. Eliza bought a roll of licorice and ate it in one night, circling the supermarket like a predator hunting for "iconic Dutch things" for her Insta.

They wanted to visit the Rijksmuseum—but only if the tour was in English, since their Dutch was "even worse than their jet lag," Eliza claimed. So he dragged them past stately paintings and let the audio guide do the work.

Evenings, at his mother's house, time seemed to contract: half a day, and it was as though he'd never left. His mother popped up everywhere with her clippings and chilled custard, everything as it always was. She watched him with a kind of double-edged sarcasm, as if to see whether he still couldn't manage fatherhood. She didn't need to say it— Matthijs could read it in the slow sweep of her hand across the table, half a millimetre slower than before.

The girls had a routine for sleepovers: sharing a blanket, watching videos too late, whispering about American issues that sounded too oversized in Amsterdam. When they slept, something in their faces struck him like a gust of freezing air—Geertruida's eyebrows in tight arcs, Leah's mouth not quite closed. With their hands on the duvet, their bodies in diagonal sprawl, they made no effort to fake that they didn't belong here.

Matthijs watched them from the doorway—they were his, and yet entirely beyond reach.

Sometimes he thought about what it must be like for Abby, in her Manhattan apartment with all its structured chaos, to allow that looseness. Whether she felt jealous, not being here; whether she looked through his mind into this borrowed night's success.

In the morning, he made pancakes—too thick, just like they remembered. Leah wanted Nutella, Eliza pure syrup, he himself plain butter and sugar. The kitchen smelled as it used to—milk fat and burnt edges. The girls laughed at his *pannekoek*-skills, at his dumb jokes, at everything that meant nothing back home but here, in this temporary house, stuck to the day like a sticker on a cupboard door. For a moment, he felt powerfully helpless—and content.

On day four, it poured, and their shoes filled with rain the moment they crossed the Kiss & Ride. The taxi driver made jokes that the girls didn't understand, not even in

English. It helped that everything in the Netherlands gleamed with moisture, holding itself as though the world had always been this way—unbothered and small. Abigail was instantly brought back by the smell of it all: smoked eel, damp rot, petrol fumes at the bus stops.

Here, there was no perfume of *new beginnings*—everything breathed the logic of staying, even when you'd long since left it behind.

Matthijs's mother's house stood at the end of a dead-end street, in the shadow of a grocer's that still sold *King* candy. This was no Manhattan. Here, shutters came down at five-thirty, and entering the house was a ritual so barbed that even Eliza fell silent.

They took off their shoes in the hall; the air smelled of old newspapers and eighties smoke. In the living room, Geertruida sat waiting, her legs in compression stockings, the table set for cake and tea—she didn't like planning; everything had to happen now, with pastries, or it wasn't worth the time.

The girls submitted politely to inspection and commentary—was their hair always this long, were their knees still bruised from hockey, did they have "normal milk" *there* in America?

Leah was the first to strike back with a joke: "In America, you get milk in boxes, but if you're healthy, you just drink Starbucks."

Geertruida sniffed disapproval but poured more tea. Eliza hid behind her phone, took pictures, sent them to herself—as if to make sure they wouldn't evaporate later. Who knew if she shared them with anyone, or if anyone even cared. But Abigail saw that fever of recording—it was exactly what she used to do, with scrapbooks and film rolls full of faces now reduced to pixels.

Pea soup didn't come until the next day. Nights were restless; the jet lag tormented her body like a torn nerve.

By four a.m., she was already pacing the hallway, where the lights stayed on until the last old neighbor hobbled to bed.

Nothing had changed except the carpet, and even that still smelled faintly of the cleaning products from twenty years ago.

She had thought the hardest part of coming back would be looking into her ex's eyes, but that turned out fine— Matthijs had grown so accustomed to his role as the "weekend father" that he now repeated everything with an apologetic precision: straightening cups, checking shoelaces, rephrasing jokes six times over. He remained endlessly warm with the girls, without any need to exaggerate. Even that felt like a small victory.

The girls were now the version of themselves they had learned to become at home in Manhattan. Maybe it wasn't something one could make or fix, he thought—maybe everything always returned to tilling the same old soil.

By the end of the week, on a Wednesday evening, they were sitting in the kitchen playing cards. His mother didn't join; she was watching an English soap on TV. Leah asked then, without looking up from her hand, "Why did you two actually split up?"

She sounded so casual that it became dangerous.

Matthijs put down his cards, turned the sentence around in his head. Explaining anything to a child always felt like a nerve shot into a sleeping limb. "Sometimes it just doesn't work," he said, "no matter how many times you try."

It was the best he could do.

"And then we moved?" Leah asked.

"Then you and Mom moved to New York, yes."

But in his mind, he scrambled everything—the time, the pain, the order in which you decided whether to keep fighting or walk away.

Eliza sighed—not unkindly, but with that faint, sleepy pity that chilled him.

"You don't have to keep us happy, you know."

He almost laughed at the reversal of it.

"Really," Leah added, as if performing a rehearsal. "We can choose when to laugh."

She looked at him, suddenly so open it made him dizzy.

Maybe that was the difference—between being able to stay and daring to stay.

They now decided how and where they wanted to laugh.

That the house didn't revolve around him, not even this week, but around whoever was still learning to belong in it.

The next morning, they woke to real snow. Everything in the Netherlands was suddenly white, the street silent. The girls took photos of their footprints on the driveway and sent them   straight   to   their   mother.

Matthijs stood in the doorway holding warm coats, himself half a silhouette.

"Going outside?" he asked.

"You're not coming?" Eliza shouted over her shoulder, laughing.

He followed them into the garden, the air full of sharp crystals.

They made snowballs; Leah hit him square in the back and burst out laughing. He refused to throw one back, but they chased him until he stumbled, and when he got up, he almost thought he wouldn't mind freezing right there— because these seven minutes were more than he'd wished for.

Eliza pressed a snow heart onto the kitchen window; Leah tried making an angel in the grass. He took photos, but none came close to what he carried in his mind of their faces.

Later, at breakfast, he noticed that the silence had vanished completely.

They talked about the frosting on the trees outside, about American Christmases, about who could decorate the best tree. Everything now had a different tone—lighter, less like a relay of obligation. During the meal, he asked if they wanted to stay a bit longer. The question lingered quietly, unspoken in its hope.

That night, in the guest bed, the lamplight from the street carved orange circles on the walls. Outside, a train hummed past in its early rhythm.

In this house, everything had a fixed place—even her memories seemed to stand upright on the windowsills. No houseplant dying ahead of time; even the old thermos on the counter made the same small, homely sounds.

The girls slept on, steeped in a cocoon of jet lag and clean air. Sampling old Dutch snacks the day before had finished them off.

Abigail laughed at herself—she'd thought before coming that in the Netherlands they'd finally leave her alone, that she wouldn't have to organize anything. Which, of course, wasn't true. Here, everything was held together by coffee and logic.

After breakfast, she hurried to the bakery on the corner—loyalty to the old neighborhood compelled her to buy overpriced raisin buns and currant bread.

While she stood in line, the woman in front of her was talking about "the Americans," not unkindly, more as a statement of fact: they could do anything, except ride a bike. Abby tightened her accent and ordered in plain Dutch. No one laughed; everyone fought the morning as they always did—zippers, plastic bags, exact change. In America, overpacking was seen as a lack of trust in the future, she thought.

Here, it was a matter of decency.

Back at the house, the hallway smelled of stale bread and damp cardboard—a scent that had never quite detached itself from her Manhattan life, only been covered up for a while.

The girls were already in the living room, playing Nintendo on the big screen—normally forbidden, but in grandmother's domain, every privilege was reinstated. Eliza sucked on a tulip-shaped piece of licorice; Leah stacked her bread without crusts. "What are we doing today?" Leah asked, as if every possibility in the world were on the table.

Abby thought of the schedule she'd set for herself— they still needed to see the notary for paperwork, maybe take an old-fashioned walk in the park if it didn't rain.

She wanted to do everything, and fast. She would have preferred to go alone, to act with the efficiency that had made her a regular at New York's monthly performance reviews.

But now she was here, and her daughters wanted to share everything, even while pretending not to.

"We'll do whatever you want," she said, and felt at once the weight of the lie.

Leah looked up, mouth corners pinned to her face like tacks.

"Then I want to climb the stairs of that weird church."

Eliza raised her hand. "And I want to go to the city. And take a picture at the market, with the cheese girls." They both had to, as quickly as possible—their way of stretching time, looting the daylight.

Still, they looked together—because it was an excuse to stay silent without it feeling awkward. Leah hunched in her chair, head turned away, but ear tuned to the conversation.

Eliza pretended a video was more important, earbuds just a touch too loud.

Matthijs sipped his lukewarm beer and shielded himself with jokes no one in this room really needed.

The rest of the stay fell into the rhythm of Geertruida's household: up at seven-thirty to the smell of instant coffee and sweet yeast from the open freezer. Eliza complained about the early hour; Leah wore her grandmother's bedspread to breakfast as an accessory. Matthijs shuffled to the bathroom in sweatpants, splashed water on his face, and was relieved to be invisibly ordinary for a while.

The girls barely looked at him, as if he, too, were only temporarily tolerated.

Abigail adjusted easily, slipped back into the vegetative rhythm of the past: passing the time with the newspaper, old photo albums, venting the dishwasher, or fixing the broken *Senseo* machine. There was comfort in the predictability, in the way Geertruida clung to the small details of a fading life—how, even years after retiring, she still began every conversation with a casual statistic about births and deaths on the street, as if everything that faded in Amsterdam was automatically relayed to Manhattan.

Leah and Eliza navigated the obstacles of their Dutch childhood effortlessly.

They switched smoothly between English and a softened Dutch, adopted their grandmother's hoarding logic (three types of sandwich spread on the table, always three, even with only two children).

In their posture, in their shrugs and the corners of their mouths, something of the Turner side was there—expertly mixed with the Dutch stubbornness of the de Vries clan.

In the mornings after breakfast, the four of them walked to the park—the first day filled with jokes, the second already routine.

Abigail noticed how well Geertruida got along with her daughters, as if her very stiffness had become porous, like a fungus welcoming new growth.

She walked beside Leah—not awkwardly in the middle, not too close to the edge—listening to fragments of their talk and filling in with half-sentences. Everything she'd once condemned in her mother—that stubborn downplaying, that refusal to let anything truly land—was now deployed like a tactical weapon in the soft warfare of grandparenthood.

Even her voice, if you listened closely, was less sharp than it used to be—trained more for steering than for punishment.

Abigail kept to the background.

She watched Eliza's eyes roll when Leah mispronounced another word.

She caught Matthijs's quiet sigh whenever his mother got her way.

In the past, she would have fought back; now she simply observed, as if it no longer concerned her. Maybe that was the only true gain of growing older—that you finally knew when to lift your hands from every power struggle.

On the fourth evening, after skating and custard, they all sat around the table as if it were a session of parliament. Eliza scrolled through her phone until Geertruida poked her. "Not at the table."

The silence that followed was one they all knew—a vacuum between four generations.

The faintly sour scent of cleaning agent hovered above the lace tablecloth.

Matthijs talked about his job, a project in Rotterdam that no one quite understood beyond the vague idea of "international."

His mother nodded briskly.

Leah tried to start a conversation about her new books, but the Wi-Fi was so weak she accidentally blurted the English title.

Geertruida raised her eyebrows and lamented the decline of the Dutch language.

Abigail heard it all filtered—voices in an overlit elevator, each one desperate simply to be heard.

Later, in the hallway where the carpet rippled softly underfoot, Geertruida pulled her aside.

"It's good you're here, Abby."

She said it as both observation and warning. Abigail nodded, knowing that every compliment here was packed in cardboard—too hard, and it would break anyway.

"Thanks, Mom," she said.

Nothing more.

Footsteps echoed above the stairs; Leah and Eliza came running, fighting over who would get the bathroom last. Geertruida sighed, but her gaze lingered on Abigail, as if she had only just become visible in the house. "They look like you." She said it softly, as if only now permitted to acknowledge the resemblance. "More than you think."

There was no triumph in it, only a dry instinct for registration.

Later, Abigail lay in the guest bed, the room filled with the smell of old linen and the faint mold every house past fifty seems to carry. It settled over her thoughts like a mantle: her girls were growing up like her, in ways large and small, and she wasn't sure whether that was a blessing or a slow-motion disaster. She tried not to think of Manhattan, of meetings, of the CEO she still had a battle to fight with over the new project. In her mind, she strung together photographs of the week like beads on a necklace: the first breakfast, Leah's laugh with a cookie in her mouth, Eliza in a hoodie pulled up over her coat collar, the afternoon walk beneath an oversized umbrella.

That evening, they all sat together on the couch—inevitably, family. Leah nestled against her mother's side; Eliza slept, folded against the armrest. The television was on, but no one watched. Matthijs spoke in the background, his hands busy constructing the story midair. Geertruida sat with arms spread, monumental, dangerous, stone-cold—" Instagram-proof," Eliza had called her again.

They climbed the church tower, step after step, until the girls reached the top, breathless and laughing at their own echoes among the bells. Abby stopped halfway; her knees had long since lost their tolerance for altitude, or maybe it was the memory of Sunday climbs with her own mother years ago—almost the same view, only now her children were the ones ahead, and she herself the middle link.

Up there, nothing moved; everything was taut in the light. Leah shouted joyfully toward the roofs and skylights of the city, her hair crackling in the static wind. Eliza tried to take a group selfie, cropping her mother out of the frame. "Sorry, small screen," she said, but Abby knew she was mercifully editing out the awkward poses—an oversensitive urban soul with no room left for shame. She let herself be photographed anyway, proof that she had been there.

Everyone needed to know: look, they were here, for these seconds, these splinters of a day.

They descended the tower. Back on the street, the light flattened, the sky peeled loose from the shimmer of the moment. They ate warm doughnuts from a stall, their breath rising white as they laughed. Leah and Eliza ate faster and faster, each in her own rhythm, as if they could stoke the day into lasting longer. Abby felt the urge ripple through her—the same haste, the same hunger to turn every joy into reproduction. You had to experience something to pass it on; that, after all, had been her mother's creed.

They bought tulips from a stand and walked home with them. Abby wondered whether a bouquet ever made a lasting difference, or if everything, inevitably, wilted. The girls walked ahead, each with a paper cone in hand, their silhouettes melting into the narrow beam of February sun stretched across the canal. The image was too simple to capture, so Abby left her phone in her pocket.

That afternoon, they drove to the notary. The car smelled of cold polyester and old plastic—a scent found in no American Uber. Eliza sighed every few minutes; Leah kept asking why everything had to take so long. Abby explained that it was for her grandmother, who wanted to settle things before moving into a care home—" just in case something happens." That, she thought, was the Dutch way of saying goodbye: procedural, drama-proof, no gaps in logic.

The notary was young, barely older than she had been when she left for New York. He spoke with a soft Brabant accent, wore Nikes under his tailored suit, mispronounced her name, yet was efficient and kind. She signed without reading; once you'd learned to approve by instinct, you gladly left the details to experts. She almost laughed when he asked if she wanted coffee. "Real or instant?" she said. For a second, she thought she saw pity flash across his face, but no—it was just professionalism polished to neutrality.

On the drive back, the girls sat whispering and texting in the back seat, their heads bent together. Abby sensed they were slowly, definitively excluding her. Did it bother her? She thought of Matthijs, of his lanky in-between jokes, the weightless tone of their messages, always skimming the surface, never revealing what lay beneath. A skill he had handed down perfectly to their daughters, whether they liked it or not.

At home, Geertruida was crumbling spirits over custard; her brain demanded dessert daily, as if sweetness were the only valid closure left. This, Abby thought, is what happens when you never discuss anything but the practical: your descendants grow allergic to grand narratives, yet fluent in small pleasures. It wound her. Here she was, years ahead of Manhattan in restraint, ending up among the only people who could reduce life to coffee, cake, and a walk.

That night, she lay between her daughters in the guest bed, their legs tangled, her heart surprisingly calm. She counted their breaths—the irregular rhythm of sleeping and half-waking. Leah dreamt aloud, Eliza kept turning, and the mattress creaked. The day rested inside her like a warm coat. That was all.

The return flight left Saturday morning, precisely on time—neither the Dutch railways nor Geertruida tolerated delay. At the airport, his mother handed her the tulips, wrapped in plastic, and half a kilo of pea soup in a Tupperware box. "For when you get homesick," she said, dryly. Abby laughed, wondering which of them would last longer without a home. She hugged his mother, this time with a touch more conviction, and felt something pass between them in the way they let go.

The girls peeked from around the corner, already set to depart. They snapped a quick selfie with the gate behind them, their faces pressed together. Abby looked at the screen and thought: *So this is it.* The inheritance is always digital—except for the stories you don't carry with you. His mother would have predicted as much, though it only now became true. Abby watched her girls slip back into Airport America—oversized Disney mascots, expensive luggage brands, doughnuts on every corner. Holding the tulips, she felt like a museum piece, an artifact with a built-in expiry date.

At the gate, the girls fidgeted. Leah held the bouquet tight, afraid the stems might snap in transit. Eliza laughed, claiming customs or humidity would kill them anyway. "I bet they'll end up in the trash," she said, and Leah shrugged in that unbothered, twelve-year-old way—half anarchist, half survivor. Abby tried not to let her face collapse. Truth was, she almost hoped the tulips wouldn't make it through U.S. Customs; then she'd have an excuse to leave them behind, a brief, merciful offering.

Boarding went as always—too fast, too loud, too cramped. On the plane, she pretended to sleep while every image of the week replayed in her head. She could still hear his mother's voice, long after it had faded, that background hum of parental certainty—never entirely quieted. She laughed softly to herself that she missed it, even here, high above the ocean.

After landing—jet lag instantly back in full effect—she gathered her daughters and inhaled Manhattan again. Did she expect it to feel different, to have left something behind? Within an hour, the chill of the old country had evaporated; habits returned with alarming speed. She made pizza, set milk on the table, folded herself back into the rhythm of American domesticity as if she'd never left. Even her inbox offered no reproach.

Later, when the girls slept, and the apartment felt tight but truly hers, Abby placed his mother's tulips in a vase. They did their best—the stems already bruised, the leaves limp—but the blooms held their ground, stubborn for a few more days. *Maybe things need to wilt,* she thought, *before you can try them again.* Between worlds, between times, all you could do was let everything drip through and make the best of what remained, even when no single moment stayed intact.

She'd call his mother later, send a voice message, the way she always did when visits fell short of what they should've been. But first, a glass of water, a laptop, and a little catching up. As long as her daughters slept and the flowers held out, nothing could touch her. She scrolled through old messages from Matthijs—where he was now, whether he truly missed the girls or only himself reflected in their memories. That's how it went, Abby knew: in the end, all that remains are the fragments you pass on, and a future of daughters just like their mothers, pushing them gently back into recognition.

She looked at the tulips and decided: next time she'd bring them again, if only to see how long they'd last. She closed her laptop, slipped under the covers, and felt the city around her not as pressure, but as the only way to keep everything moving. Half an hour later, Leah spoke in her sleep, her voice hoarse, as if she hadn't quite left the Netherlands behind. Abby smiled in the dark; even in America, something kept calling them back.

In the morning, they sat at the kitchen table, three suitcases still unpacked, tulip petals scattered on the counter. Eliza pulled her breakfast closer; Leah spilled juice across the table. Abby asked if they were all right, if it felt strange to be home again.

"Everyone's the same," said Eliza, her mouth full. Leah nodded, trying to smile with apple slices in her cheeks. No drama, no grand narratives—just the rhythm of return. Abby felt relief settle in her chest. Maybe that was all a mother could do: make sure landings were never completely painful.

She cleared the table, tossed the first wilted petals into the trash, and felt calmer than she had in weeks. There were no lessons to draw. Maybe it was enough to repeat the pattern—to leave, to return, and to live enough in between to pass something on to your daughters, and maybe, one day, to theirs.

A new day. It simply began again. Abby switched on the kettle. Manhattan was exactly as she'd left it. She smiled to herself, turned around, and watched her children, growing faster and faster while she herself kept circling back to where it had all begun.

The rhythm resumed with practiced ease: morning, frying pan, the near-argument over who got the bathroom last. Abby tried, as the days fell apart again in rapid sequence, to catch the current of her working life—meetings over the children's noise, Singapore questions during the dishes, preferably without visible interruption. But it was no use; her head lived on two continents at once—and so did her daughters.

She wondered if Leah and Eliza carried something from the trip, a relic of home tucked inside them. She would say,

"You must be homesick," but got back only half-filled school planners, deadlines, and demands—a miniature bureaucracy, just like before. Only at night, in a small pause, when Leah opened her atlas and traced her finger along the IJsselmeer, did something flicker beneath the skin: a sliver of the Netherlands hidden between the pages.

One Tuesday afternoon, as rain licked Manhattan with the seriousness of an urgent job, Leah stood by the window, staring through the double glass. She picked at her sweater, pressed her shoulder to her mother's, as if waiting for a secret transmission.

"Is it weird," she asked after a while, "that I don't know where I like it best?"

Abby nodded—not out of empathy, but because she didn't know either. Or rather: she knew exactly. But the answer was too small, too plain, too American, perhaps.

"You don't have to choose," Abby said at last, half-embracing her daughter — an arm, a bit of shoulder, a head tucked beneath her chin.

It felt like a change in law — that she didn't have to choose, that two stories could coexist, both equally true. *Who writes this down?* she wondered. *Who keeps a record of a family in motion?*

That night she opened her laptop and worked through the hours, clearing mail after mail, pushing herself through a thick sediment of caffeine and fatigue — anything to avoid the question of whether she still had roots anywhere. Somewhere in between, she patched the gap with plans for next year: another trip, another flight, best of both worlds. A hypothetical balance, a fine piece of projection, a perfect athlete in detached parenthood.

By the end of the week, she noticed the tulips were still standing.

They'd lost all color; their leaves threw angular shadows across the counter, but somehow they kept together, like a failed line-up. She thought of his mother, who, with her clear, unsentimental logic, would have thrown them out days ago. Sentiment didn't belong in a household that ran on repetition. Still, Abby let them stay a while longer. For form's sake. For process.

No day was quite like the last. The girls were two weeks back into rhythm; Leah had lost her fear of tests, Eliza's hair had grown too fast again, which turned every morning into a cold war over the bathroom. Abby finished work fifteen minutes later than planned each evening, yet the panic over those minutes had somehow dissolved. She was surprised at how quickly the trip had flattened into a desktop folder, a half-memory in her children's timelines — and nothing more.

Until one spring week that arrived like a coat a size too small, a sliver of the Netherlands slipped through her day.

She came home with groceries — too much comfort food, because it was raining and the messages from Singapore weren't kind. The girls were bent over their homework, relaxed, half whispering to each other. For a moment, Abby felt like an intruder, as though she'd interrupted their quiet world. Leah whispered to Eliza, who raised a hand without looking up. They'd been like that lately — conspiratorial, self-sufficient, barely leaving room for her.

On the counter stood her mother's tulips, now truly dried to paper — once meant to be thrown away, now too cowardly to part with. She ran her thumb along a brittle petal and brushed the flakes into the sink. *Might as well*, she thought. *If only to make space again.*

From the kitchen came Eliza's soft singing — not a real song, just a phrase looping without beginning or end. Abby stayed quiet; interrupting children in their flow always broke something. Eliza had tied her hair up and half-turned. "Is Dad coming this summer?" she asked, not really to anyone. Leah ducked under the table as if she'd dropped something.

Abby set down the milk carton and said, "Maybe. Depends on if he's working."

She felt the line too much, tasted its defense, but it needed to be said.

The girls nodded. Even Eliza. It felt like an agreement.

In the hallway, Abby looked for her planner. She flipped through it, reading what she'd promised herself for the month: routines, progress, deadlines. No space for visitors, no space for fathers who treated time like an amoeba. But the thought lingered — maybe the girls needed him as much as they needed her.

She opened a new email, typed his address, watched the blank field breathe for a few seconds, then wrote: *We could plan a week in July, if you'd like. Let me know.* She kept it bare. No extra punctuation, no photo of the flowers — though she wouldn't have minded sending one.

Her finger hovered above *send*, as if she still needed approval from an older version of herself.

Then she pressed it. Wiped her hands on her jeans. Drank a full glass of cold water.

Strange how little it took to shift direction — a few words, a date, the quiet threat that summer might unfold differently than expected.

That evening, after dinner, Abby worked through her inbox, lingered over a chart of faltering quarterly results, and wondered about the day when none of it would matter anymore. Not yet, but someday, when her daughters would have entirely replaced her part in recording memories. She wondered what their version would look like — this week, this spring, this peculiar mix of countries in their veins.

The next morning, she found Leah in the living room, buried in an old atlas.

Leah looked up briefly and asked, "Can you remember everything from when you were little?" Abby hesitated in the doorway, afraid to step too close, as if her presence might turn the question into something heavier.

"Not everything," she said. "Some of it you invent to fill the gaps. But most of the magic stays."

Leah turned a page, tracing a faint pencil line along the edge of the North Sea.

"Maybe you only remember things once you know they'll disappear," she murmured — soft enough to make it sound unimportant.

Abby closed the door behind her, the ghost of her mother's hand echoing faintly in her own. Maybe Leah was right: you only remember what you can't hold, or what you long to miss.

She thought of his mother, who never said *I miss you,* but passed it on through a poorly timed bouquet, or a half-sentence tucked between the lines. Maybe the trick was to keep longing from hardening into regret; to let it flow, even when the details washed away.

By the end of the week, everything had settled again — hurried, taut, but steadier somehow. The girls argued over homework, Abby lost herself in work, and at night they ate pizza on the couch, watching a series nobody truly cared about. Yet it didn't feel like transit anymore; it felt like staying, at least for now.

Before bed, they each wandered down the hallway — Eliza brushing her teeth too loudly, Leah drifting with her book. Abby paused outside their door and listened. She caught just a fragment: *"Maybe you can have both, and that's enough."*

Maybe that was true, Abby thought — that you didn't have to choose, as long as you left room for everything to be equally real. As if it didn't matter where you took root, as long as you dared to grow.

Later, when the girls slept, and she loaded the dishwasher in the dark, Abby thought about summer. How the light in Manhattan would soon pour out like liquid asphalt, how the heat would thicken between their bodies until everything they did slowed to syrup. Maybe — just maybe — they'd really spend that July week with Matthijs, some inverted form of family no one yet had a word for.

She checked her phone: a new message from Matthijs. Four words — *Yes. Let me know.* No punctuation, no emotion. Abby waited before replying. She didn't need to release everything at once. Better to hold it a little longer, inside her own version of home.

She noticed how much softer the city sounded now, after a winter that had clung to her like wet fabric. The girls were growing, the days crowding, yet for the first time in a long while, Abby felt one step ahead of her mother's shadow — not behind it.

The next morning, she chose a vase from the cupboard, filled it with new flowers, and smiled at herself. It was nothing. It was everything.

And maybe that was what made it a good story.

Afternoon in Manhattan.

The girls were delirious over a new TikTok trend: Eliza had duct-taped a fake mustache to her lip, Leah coached her in exaggerated English like a deranged flight attendant. Abby had to admit — it made no sense, yet Eliza's voice was eerily close to how certain CEOs opened their calls: abrasive American tones, glitching subtext. Within minutes, the girls had cleaned the floor (hair stripped from the tape) and laughed their mother's morning stress away.

By breakfast's end, the impressions of the Netherlands had already drained from their systems. A week later, they were fighting over weekend plans — who could hang out at a new friend's penthouse above Central Park ("but her house has its own elevator!"). Abby said yes, as long as the homework got done, but something in her tightened — a strange ache for simplicity, perhaps, for a time when their greatest joy was a bowl of custard and a bedtime story.

She thought of summer again. There would come a moment — somewhere between Matthijs's third beer and the carton of chocolate milk on his mother's balcony — when more would be said than in all those weeks of email. Maybe it wouldn't even need to be profound: a talk before bed, something about roots, about remembering, about how you don't always have to know where you belong.

She just hoped she wouldn't fall short — that her daughters would feel free to decide which parts of their story to keep, and which ones to let go.

…the parts of their story worth keeping.

That evening, Abby sent her mother-in-law a photo of the girls — both with vacuum-tight face masks, their skin porcelain-white. *"Techniques don't change much over generations,"* she typed beneath it.

Geertruida replied faster than expected: *"As long as your face remains visible."*

That was it. No emojis, no elaboration.

She placed the vase — now filled with plastic lilies from the dollar store — at the head of the table, slightly out of sight. Out-of-season tulips, but at least these would last. She noticed the girls no longer even looked at them. Perhaps they were relics. Perhaps routine. Or maybe just practical, in case the table got messy.

The week swelled toward a crescendo of deadlines and parent-teacher meetings. Eliza had to do an *oral history* project for history class — about family. Abby thought about the subtleties: the hinge moments, the migrations, those European roots that had never quite taken in New York water. She decided not to interfere, just to see what Eliza would make of it.

The result came as a PowerPoint — four slides, hardly any text, but full of photo collages. First slide: a selfie beneath the Gouda cheese market.

CHAPTER 3
BELIEFS AND CONSEQUENCES

Every morning, Miriam Goldstein woke with the suffocating sense that a world needed saving again—if not the entire world, then at least one crumbly square meter of Tel Aviv. She sank into the worn-out armchair facing the window, where the daylight poured through like rough sand, and checked her phone.

No new messages from the Activist Collective.

Three missed calls from her mother.

Five classic "witness reports" from neighbors warning of yet another stray cat terrorizing the street.

One contamination alert.

And—oh yes—a text from Naomi.

"At the garden. No coffee left. x"

Miriam cupped the cold espresso mug from last night. Empty. Of course. Naomi was always a few minutes ahead in everything—coffee, confrontation, even the kind of awkward morning conversations that serious activist types weren't supposed to have. Like mother, like daughter.

She opened her laptop. The blue-white homepage light blinked awake, and headlines loaded like incoming disasters: Member of Parliament threatened. Women's March dispersed. Housing crisis deepens. The dollar drops again. Miriam nodded grimly, shoulders tightening, as though her acknowledgment alone could validate the chaos. She shared the articles on her feed, typed a few polemical tweets, and closed the laptop. The day now had its battle lines drawn.

In the kitchen, Naomi was bent over the counter, curls tied in a messy knot, hands buried in the soil of a cardboard box filled with half-forgotten bean plants. The scent of damp earth, of coffee grounds, of her chamomile shampoo drifted through the air. No makeup—never had any. Her skin glowed with the defiance of youth and the stubborn optimism that came with it.

Miriam watched her daughter scrape dirt from under her nails. Those hands—she knew them. They had once been small, grasping for her own index finger in the dark. Now they looked like hers: sinewy, restless, always working.

"Want some tea?" she asked, trying to sound casual.

Naomi shook her head, a quick, colliding gesture—her default form of resistance. "I'm going to the district office meeting. They want to tear down the garden for another parking lot."

Miriam nodded. "I'll come too, after my interview with Channel 12. They want to know if I think the university's shifted too far to the right."

"Do you?"

She shrugged—half performance, half genuine fatigue. "They've all shifted right. That's the disease these days."

Naomi transferred a seedling to a smaller pot, tucking it in with a thin blanket of soil. "Then maybe we should do something radical. Go social media?" Hands on her hips now, her posture turned into a small fortress.

Miriam smiled—a flicker of relief sparking in her chest. Born negotiator, she thought. "You know how that goes. They don't listen."

"That's why we have to shout louder." Naomi wiped her hands on her jeans, splattering already dry mud with fresh smudges.

Miriam sat down at the kitchen table, arms crossed in that old activist pose that felt too formal at home. Without the cameras, she always felt exposed. She grabbed a mandarin from the fruit bowl—food for thought—and began peeling it with unnecessary vigor.

"You didn't read my message to that guy last week," Naomi said suddenly, in that tone that balanced perfectly between complaint and reason. "We agreed: no more poster campaigns. We'd make it performance art this time. Guerrilla, not graphics."

"And?" Miriam asked sharply, the citrus scent biting at her thumb.

"And you posted a picture of the posters anyway. With my name tagged."

Silence. Miriam tore a wedge from the fruit and pressed it between her lips. How many of her battles had she sacrificed to bad communication and half-baked hashtag campaigns? She swallowed.

"They found it immediately at the university," Naomi said, quieter now. "I'm not scared, but… sometimes I wonder if you realize that I'm the one who gets the backlash now."

The room turned colder. Above the fridge hung an old Polaroid of a smaller Naomi—her first protest, cheeks red with pride, Miriam beside her, one heavy hand resting protectively on that miniature shoulder. Everyone had to learn to fight somewhere.

She pushed her chair back, got up without a word, and rummaged through a cabinet for the right tea—the calming kind Naomi always mocked. Chamomile, of course.

"You just have to stay yourself," Miriam said finally. "Let them call you radical. You're not your mother."

Naomi sniffed, almost smirking. "Maybe I don't always want to be myself if it hurts, you know?"

The kettle shrieked. Miriam poured two mugs, the air filling with the faint illusion of calm—a small infection of peace, she called it, when she tried to hand her daughter something soothing, like a stuffed animal that had lost its fur. She blew on her tea, impatiently, until the surface trembled.

Sometimes she wondered if all this inherited rage amounted to anything, or if it was just their way of giving powerlessness an acceptable soundtrack. Everything lately felt like a variation on survival—the fight, the noise, the shutting out of dust and headlines.

"Mom?" Naomi cupped her mug with both hands, her nail beds packed with soil—new life wedged under the skin.

"I was thinking of calling that community bank. They're looking for young representatives for their social project."

Miriam paused mid-sip. She weighed the words, then nodded. "You'd be great at that. But you know they'll screen everything—every protest, every sit-in. They'll want your entire history."

"So?" Naomi's chin lifted, that familiar defiance hardening her jaw.

"So nothing. Just be ready for the questions." Miriam set her mug down gently, as if too much honesty might crack it.

They never meant to wound each other—or so they told themselves. But every conversation felt like a sparring match no one wanted to win, and still, there were bruises. Miriam thought of her own mother, sneaking home after midnight protests, silence thick as judgment until morning.

"Maybe it's time we did something practical," she said. "Something that doesn't need a megaphone."

Naomi grinned, bright and sharp in the backlight. "And if I do want a megaphone? Can I borrow yours?"

"Always," Miriam said, laughing for real this time, her shoulders finally dropping out of fight mode. The porcelain cup was warm against her cheek—a tiny reward.

The conversation didn't end so much as dissolve, the way peace sometimes does when neither side insists on winning. Naomi tidied the soil and wiped the counter. Miriam looked out the window at the pale light spreading over the city, trying to see the day as something still colorable.

For the first time in weeks, she wanted to call her mother back. Maybe that, too, was a kind of resistance—refusing to play the role history had written for you. She winked at Naomi, who rolled her eyes and grabbed her bag, already halfway out the door to the next meeting. You have to dare to take root, Miriam thought. Even if you're afraid the wind will find you.

The day unfolded looser than she'd expected. Miriam moved through her appointments, interviews, group chats— a swarm of causes. Sometimes a name would flash across her screen and jolt her: an old lover, a once-friend turned political opposite. The same chill that had crept through the kitchen returned each time, easily masked with irony.

By mid-afternoon, she stood outside Channel 12, a steel box lost between half-demolished buildings in South Tel Aviv. She lit a cigarette—her first in months—and waited for her name to be called. Two young producers, barely older than Naomi, greeted her with that hybrid of admiration and suspicion reserved for the once-relevant. She followed them down narrow hallways, nerves slick under her blouse.

The interview was gentler than she'd feared; sometimes it was easier to talk to strangers than to convince your own child. When it ended, someone offered her a strong coffee— the kind that doubles as both gratitude and dismissal. She drank it outside among the rusting bikes and torn flyers, then texted Naomi:

"What time's your meeting? Good luck. x Mom."

Five seconds later:

"Six. They're bringing shirts. Break at 7:15. See you?"

"I'll be there. Bringing baklava."

She held the phone in her hand a little too long, as if it might reply on its own.

The walk home was slower than usual. Miriam moved through the soft chaos of the city—the half-built towers, the scent of falafel oil cooling on the evening air, the muezzin's voice melting into the shrill hum of traffic. She let herself be carried, step by step, until the words from the interview began to fade, replaced by something quieter, something domestic.

When she reached her street, the light had already shifted to that mild orange hour when everything seems briefly possible. Through the open window, she could hear laughter—Naomi's, unmistakable, bright and stubborn.

Inside, the apartment smelled of garlic and laundry detergent. On the table, a vase stood like a witness: filled with plastic lilies from the dollar store, their white petals catching the last sunlight.

For a moment, Miriam stood there, uncertain. The lilies had been Naomi's idea, a joke first—" eternal flowers for eternal causes"—but they'd stayed maybe because they required nothing, maybe because they outlasted everything real.

She moved them slightly out of sight, to the corner of the table. A tulip out of season, but at least it stood straight. She smiled to herself; some compromises were just the shape of living.

"Hey," Naomi called from the kitchen. "You were great on TV. Grandma texted me—said you looked tired but 'convincing.' Whatever that means."

Miriam laughed. "It means I didn't say anything she disagreed with."

Naomi appeared in the doorway, barefoot, phone still in hand. "She said she might send you that old photo of the protest in Haifa. The one with the red flags."

"Oh, God," Miriam muttered. "That one should've burned with the archives."

Naomi grinned. "Too late. She said she's keeping it for Eliza's history project."

"Eliza?" Miriam blinked. "Who's Eliza?"

"My cousin," Naomi said, mock-dramatic. "You know, the overachiever who builds PowerPoints like she's coding the revolution?"

Right. The family project. Oral history. Roots that never quite took.

Miriam leaned vagainst the table, rubbing a spot of dried tea from the wood. "And what's her angle?"

"Four slides," Naomi said, counting on her fingers. "One: a selfie under the Gouda cheese market. Two: Grandma with the tulips. Three: You at some rally with a bullhorn. Four: Me planting beans in the community garden."

"Multigenerational trauma chic," Miriam said dryly. "Very 21st century."

Naomi rolled her eyes. "You could at least be proud."

"I am," Miriam said, softer now. "Just surprised she found a story at all."

Outside, the sky was bruising into blue. Somewhere a siren began its lonely spiral, rising, falling, as if marking time.

They sat down to eat—the kind of dinner that wasn't really a dinner, just pieces of bread and leftover lentils. Naomi talked about the community meeting: the endless arguments, the way people circled the same fears like hungry cats.

"They want to pave over everything," she said. "Even the fig tree."

"Then you'll have to climb it first," Miriam said, smiling.

Naomi laughed, then grew quiet. "Sometimes I think you already fought all the good fights. What's left for us are the ruins."

Miriam looked at her daughter and saw, in that face, the echo of her own at twenty-two—defiant, exhausted, luminous. "Then build something on the ruins," she said. "That's the only thing we ever really get to do."

A pause. The silence between them wasn't cold, only full.

After dinner, Miriam washed the dishes while Naomi scrolled through messages. Every so often, she'd read one aloud—a meme, a protest update, a rumor about a new policy—and they'd share a look that was half disbelief, half amusement.

By the time the plates were stacked, the world outside had slipped entirely into night. Miriam felt the familiar weight of fatigue, that strange mix of duty and tenderness that came after too much talking.

She thought of her mother again, and of all the women before her—each convinced the next generation would fix what they could not. Maybe inheritance wasn't blood or ideology, but the stubborn insistence to keep trying, even when the effort itself felt absurd.

Naomi yawned, stretching like a cat. "I'm meeting the team early tomorrow. We're making shirts—'Save the Soil,' I think."

"Good slogan," Miriam said. "Short, honest, impossible."

Naomi laughed, already halfway to her room. "You sound like my editor."

When she was gone, Miriam stood for a while by the window. The plastic lilies reflected faintly in the glass, almost real in the dim light. She touched one of the petals; it was cool, perfectly still.

A single line beneath it:

"Techniques don't change much over generations."

Miriam typed back before she could stop herself:

"As long as the face remains visible."

Send.

That was it. No emojis. No elaboration.

She turned off the light, leaving only the city's glow to color the room. For a second, everything looked paused— like an unfinished thought waiting to be named.

Miriam lay down, eyes open, the weight of the day softening against her skin. Somewhere, faintly, she heard Naomi laugh again, from another room, or maybe just from memory.

She smiled into the dark.

"Beautiful," she whispered to no one in particular.

The silence was too heavy; she regretted it the moment it left her mouth. But it lingered for a second, long enough for the woman with the red glasses to smile, amused, and for the man beside her to nod slowly, spinning her words further.

"Brave," the woman said unexpectedly. "Radical transparency. You don't hear that often from your generation."

It wasn't quite a compliment — more curiosity than praise.

There was more talk after that, but what Naomi remembered most was the tremor in her hand as she reached for her glass of water. She could still hear her own words echoing when she stepped outside into the cool night. Rain clattered against the roofs; her phone buzzed like a nervous bird.

Two missed calls from an Unknown Number.

One message from her mother: So proud. And I brought baklava — vegan, don't worry.

She laughed at how predictable it was, yet her nerves still quivered down her spine. Pulling her coat tight around her ears, she crossed the square. Just as she ducked under an awning, her phone vibrated again — not an unknown number this time, but Dad (NL).

She stared at the screen until it stopped, but kept looking until it started again.

She answered.

"Hey, it's Matthijs."

Silence. She could hear the echo of his kitchen cupboards on the line, maybe the tap of a ring against a glass.

"Hi," she said, briefly. She'd almost forgotten how he sounded — that half-cracked tone, as if every word stumbled into existence by accident.

"I saw your talk, you know. Really good. You owned that room."

He said it so easily, as if they'd spoken just yesterday.

Naomi said nothing. She thought of the evenings at her grandparents' house by the Amstel — how Matthijs always arrived late, then charmed the whole family into forgiving him within three minutes.

"What did you want, Dad?" she asked faster than she meant to.

"Your mother sent me the clip — that meeting with that odd woman in the red eighties sweater. You were the only one still sitting upright."

"She's my supervisor," Naomi said. She hated how quickly he could turn her world into parody. Yet somehow it felt familiar, almost comforting.

"You're right, though — about that radical transparency thing," he said, pausing long enough for her to imagine him rolling a cigarette. "In my day — God, I sound ancient — in my day, we thought you had to hack the system from the inside. But you lot... You just want to start over. Out in the open. That's not cowardice, that's—"

"Stupid, according to most people," Naomi cut in.

"Nah. You just need allies who can listen as well as shout. Listen — I'll be around tomorrow. Maybe we can talk, no audience this time?"

He must have heard her hesitation, the held breath that meant I don't know, but there was no click, no end.

Instead, she felt her shoulders drop.

"You gonna call more often?" she heard herself ask, half-joking, half-testing.

Matthijs laughed softly. "Only if you pick up. And only when you say something that annoys me this much. Tomorrow then?"

She wanted to say something like we'll see or probably not, but what came out was a simple, unguarded: "Yeah."

Then the line clicked.

Her socks were soaked through. Waiting for the bus, she jammed her hands into her coat pockets. The neighborhood seemed to breathe — inhaling damp, exhaling through vents and cracks. Even indoors, the walls looked wet. She thought of evenings long ago, that dark core of the living room where adults folded themselves around her, their voices a kind of blunt cushion — loud, but safe.

She didn't know if her mother was cooking now or stuck in another meeting. She scrolled through her phone — it felt like touching the skin of the world. Sometimes she wanted to delete her entire profile, let every trace of herself dissolve like vinegar loosening chalk. Why not? Someone would screenshot her anyway.

Home in 15, baklava's in the fridge, she typed to Miriam, adding an X out of habit, not affection.

In the kitchen, only the light above the sink was on. The box of baklava sat on the counter, its soft, sticky scent mixed with leftover falafel warmth. Miriam was in her office, perched on her chair with a headset on, her voice firing like a machine gun through the glass panel. Naomi couldn't hear the words, but the rhythm told her enough — her mother's voice always took on that granite edge when it mattered.

She made two cups of tea and set them down. There was no point trying to talk mid-meeting; Miriam could rage on for hours without a pause. Naomi cut two squares of baklava, ate them both, the sugar pressing against her teeth like furniture.

She scrolled again — old photos of her father, interviews, half-forgotten essays. In every picture, he was laughing as if he'd just dropped something valuable off-screen, always on the move. She tried to remember his smell, but it was too vague — blurred into other people's stories.

"Even in Israel," he had once said, "you can get lost in your own house."

She smiled despite herself — that same dry laugh of his, half smoke, half wine.

He'd laughed the same way tonight, she realized. Maybe he hadn't changed much. Maybe none of them had.

Even the rain had begun to slow when she reached home. The apartment smelled faintly of cinnamon and crushed sesame, the hum of overheated laptops filling the silence. Miriam stood at the counter, hands covered in crumbs, her face caught between worry and relief.

"How was it?" she asked without turning around, her voice carrying a small tear in it.

"Good. Actually… good."

Naomi hung her damp coat over a chair and snatched a piece of baklava from the tray — sticky-sweet, but solid underneath.

"And I've got news. Or, well, something weird."

Miriam spun around, as if she already knew. Her eyes flashed, then softened.

"He called you."

Naomi nodded, mouth full of syrup. "Yeah. It was… okay."

For once, there was no need to turn it into an argument. They left it hovering between them — a shared quiet, suspended somewhere between sugar and screenlight. Miriam leaned back against the counter, a faint shadow under her eyes, her face open, rinsed clean after the storm.

"If you want," she said, "you can bring them to the Forum.

"Both?"

"Both. Why not? Maybe we'll get more out of stroopwafels than opinions."

Miriam smiled — brief, secretive, like a private joke between exhausted allies.

Naomi listened to the static hum on the other end —
wind, a flicking lighter, the muffled chatter of Dutch news
radio. His voice had aged: rougher, slower, no longer afraid
of silence.

"Is something wrong, Dad?" She caught it herself —
that odd hitch in her voice, the tiny pull of a child's hope
tightening her muscles.

"I just wanted to know how you're doing, Naooms.
That's all. Your mother said you've been…" He swallowed
the rest of the sentence, hiding it somewhere behind his
teeth. "Those things have been hard. Are you happy there?"

She thought of the kitchen table, her curls damp with
rain, the leaking vegan falafel in her bag, her mother with a
box of baklava on the way home. Sweat was clinging to her
shirt.

"I'm fine," she said. "It's just… a lot sometimes."

"That's how it goes."

She swallowed the flimsy comfort, wishing he could
blast her world open with an old-fashioned father's gesture
— a rescue, a ridiculous souvenir from the NEMO museum,
anything. Still, it felt good to hear his voice, even if it fixed
nothing.

"I'll be in town next month," Matthijs said after a pause. "For work. Maybe we could have coffee? You pick the place."

"Deal. But only if you don't start on the whole 'you're an adult now' speech."

"Never!" He laughed, a cough breaking through. "I'm proud of you, idiot. Your mother thinks I'm cynical, but I'm just jealous — you actually dare to be radical. I never did."

A strange calm settled over her. Nothing had changed, but the tension dropped a notch, like a bass line gone soft.

"See you soon, Dad."

"Till then, sweetheart," he said — and the line went dead.

She kept staring at the dim glow of her screen, little blades of grass leaving wet streaks across the glass. Then she braved the last stretch of rain home, the pomegranate seeds rattling in her bag, the falafel box sticky with false promises.

At the door, Miriam was wrestling with a box of baklava — her fingers honey-glued, a smear of mascara on her cheek.

"Tough day?" Naomi asked, no sarcasm this time.

"Standard. But two Gen-Z kids at Channel 12 called me inspiring."

Of course they did. Only your own generation could truly overtake you. Miriam wrapped a strip of paper towel around her finger, dabbing at the sticky edges of the box. Naomi leaned on the counter, watching her mother give herself half a minute of permission not to look indestructible.

"Channel 12?" she asked, tearing off a syrupy piece of pastry.

"I attract the modern kind of groupie these days. Seems practical, until you realize they review everything in emojis."

"You should try it," Naomi said. She knew that kind of irony — a balm disguised as banter, a dusting of humor over an open wound.

Miriam snorted, eyes fixed briefly on the tiled floor. "They talk about a generation gap, but I just see a small step. I understand your instinct. Theoretically." Her voice tilted — a flicker of softness before snapping back to its usual wit.

Naomi prodded the center of the baklava with her fork, as if to prove she could pinpoint the core of everything herself. She wondered whether her mother had ever wanted a father figure — not the real one, but the kind who sits with port and quietly absorbs the news.

"He called you a lunatic," Naomi said with a grin. "Matthijs. Said he never dared to do what you did."

"That sounds exactly like him." Miriam's smile was too practiced, as if already rehearsing for disappointment. "Think it'll be worth it tomorrow? A forum without cameras?"

"There'll be pizza slices. That guarantees an audience." Naomi pictured herself at one of those overfilled tables, her mother's arms a mix of anchor and engine. The friction between them — eternal, exhausting — hurt less tonight. More like the ache after a long run.

Miriam scooped tea from a faded tin. "You know where we'll crash halfway through, right?" She didn't expect Naomi to understand, but her daughter's look said she already did. Maybe that was the only way family worked — constant mutual translation.

"If he gets annoying, I'll tell you word for word," Naomi said, her tone light, hands clasped around her mug. "Same goes for you."

They sat at the kitchen island — not as opponents in a ceasefire, but as witnesses to each other's stubborn endurance. The silence had a new flavor, less bitter, more like something baked and cooling. Miriam felt it as a fragile advantage: if you belonged nowhere, no one could exile you.

"Good," said Miriam. "Then we'll make sure there's always food."

Naomi laughed softly — cold still in her hair, syrup on her fingertips. For a moment, their Tel Aviv apartment didn't need to save the world. They simply held their mugs, as if morning would never again catch them off guard.

Then — a shuffle in the hallway, the rattle of the pipes, and an eager ringtone out of nowhere.

Miriam rolled her eyes — probably another building group chat, the thirty-ninth emergency of the day. But Naomi was quicker, snatching her phone, reading in silence.

"They suspended the meeting," she said finally. "People are angry. Someone made my quote go viral. They're all fighting in the thread."

Miriam burst out laughing — not meanly, but with an old glimmer of pride breaking through scar tissue.

"Then tomorrow you'll be twice as good," she said. "Extra baklava if needed."

Naomi thought of Matthijs, of his cardboard hotel rooms and too-early nostalgia; she thought of her mother, her comfort in conflict, the soft floor beneath every word-war.

She wiped the syrup from her fingers, smiled at the dim kitchen light, and let the evening settle. Tomorrow would come — inevitably — but for now, that felt like a damn solid accomplishment.

She looked down at the papers on the counter, their colors bleeding. "You know," Naomi said quietly, "I think I get him. And you. Maybe we're just weird mutations of the same gene." She grinned, wiping sticky fingers on her jeans.

Miriam tilted her head, half amused. Mutation — it sounded like a diagnosis that grew mushrooms on your tongue. Still, she watched her daughter's hands, steady now around the mug, no longer trembling.

"As long as you know you can do anything," Miriam said. "You can even skip the future if it doesn't suit you."

Naomi nodded — a small, almost kind gesture. She packed the rest of the baklava into a Tupperware, as if it were a task with a beginning, middle, and end. Then they slipped together into the night. No more words. Miriam scrolled through a drained Twitter feed; Naomi watched videos that lit her face from within.

That night, Miriam lay awake, her back carved into the mattress, a restless itch in her legs. She thought about what Naomi had said — mutation, not gift, not flaw. She loved the quiet that settled when her daughter slept; the certainty that no new disasters would bloom before morning. Even the air in the house felt newly washed.

She heard Naomi whispering on the phone in the hallway — her voice unguarded, soft, almost like a spell. It was a comfort to know that connection still existed, that the history of generational wars hadn't yet consumed the small things.

Miriam got up, made tea, and perched on the couch with a blanket around her shoulders. She thought of her own mother, who used to peek into her room at night, always setting an extra plate in case someone came home hungry. Everything is prepared in advance, and nothing is wasted.

She typed a short email: "Some days I don't manage so well. But today felt surprisingly light. Can you come for coffee?"

She sent it without rereading. There was peace in that kind of vulnerability, she thought — maybe you had to be older to stop finding it embarrassing.

By morning, a little later than usual, Naomi stumbled into the kitchen — eyes puffy, hair a tangle. But something in the air was different, lighter somehow.

"You know what's weird?" she said. "I dreamed I was gardening. But every plant I pulled from its tray had grown back by nightfall. Like none of them wanted to root."

"Maybe they were homesick," said Miriam, wiping the corner of her mouth and looking up.

"Can I pick the tea tomorrow?" Naomi asked, like it was a test.

"You can even pull mint from the garden," Miriam shrugged. "That's how radical we are here."

The evening, despite everything, stayed soft. Naomi slid her feet under her mother's lap, wasted twenty minutes on TikTok, and read her the comment section of the university news in exaggerated voices. Miriam snorted, clutching the counter for balance as Naomi mimicked an ex-Knesset member. Their laughter shook the apartment until the neighbors stomped, which only made them laugh harder.

Naomi fell asleep with her phone pressed to her cheek. She dreamed of opening a protest march that turned, somehow, into a garden party. Instead of banners, there were streamers. Miriam shouted through a megaphone for people to dance harder. At the end of the parade sat her father, sharing a stroopwafel with a low-profile minister, waving at her. Normally, such dreams stuck to her like syrup, but this one floated — a marshmallow after a war of lemon drops.

By morning, Miriam was already bustling about, windows open to air out the previous day's smoke. Naomi stayed in bed a minute longer, listening to her mother's quiet footsteps and smiling at the choreographed silence of their home.

She found Miriam at the kitchen table, surfing on her laptop. The kettle clicked off. Miriam tapped her mug against the ceramic a few times — a nervous, thoughtful rhythm.

"Your father says he's forwarding your forum idea to all of Amsterdam," she said without looking up.

"He's bluffing," Naomi replied, though the thought warmed her.

"And he's sending stroopwafels. Vegan ones, from De Pijp — apparently the place to be."

"As long as they're not stolen from a supermarket."

"You know him." For the first time, Naomi heard no judgment in her mother's voice — just a hint of conspiratorial fondness.

Then, sooner than expected, came the forum: dirty office chairs, the stale breath of old coffee. Naomi pictured herself sharing the stage with people who understood everything just a bit too well — and she wasn't afraid. Her mother cycled beside her, baklava strapped to the carrier, the smell already soaked into their clothes.

During the forum, Miriam held back — not her wit, not her urgency, but space. Sometimes she just looked, jaw working silently, but every time Naomi glanced sideways, she caught her mother's eyes. Not approval, exactly, but a proud sort of sport.

Afterwards, Naomi lingered by the door, a warm glass of cola in her hand. She wanted to fast-forward to the next moment — the one where her father waited on some anonymous curb, no audience required. Still, she let the ritual play out: the aftertalks, the compliments, the near-embarrassing respect from peers who never dared to speak.

The train rocked her toward the other end of the city. The towers outside repeated themselves like tired lines of code. Just past the final stop, her phone buzzed. A text from Matthijs: "Here early. Sitting in a café opposite the exit, looking like a stowaway."

She spotted him immediately — a lamppost of a man in a too-light denim jacket, face five years older than memory allowed. He was arguing with the barista about the vegan menu, but grinned when he saw her.

"Hey, old man," she said, half-teasing. He laughed.

"I had falafel. You're not missing anything."

He ordered her a ginger tea, himself a dark beer. They sat by the window, their reflections overlapping. The first few minutes were about her mother — how she could leap from argument to argument before the previous one had even cooled.

"She says I'm not afraid to speak," Naomi said, hand hovering over her mug.

"You're not," he replied simply. "But you hesitate. I used to, too. Must be in the name."

She tried to read his intent. There was no nostalgia in him, no longing — just the plain recognition of shared DNA. Still, Naomi's body tensed, bracing for impact.

"Why are you only showing up now?" she asked, more bluntly than she'd meant. The question cracked between them like dropped glass.

He laughed, shrugged, eyes on his hands against the white tabletop. "I thought you didn't need me anymore. Or — better said — that you'd figure yourself out without me."

It wasn't an answer, just the same evasive precision her mother used. Naomi felt the energy drain from her shoulders.

"I could still use a father," she said. "Even if I'm not a kid."

"Yeah," he said, this time with nothing but truth. "I get that."

They decided to walk outside, leaving the station behind.

At a corner, Matthijs stopped, brushed a bit of lint from her shoulder.

"Sorry it took me this long," he said. "But you really do look like your mother. Not just in your face — in your… hope."

"She's not hopeful," Naomi corrected him. "She just believes the world's going to shit."

"That's art," he said. "Staring into the abyss and still insisting the glass is half full."

The wrinkles around his eyes folded twice, an old habit that must once have been meant as comfort.

They kept walking, though the pace had gone out of their talk. It could be slow now. Naomi no longer felt watched, tested, or half-admired; only normal for a moment. Just someone's daughter, in a city where no one could interrupt them.

In a bookstore, they were startled by the crash of falling cardboard boxes. The clerk, a nervous boy with cropped hair, nodded at them in a way that immediately cast doubt on his own expression. Naomi had to laugh. They were exactly the kind of people you'd expect here — ex-journalist and semi-activist, both too far in their own heads ever to be fully present.

"Do you ever buy anything?" she asked, sliding along a shelf.

"Never," Matthijs laughed. "I'm a browser. But you?"

She turned, holding up a red-covered book.

"This one's for Mom. Full of unbearable rebuttals." She flipped through the contents, her finger ticking down the list. "You two can compete for another week."

She bought it without hesitation, paid with a debit card still damp from the rain. Matthijs swore affectionately about the price but waited outside by the window display, hands in pockets, shuffling cigarettes into a small cardboard box.

"Heading home already?" he asked, shoulders squared and still.

"Tomorrow," she said. "Today I'll stay with you. That's okay, right?"

"Always."

Nothing dramatic about it, no embrace, no performance. Yet they walked on together, slowly — Naomi with the book under her arm, Matthijs with his head slightly turned away, thinking about nothing, or perhaps everything.

He talked about Amsterdam, about how everything had been sealed shut with the same layer of coffee foam. Naomi listened, absentmindedly peeling the paper off her straw, watching it flutter away and stick to her wrist again. She thought about the baklava at home, about her mother who was surely planning three new protests by now, but also that this, this right here, was another kind of home.

They passed time without an agenda — something that actually suited her better than all the running and rallying. At one point, Matthijs told a strange story about his childhood, a secret boys' club, and a forbidden swing above the dike house. Naomi laughed, but saw on his face that it was more than a joke. There was space in the way he spoke — not to teach her, just to share the air.

By twilight, they were hungry. They found a Chinese place where the menu was mostly pictures. Matthijs ordered vegan noodles, let Naomi pick whatever she wanted, and smoked by the door while she wondered whether his behavior annoyed her or calmed her.

They talked about everything — gardening without pets, what kind of insect they'd be if humans vanished, and why some people found it so hard simply to stay. Naomi told him about the blunt questions at the forum, about how sometimes it was easier to talk to sixty-year-olds than to her own peers, and how it comforted her to know that no generation had ever managed to save itself completely.

When the meal was done, no one suggested who should pay. They split the bill in half — coins sticky with soy sauce. Outside, it had stopped raining.

They sat another half hour in a bus shelter, watching the dark city as if it were a sleeping dog: harmless, as long as you didn't wake it. Naomi asked when his flight was, thinking this would be the moment they said goodbye — but neither of them stood.

"It feels strangely easy now," she said, voice no louder than a muted TV.

Matthijs nodded, that same small, crooked smile. He clicked his pink lighter open and shut. "Maybe that's how it's supposed to be. No grand reunion, just… this."

Naomi thought of how her mother would ruin such moments — a joke, a political statement, anything to keep it from turning too sweet.

So she said, "You can stay next to me a bit longer."

And he did.

"I'm heading back tomorrow," he said casually, "but sooner next time."

"You don't have to promise. This is fine."

He lit his cigarette, offered her a drag. She took it without hesitation. The smoke tickled her cheeks, clung there like a nervous warning.

"You know what it is," he said after a while. "People who think the world must change all at once never appreciate the in-between. But this—" he spread his hands, as if to part the air between them — "this nothingness, that's the good stuff."

Naomi laughed, kicking her heels against the aluminum bench.

"Seriously. My mom would send a meme right now. Something with a retreating penguin."

"And she'd be right. They're the only ones who keep warm."

They leaned into each other in a silence that was finally unawkward. He slipped an arm loosely around her shoulders, and she let it stay, simply because she could.

The bus never came. They walked the last few streets, no hurry, the asphalt still slick beneath their shoes.

Naomi felt nothing holding her back now — not the vague urge to escape the city, not the fear that her mother would shut down whenever her father came up. Everything was simpler than she'd thought: you could just sit, just laugh at your own mistakes, you didn't always have to start a revolution.

Before they parted, on a nearly empty street, he pulled a yellow notebook from his pocket — pages full of spiky handwriting and too many commas. He tore out the front page and folded it into her palm.

"Read it when you can't sleep," he said. "I'm curious if you'll get it."

She tucked it, unread, into her jacket. When she looked back, he was still standing there — no cinematic wave, just a short nod, a cigarette stump between his fingers.

At home, she couldn't sleep. She drank the flat cola from the frosted glass, turned off the lights one by one. It wasn't until morning that she remembered the note.

She pulled it from her pocket, unfolded it. In jagged letters, scratched over and over, it read:

"It takes courage to stay behind. The rest is child's play.

x"

Naomi laughed. It was such a half-baked bit of man-wisdom — and yet, somehow, it felt like a compliment. She set the note on her nightstand, between the plant cuttings and forgotten memories.

In the morning, she woke to the sound of potato peels hitting the sink and the smell of burnt tahini. Miriam sat at the breakfast table, the red book open before her, underlined and marked in pencil.

"Home on time?" she asked, without looking up, hands still peeling mandarins.

Naomi slid into her seat at the table, her coat hanging off the chair, the yellow note pressing softly against her thigh. She nodded — not tired, not awake, just there.

"It was nice. Quiet," she said. "We went to that park."

"You didn't listen to the news? Or protest? Or spy on people for sport?" Her mother's tone was mockingly cheerful, the kind of brightness that tried to prove she could go a day without interfering.

"We talked," Naomi said. "About nothing. About dogs and coffee and half the city."

She ate in small bites, pushing the mandarin pits into a perfect little circle on her plate.

Miriam laughed — not sharply, but with that blanket-warmness of firm opinions. "You think your generation has nothing left to prove. Just wait. You'll run into yourself sooner than you think."

"Probably," Naomi said. She knew her mother was right, but it didn't sting. Maybe it was the rain, maybe the scraps of baklava she'd eaten out of midnight hunger, or maybe the thought that some days didn't have to add up — and that that was enough.

Miriam went back to her book. Naomi brewed tea, picked the flavor with the most unpronounceable herbs, and filled two mugs to the brim. She sat across from her mother, their legs just out of sight from each other's line, and felt a kind of stillness she hadn't known existed when you're always in motion.

"What are you going to do today?" Miriam asked — a little too early, as if already turning the page of the conversation.

"Maybe I'll work in the garden. Maybe not talk to anyone. Maybe sleep," Naomi said. "You can pick."

Her mother turned the page. The cover cracked softly under her fingers, but the book stayed closed.

"Not everything has to be for the world, you know that?"

Naomi nodded, leaned back, let the warmth of the tea climb slowly through her fingers.

She reached into her pocket and unfolded the damp piece of paper. The ink had bled from the rain, but the words still stood — exactly as they were meant: staying behind as an act of courage.

She thought of her father — somewhere in the air or behind a newspaper — and how different he felt now. Or maybe simply how little it took to exist quietly, without trouble, without fight.

She laid the note on the table and pushed it toward her mother.

For half a second, Miriam hesitated — as she always did when something unknown came from someone she loved. She read it silently, no nod, no comment.

But the corners of her mouth lifted — the kind of smile no one else would have dared.

"Nicely said," she murmured.

She folded the paper once and laid it beside her mug, as if it deserved to stay there a while.

The rest of the day went by without any real peaks.

Naomi ran her hands through the soil, wiped rain off the garden chairs, caught her reflection in the window, and saw a crumb of adulthood in her profile.

Her mother called between tasks, worked through sheets and tables, but in a way that no longer felt rushed. There was calm in the idea that nothing ever had to last more than a day.

That evening, they ate together — falafel and salad — Miriam seated at the head of the table, Naomi halfway toward departure.

"Do you think you'll stay?" her mother asked, not as a demand, but as a possibility.

"For now," Naomi said. "Tomorrow might be different."

Miriam laughed that inimitable laugh of hers — that short, breaking sound, like a glass deciding whether or not to crack.

"Everything changes faster than you think," she said. "So enjoy the in-between."

Naomi pushed her plate aside and looked at her mother.

So much fell away in that gaze — the struggle, the generations, the stories of other people. Just two humans, a table of food, and the rest of the evening left to fill.

She thought of Matthijs — maybe already back in that other country, or simply one stop further down the road. She hoped he felt it too: that there was power in doing nothing, that staying could be an act of grace.

They cleaned up together, fed the scraps to the neighbor's cats, and put water on for tea.

When darkness finally settled, and the city lost its sense of direction in the padded quiet, Naomi suddenly laughed.

"Ma'am, remember how you used to say everything is political?"

"Yes. You think I'm taking it back now?"

"No," said Naomi. She folded her father's note around the edge of the teapot. "I just think—sometimes everything's just tea."

And Miriam nodded — maybe as a mother, maybe as a woman, maybe simply as a person.

"That's fine too," she said. "That's fine."

They passed the evening like that — no future needed, no roots demanded, only the warmth that stayed.

Miriam looked at the letters, raised her eyebrows, and instantly recognized the hand — the not-quite-moderate sharpness of Matthijs de Vries.

"Courage as deviation," she read aloud. She pinched the corner of the page and set it straight before her.

"Not bad," she said. "Your father's finally grown up."

"Or I have," said Naomi.

The silence that followed wasn't heavy, not accusatory.

It was the kind of quiet that holds a small nod between two people.

They ate breakfast. The tea smelled stronger than ever, and the city pulsed faintly in the background — like an idea you could almost, but not quite, reach.

Naomi thought about the night ahead, about how life could, in fact, become familiar.

How no one called her Naoms anymore, girl with the future tied to her shoelaces.

Maybe that was enough. The baklava was nearly gone; her mother lifted the last piece as if to toast whatever this was.

"To everything," she said simply.

"To everything," Naomi echoed.

And for the first time, it didn't feel like victory.

It didn't feel like a loss.

It felt like staying.

And that was exactly enough.

Her phone lit up in her pocket: unknown number, with a +31 beside it — as if her old life were suddenly chasing her new one.

She watched the digits pulse. Dutch morning, here nearly midnight.

She could already hear the voice — that slight rasp, always a little too light or too heavy.

She declined the call.

The screen went dark again.

The room was filled with the dull percussion of rain against the window.

Her mother upstairs — probably with earplugs and half a mug of weak tea — while everything drifted through the stairwell like leftover smoke.

Naomi tried to anchor herself to the carpet.

Nothing to fear. Nothing waiting.

And still, her finger hovered above the screen.

Another call.

This time, she let it ring until the voicemail cracked under the weight of silence.

Hey, Naoms, said the voice.

He'd always said it like a joke, as if he could let it roll off her like sunscreen.

Hey, Naoms. Don't feel like you need to call back or anything. I just wanted to hear how you're doing. I'm in some hotel with weird carpet and too much in my head, I guess. Anyway—hope you're okay. Love you. Dad.

The silence that followed was the silence of cardboard with too much air in it — something you want to press your fingers into, knowing it will never press back.

She listened to it three times.

Three times the same, each time faster, then slower again, then right on the edge of laughing. Absurd, how that voice could still reach her after all those years of pretending it meant nothing, that it didn't count. She wondered if her mother ever took it seriously anymore, or simply blocked it out like a pop-up window.

She decided not to do anything. Or no—she decided something else entirely: she would let the voice sit there until it turned into a fossil, until it stopped kicking or glowing. And then maybe, when she was finally too old to find it childish, she'd call back just because it would hurt less that day.

There was music thrumming in her head, directionless. She opened the baklava, drank her tea cold, looked at her mother's slippers by the door, and imagined how, by tomorrow, they'd be in exactly the same place—or a few millimetres further—to prove that life did in fact keep moving.

She half-dozed on the couch, the voicemail still echoing faintly, rainwater sticky beneath her shirt. She dreamt she was crossing a bridge, a bridge soft as sponge cake, while her father waved from the other side with both hands. Her mother stood beside him but didn't nod, just watched and waited for Naomi to cross, as if it were nothing.

By morning, when she switched her phone back on, the voicemail had vanished from view. Just punctuation.

She slumped into her worn chair; before she could even exhale, the phone lit up again—this time not some anonymous number, but Pappa (NL). A leftover joke from her mother. The name she always shortened in her head. She stared at it, feeling a strange mix of curiosity and dulled resistance, as if the device might explode or turn itself into a loudspeaker for something she couldn't yet process.

She counted to three. Let it ring. And just when she thought he'd hang up, she answered anyway. The line opened like a freshly polished floor: clean, empty, dangerous.

"Yeah?" Her voice came out sharper than she meant.

"Hey, girl. It's… well, me." Matthijs de Vries. Even his breathing sounded like Amsterdam—wet bicycles, stairwell echo. The silence on his end was clumsy.

"Heyoo, meisje," he said finally, his trial-run English cracking under Dutch vowels. Always that. "Just checking in. You okay?"

"I guess," she said. Automatic. She tried not to think about the last time she'd seen him—that night in the park, wet bench, their conversation stretched like elastic. There was a tone in his voice now that unsettled her.

"I saw you," he said. "In that video. You did great. I think your mom was proud. Or jealous. Or both."

She laughed once, too quickly, caught off guard—like he'd sensed how she never managed to cut them loose, not from duty, but from a strange, stubborn comfort.

"What did you want, Dad?" Her tone was sharper than she intended—half armor, half test.

"Nothing special. Just—missed you, I guess. And I was thinking of coming next month. Would that piss you off?"

She heard a car swish past on wet asphalt. Heard the scratchy laugh he used whenever he got too close to honesty.

"Fine," she said. "You can try buying baklava again."

"I will. Vegan stroopwafels, too, promise. We'll eat out, old-school. Like we used to."

"Sure," she said. He didn't know that they used to barely exist.

"Give your mother a hug from me," he said, voice now half-buried under café noise.

"I will," she lied.

"Take care, yeah?"

The line clicked off, a clean slice through the air.

She sat there for a long moment, the phone still glowing in her palm, her reflection warped in the black glass.

Later that morning, the smell of burnt tahini drifted through the kitchen. Miriam sat at the table, newspaper open, a bottle of mineral water beside her. She looked composed again—in control, but softer, as if she'd finally stopped acting the part.

"Sleep well?" she asked.

"Yeah. Didn't, but yeah."

Miriam turned a page; the sound cracked through the quiet. "Was he annoying?"

"Surprisingly not. He gets more than you'd think."

"I've been saying that for years," said Miriam. No triumph in her voice, just mild satisfaction, as though the past had finally earned itself a coffee break.

Naomi set the kettle to boil. She thought of the note, the small yellow scrap folded in her pocket—how certain fragments of life could be torn loose and still belong to you. She wondered how long it took to see your parents as people, not as half-burnt myths from a stage play. No roots tugging, no guilt. Just two people, half-botched, half-alive.

"Should I water the garden today?" she asked, picking at the window latch.

"If it doesn't rain, sure."

Naomi looked outside. The city looked remarkable in its inaction. Had it always been like this? She thought of yesterday, of how easy it was to choose the loud things— protests, noise, causes—and how maybe the real fight lived in the quiet. In the decision to stay.

"Hey, Mom," she said, her shoulders loosening, her neck finally untangled. "Maybe I'll skip tomorrow. No energy for the future."

"Good idea," said Miriam. "We'll make a new one ourselves."

They both laughed, briefly but sincerely. For the first time in a long while, the house didn't feel like a trench, but a place where even detours could root.

She poured herself tea, sunlight crawling up the tiles.

By midmorning, Miriam was typing again, the garden shimmered damp and alive, and Naomi felt a kind of softness she hadn't expected. Maybe it was the sugar, maybe the folded paper in her pocket, maybe just the thought that some days could exist only as pauses.

She pictured her father now, already in an airport seat, cardboard coffee in hand, a restless drift in his bones.

And that, somehow, was enough.

She thought of her father, already back in an airport chair at Schiphol, cardboard coffee in hand, and that quiet urge to disappear. Maybe he'd always been that way—sunken into his own cup—, but somehow she now knew he was fine there. She could resent him for not staying, but she didn't: when all you've ever known are people balancing on edges, it feels only natural to keep standing there yourself.

Not falling, not jumping—just staying.

The house smelled of cinnamon and bleach, the garden of wet citrus and husk. In the background, she heard Miriam talking—on the phone with a colleague, or her mother, or both—her voice ping-ponging between the walls. You could hear in her tone that today didn't need to be a fighting day. No rush, no flame in her chest, no urge to tweet or dissect the news. For the first time in weeks, Naomi looked at the headlines without a filter:

"Protest Group Splits." "University Swaps Headscarf for Hoodie." "City Claims Itself." "Avocado Prices Stable Again."

She set her mug on the edge of the sink, let the tea steep, and watched her reflection in the glass: dark circles like camouflage, curls like armor. She didn't suddenly feel grown up—just less like startled game.

Maybe staying was a kind of movement too—a motion inward, toward the quiet.

When Miriam walked into the kitchen, fingers still damp from morning emails, her eyes immediately landed on Naomi. She said nothing, just poured out the rest of the coffee like a bartender at the end of a shift.

"You could plan something today," she said. "We don't get many days where we can just sit home and hope the future sorts itself out."

"Maybe I'll just do it your way," said Naomi, propping the little note upright beside her cup—her small protest in a sea of domestic logic.

Miriam grinned with one corner of her mouth and bit into a banana. "Does it work?"

Naomi shrugged. "Feels less awful than expected. Even if it leads nowhere."

"Good. Tomorrow might be war again," said her mother, immediately diving back into her phone. "But today, you can stay."

It only needed saying once. Naomi dipped her cookie into the tea,

felt the sensation: relief tinged with melancholy, like sleeping in a drying house after a storm. Things could always blow back to where they'd been if you weren't careful. She tried to believe that maybe, finally, this time was different.

The day stumbled forward: Miriam closing her laptop and sparring over semantics on Zoom; Naomi weeding the hallway plants, scrolling through meeting notes on her phone. The morning sun fought its way through damp windows but glowed bright enough to paint the house in citrus light.

She thought of tomorrow's forum, of her father's arrival, and tried to imagine the meeting not feeling like some low-budget reunion quiz show. What she felt wasn't quite nerves—maybe just curiosity. Something was tugging gently at the anchor of her routine.

Around noon, a text from Matthijs:

"Remember: if you say nothing, they don't listen.

But if you say everything, you lose them just as fast."

Naomi read it three times. Her brain looked for the trap, but for once it seemed like he saw the world the way she did—dryly amused, economical with words, always slightly ahead. She didn't reply. Silence felt stronger.

In the afternoon, rain danced back across the roof—heavy drops smacking the attic window like pebbles. Naomi sat in the kitchen, feet on the table, dreaming of the day someone would answer her call without it feeling like a jolt. The phone stayed silent, but the house hummed with relief.

She thought of her grandmother, long ago alone, and the generations of women before her—rubble clearers of their own small wars, forever patching cracks to keep the cold out. Maybe they'd been proud, maybe just critical, but Naomi knew: if you were born a deviation, you had to build your own life from it.

That evening, they ate carrot soup—too sweet but comforting—and sat together on the couch, each holding the other's phone. They watched old clips, laughed at forgotten nonsense: Rutger in a clown suit; Miriam in the rain, her umbrella print bleeding inside out. Even her father's voice surfaced in a stray recording—his unmistakable bark of a laugh after telling a joke.

"Think he's drinking coffee right now?" Naomi asked.

Miriam looked over, no irony in sight. "Absolutely. He doesn't know how not to."

"And do you think he really gets what I'm doing here?"

She didn't know where the question came from, only that it had to land somewhere.

Miriam looked up from her phone, thumb tracing the rim of her mug, lips curling into what could've been a smile—or maybe just a tic she used when choosing words.

"Your father understands everything new," she said softly, "as long as it doesn't take itself too seriously.

So yes. He gets it. Maybe even better than I do."

"Even if he forgets?"

"Especially then." This time it was a real laugh—no restraint, no self-mockery. "You nervous about tomorrow?"

Naomi shrugged, that familiar gesture that hid and shared at once. "Not really. Or yeah. I just don't want it to be weird."

"Then be weird before it gets weird. Only strategy that's ever worked in this family."

They both laughed, and suddenly nothing felt wrong. The house felt lighter, the air thinner. They decided to sleep early—the forum started at dawn, and no one benefited from a frantic morning.

That night, Naomi dreamt of a crowded room, an echoing cycle of voices all talking at once. Her mother sat on a stepladder—not a throne, just randomly chosen—and her father leaned in the doorway, feet not touching the ground. Someone passed around stroopwafels. No one truly heard each other, yet no one felt left out. When she woke, she realized it was the first time she'd seen her parents together without it hurting.

Morning came soft, wet, barely light. Miriam had made sandwiches, filled a thermos with mint-lemon tea, her own name scrawled on the lid in permanent marker. Naomi didn't mind. The tram was on time. They sat on opposite benches, like couples traveling through a half-solved argument but still comfortable in each other's silence.

At the forum building, a banner hung across the entrance—exactly the kind her generation loved to drape itself in. Naomi no longer felt the need to critique it; she just walked in, picked up her badge, and found her seat at the table.

The organizer, a woman with a too-tight bun and permanent under-eye shadows, scanned the room with laser precision. Naomi hung up her coat, glanced around, and touched her pocket—yes, the note was still there.

The session began. Panel debates, a row of students each selling their own version of radical transparency to the crowd. Sometimes Naomi felt she'd heard it all before, but today it was different—like playing a record in a new order: some songs sounded suddenly fresh, others older than the walls.

After the first break, she saw her father by the coffee corner—ten minutes early—and her stomach tightened at the sight of his silhouette. Head too big for the narrow frame, coat badly fastened, hands buried in his pockets as if he wasn't sure whether he'd come to stay.

She didn't want to flinch, but felt herself edging toward the exit. Too late. He'd already seen her.

"Hey, Naooms."

A line so soft it hurt nowhere, as if she were a ghost he was trying to catch up to.

"Hi," she managed—no joke, no shield, just the rawness that follows a night without overthinking.

Matthijs nodded but didn't move closer. He glanced at her badge before saying,

"Playing it serious now, huh? Real name on your firing squad."

"We don't do aliases anymore," Naomi said, suddenly finding a sliver of defiance. "Or do you think that's dangerous?"

"Your mother would call it reckless," he said. "But secretly, she'd love it."

They stood there between paper cups and peeling motivational posters, unsure what belonged to them. Every part of her wanted to run, but her knees betrayed her. She imagined someone taking their picture; they'd look like travelers caught mid-transfer—two people meeting by accident on their way to different capitals.

"Want something to drink?" he asked, as if the meeting required neutral ground.

"Sure," said Naomi.

The coffee was too hot, rough against her tongue, but she kept her face still. Matthijs sipped, watching her over the rim.

"Your mother said you're working on something big— some kind of performance that shook up the university."

Was this how conversation was supposed to work after years of silence? Her mouth felt empty.

"I'm not angrier than anyone else," she said. "Just worse at waiting."

"And what do you want from it?" His eyes flicked to the badge on her chest.

She thought of the forum, of those half-lit mornings in the kitchen with her mother. She thought of the note in her pocket, of last night, of how everything always ended faster than planned.

"I think I want people to stop postponing things," she said. "To talk before it's too late."

"Sounds wise." He pulled one corner of his mouth up, grabbed a cookie from the tray, and broke it neatly in half.

"You know what the best thing about talking is? You don't have to win it.

Not always, anyway."

Naomi smiled — not broadly, but just enough to feel her face still remembered how. She looked at the crumbs on the table, the stain of too-hot coffee slowly drying. Outside, the rain was retreating, leaving streaks on the window as if someone had hurriedly wiped something away.

She didn't know if this was a beginning or just a small pause in something that had already been unfolding. Maybe that didn't matter.

Some conversations didn't need to solve anything — they only needed to exist.

And while her father said something about flights and transfers, she felt, for the first time, no urge to reply. She let the silence come, let it breathe between them, just long enough to know that nothing broke.

Just stay — she thought.

Maybe that was already enough.

CHAPTER 4

FLORENCE CREATIVE CHAOS

Florence's studio breathed turpentine, linen, and the paper scent of old books. On the counter, beside the compost bin, coffee rings layered over one another like dead-end ideas. She was supposed to be writing the text for a performative installation at the Tate, something with mirrors, water basins, and someone's unfinished self-portraits. She had forgotten to call Daisy's teacher about the field trip money, meant to text Samuel about his latest nightmare, but her phone was full of unread messages from gallerists and creditors, and her head was turning into a swamp.

In the kitchenette, Daisy was rocking two teacups together and asked, "Why are you afraid of water, anyway?" Florence picked up a lemon and treated it as a crucial tool, something that demanded absolute precision.

"Water isn't scary," she said, frowning. "It just remembers. If you look into it, you see everything again, only changed."

Daisy rolled her eyes. "That's not scary, that's just science. Or reflection. Or how things work."

Her daughter had the firmness of youthful logic, the kind that could dismantle anything simply by naming it.

Florence squeezed the lemon over her fingers. "Maybe I'm just jealous of people who don't change when it rains," she said, smiling as if it were a joke.

In the living room, Samuel hung upside down from a candy-pink armchair, his legs twisted in a strange knot. He had a Woolf novel open before him, but kept rereading the first sentence, as if it were a code waiting to be cracked. Florence felt the gravity of obligation to be a good mother, a relevant artist, to leave behind something tangible. She used to believe that being an artist was about awakening, about following threads, being led by the universe; now, everything was a battle between light and the electricity bill.

Daisy came to stand beside her, her hands sticky with honey. "I have to write about myself at school," she said. "Can I say you're some kind of wizard?"

Florence thought of her own hands, dry from turpentine, of her mother's letters that never began anywhere except with the word darling. She thought of the emptiness inside her when the silence lasted too long. A wizard was good. No one ever asked a wizard why the house sometimes felt hollow, or why she could spend whole days in pajamas without looking out the window.

"Write whatever you like," she said softly. "As long as it sounds beautiful."

The lemon was still wedged beneath her nail. She thought of the mirrors, the Tate, the water that remembered everything. Maybe she should take Daisy to the canal one day, show her everything that could go wrong, but also everything that stayed afloat.

That evening, when both children were in bed. Daisy, deep in her animal dreams, Samuel with his Beats headphones and the flicker of light behind his eyelids. Florence remained at the folding kitchen table. The light above the sink cast the faded postcards on the fridge in pale pastel tones. She tried to type a text about transparency and promise, about how the eye can't escape itself, even as everything disappears.

Her fingers moved across the keys, half-sentences dissolving before they could take shape. She quickly Googled: psychological effects of mirror water. Then she searched Florence Harper reviews and found her name buried in a thread on some obscure forum.

"Instinctively right, but overcast," someone had written, and the words clung unpleasantly in her mouth, like lemon zest, too bitter to swallow.

By midnight, she still hadn't sent an email to the Tate project lead.

But somehow she had texted her mother without realizing it: "How are the tomatoes this year?"

That kind of thing.

Outside, rain tapped against the window—not furiously, not tenderly, but with the precise irritation of a drop that refused distraction. Florence propped her elbows on the table and tried to picture Daisy's face at the moment she'd said wizard. Even her daughter could see through her; that was the frightening part. The child sensed her absence without needing to name them.

She often thought about the first time she'd bathed Daisy, how she'd held a hand beneath her back, the baby surrendering with the joy of someone who had never fallen. Florence had said, You never fight water; you let it carry you.

It was still a mantra she repeated to herself, though it felt like nonsense on the mornings she turned on the shower and the water simply ran down her shoulders without washing anything away.

Maybe it was too late to become someone who had everything under control. She sent Samuel a text, knowing he wouldn't read it until morning. It came out softer than intended: You're fine the way you are. Water doesn't remember why you were ever afraid of it.

Then she drafted an email to the Tate project lead:

When the audience sees itself, it also sees how it constructs itself. Water can fracture everything, but also hold it together.

She hated how hollow philosophy could sound once it was written down, but at least it was a start.

She brushed her teeth in half-darkness, the acidic trace of lemon still beneath her nails. Sometimes Florence thought life was just a series of bad rehearsals, endlessly stretching chaos until it looked like form again. In bed, she stared at the ceiling, where every shadow seemed to hide a version of herself. In ten hours, she'd have to get Daisy to school,

Samuel to work, and show up in spaces where people were expected to display their brilliance.

She filed her to-do list into a mental ivory drawer: sanitary pads, brushes, Samuel's new medication, an email to the curator, and a reminder to text the neighbor back.

Her mind buzzed—a polyphony of trivialities—while she traced an invisible line across her bare arm, from wrist to elbow.

Somewhere, long ago, she had believed that art was a kind of escape route — a hallway leading outward, a secret door hidden in the most banal walls.

Now she sat in her own house, rooms full of half-finished things and snake-like extension cords.

The only freedom left was in her head, and even that was shrinking.

It lasted until exactly fourteen minutes past twelve.

Then Daisy texted that they'd stayed at the park because Sam's mother could pick her up after the library. Florence typed "have fun" and added a heart emoji, even though emojis felt foreign to her — like stamps on a feeling that refused to be stamped. She scraped bits of apple pulp from the coffee machine's filter with her thumbnail. Her head sounded surprisingly empty — for now.

Planning the sketches for Tate went faster than she'd expected. She used hesitant lines, left edges loose, allowed the water to run where it wanted — the way you let a child wander as long as it doesn't drown. The formal text for the curator read like another imitation of herself, but she pressed send and closed the laptop. One thing a day was enough. Maybe tonight she could finally cook — something slow, something that allowed the house to fill up with its own scent.

That afternoon, Florence pasted fragile papers on the window in a grid that reminded her of her mother's kitchen — always a scrap of lace curtain somewhere, always a draft along the floor. She wondered if her mother, right now, was also cleaning her nails after harvesting tomatoes. That woman was always doing something — never with Florence, but always around her. The longing for that cosmically useless nearness stayed strangely intact, even now that Florence was a mother herself.

Daisy came home with damp hair and a pile of shiny library books, and for the first time that week, Florence didn't feel that stab of inadequacy. She made tea, listened to the day's report, and asked questions without thinking about their purpose. Her daughter admired her — but also the mothers of her friends, the ones who could make intricate cupcake fillings or sew buttons on winter coats. It was comforting that even heroism was relative.

After an hour, Florence tied a plastic apron over Daisy's jumper and cut her hair just above the shoulders.

"So your reflection won't always be in your face," she joked, and Daisy actually laughed. Florence discovered, with mild astonishment, how sure her hands could be — even when they didn't know what they were doing.

While cooking, she lost herself in the rhythm: chopping, frying, waiting, tasting, adding a little more salt. Potatoes and onions and garlic and peppers — and as she lifted the pan, it felt as if every thought she'd ever had about food collapsed into one gaping desire: to satisfy someone, to be good enough that hunger would briefly subside.

It wasn't until dinner that Florence noticed how Daisy let her fork rest longer than usual, staring into the pool of gravy, downward, where the table mirrored her face.

"Mum?" she said.

Florence felt the hesitation — that small crack just before an important question.

"When will I see Dad?" Daisy asked. She didn't use his real name; Florence had — stupidly — turned it into an artefact, something too heavy to touch. But Daisy meant Matthijs, the incurable Dutchman, the man who drifted through a different city each autumn until some child across the Channel remembered who he was.

Florence tightened the pepper mill. In her head, she searched for the right packaging — not too much drama, not too much air.

"Next month is autumn break," she said, casually. "Maybe you can stay with him for a few days." Stay over — a phrase of moderate promise and low stakes. It tasted like plastic forks and liquid pudding. Daisy's eyes refused to rise above the edge of the table.

"Is he ever coming back?" she asked — this time without a question mark, only the soft sag of tone.

Florence thought of the last time she'd spoken to Matthijs, how his voice always dissolved into new plans and café salads, how his attention duplicated everywhere except where his daughter was. She hesitated — wondered whether honesty belonged here. Maybe Daisy should be allowed to believe in the myth of the distant father, a man with jobs and important things to do, instead of the true version — the man who'd forgotten how to be one, and had turned himself into a role in a badly staged play.

"He's not coming back to live here," Florence said slowly. "But you can always call."

She tried a smile, hoping enough courage leaked through her voice. "And it's never wrong to know where you come from. He's not gone — just separate."

Daisy seemed to accept that; her fork made small circles again, and she took another bite without comment. Florence felt, deep in her stomach, the raw ache of failure — the inability to keep families whole, to keep her children safe from everything that quietly fell apart. She thought of the Tate installation — of mirrors that reflected without judging, and of water that could convince you of anything, as long as you kept watching it from a new angle.

The rest of the evening unfolded in the usual residue of sound: faint scrolling, the glow of screens. Florence checked her inbox fifty times, as if a reply from Matthijs might suddenly make everything less awkward. Nothing came. The kids sat at opposite ends of the couch, Daisy on a game,

Samuel doom-scrolling through TikToks. Florence wiped the table, picked up the plastic knife she always used for bread, and felt the same hollow that followed a bad review — everything built, nothing that stayed.

Later, in bed, she pulled the duvet over her ears, trying not to think about the conversation or the look in Daisy's eyes when she asked about her father. It always came down to this: no matter how long you thought about it, there were never enough words to make things whole. She remembered the same awkward void from her own childhood — the silence between her and her mother stretched just as far as the one now filling this apartment. Florence tried to imagine a version of Daisy where sadness didn't dominate — or rather, where sadness simply had a place, next to the books and the tea and the haircutting. You had to learn to carry things quietly.

She traced the cracks in the ceiling; to her surprise, it calmed her. In the dark, she heard Samuel moving in the kitchen — probably milk, or water. He wasn't much older than Daisy, but carried himself like someone twice his age. She wondered if that heaviness had come from her.

Later, they all lay under their own blankets, three separate islands in the same flat. Florence rested her hand against the bedroom wall, felt the cold concrete, and suddenly understood why people used to touch walls at night — to keep from getting lost in the dark. It gave you something to hold on to.

In the morning, Daisy was already at her bedside before she'd properly woken up.

"I dreamed I was standing on the lake and you saw me," she said.

Florence blinked, tried to hold the image. "You were standing on the water?"

Daisy nodded, hair wild from the night, eyes fixed on the curtain moving in the morning draft.

"Maybe you can take your dad to the canal in autumn," Florence said. "Show him that water doesn't have to be cold."

Daisy shrugged, but reached for her hand under the table. That was something.

She tried to lessen her expectations that day. Emailed the Tate curator a revised line — "the breaking point of reflection is that it always returns." Cooked a dinner even Samuel ate without comment.

Then came a voice message from Matthijs, restarted three times before he was satisfied:

"Hey kiddo, still saving up for the trip, but I'll call soon. Big kiss."

Florence let the phone glow in her palm for a full minute, unsure if it was good news that he'd checked in or proof of the opposite.

She played it for Daisy, who listened with her head tilted, her mouth caught somewhere between hope and relief.

The days shortened; mornings lingered in damp light. Florence worked through the project plan, edited and rewrote, titled the piece "Invisible Current," still doubting whether it meant anything. She replied politely to school and gallery emails, got stuck in conversations with Daisy about science facts — "did you know water never really stops moving?" — and dreamed more often that she was in a leaking boat, with her kids and all the things she'd forgotten to bring.

Sometimes Samuel stayed up late, shuffling down the hallway, back against the bathroom door. When Florence found him like that, she avoided too many words. Sometimes she made pancakes at 3 a.m., an act of quiet rebellion she'd inherited from her own mother. Samuel always ate, never commented. In their faltering, they resembled each other more than Florence liked to admit.

Autumn battered its way into the house.

One Thursday, Florence looked in the mirror and saw her face drawn with rough lines stretching toward her temples. Yet she also found herself beautiful — a messy kind of pride. She thought of Daisy, who mimicked her constantly, running through the house with scarves and tissues around her head like a forgotten shaman. Maybe her daughter would one day remember that being different didn't mean always getting everything right.

Daisy marked Xs in her planner and gathered questions she wanted to ask her father — "maybe I'll write them down," she said, and Florence found it tragic but also beautiful. Samuel grew quiet again, stopped appearing in her studio, ate only at night, and left YouTube videos playing too loudly. Maybe jealousy, maybe fear of being left behind — but with him, nothing was ever direct. Florence painted harder than ever, as if the Tate project could burn away every doubt. Sometimes her own intensity startled her — the way she pressed her hand against the rough canvas, needing everything to be dirty and real.

When Daisy couldn't sleep a week before the trip, she crawled into Florence's bed. Her body against Florence's shoulder felt warmer than she remembered from babyhood — softer, less certain than Samuel's angular sprawl.

Florence laughed into the pillow; the question was so careless, so full of kindness.

She thought of hundreds of things — why did you leave, why don't you call, was I ever enough — but all of them sounded foolish aloud.

She said, "Ask if he still remembers what stroopwafels taste like."

Daisy giggled and squeezed her hand.

Florence realized how small her desires had become, and how, strangely, that felt like peace.

She managed until exactly fourteen minutes past twelve.

Then Daisy texted that they had stayed at the park, because Sam's mother could pick her up after the library. Florence typed "have fun" and added a heart emoji, though emojis felt foreign to her—as stamps pressed onto feelings that refused to be stamped. She scrubbed apple residue out of the coffee machine's filter with her thumbnail. Her head felt surprisingly empty—for now.

The sketching for Tate went faster than she'd expected. She used halting lines, let edges drift, allowed the water on the paper to run as it wished, the way you let a child wander so long as it doesn't drown. The formal text for the curator sounded again like an imitation of herself, but she pressed send and closed the laptop. One thing per day was enough. Maybe she could finally cook something for dinner— something that simmered slowly so that the house could absorb its scent.

That afternoon, Florence stuck fragile bits of paper to the window in a diamond pattern that reminded her of her mother's kitchen—always a scrap of lace curtain, always a draft crawling across the floor. She wondered if her mother was, at that very moment, scraping her nails clean after harvesting tomatoes. That woman had always been busy— never with Florence, but always around her. The longing for that cosmically useless nearness still clung to her, even now that Florence was a mother herself.

Daisy came home with damp hair and a stack of shiny library books, and for the first time that week, Florence felt no sting of inadequacy. She brewed tea, listened to Daisy's recounting of the day, and asked questions without thinking about their purpose. Her daughter admired Florence—but also the mothers of her friends, who could make intricate cupcake fillings and sew buttons onto winter coats. It was comforting to know that even heroics were relative.

An hour later, she tied a plastic apron around Daisy's jumper and cut her hair just above the shoulders. "So your reflection doesn't always sit in your face," she joked, and Daisy actually laughed. Florence was quietly surprised by the precision of her own hands—how sure they could be without knowing why.

While cooking, Florence lost herself in rhythm: chop, fry, wait, taste, a little more salt. She knew the recipe by heart.

Potatoes and onions and garlic and peppers—and as she tilted the pan, it was as if all the thoughts she'd ever had about food condensed into one yawning desire: to satisfy someone, to be good enough that hunger itself might dissolve for a while.

At dinner, she noticed how Daisy let her fork rest longer than usual, staring into the remaining gravy, downward, where the table's shine reflected her face.

"Mama?" Daisy said.

Florence felt the hesitation—the faint crack right before an important question.

"When will I see Dad?"

She didn't use his real name; Florence had made that—stupidly—into an artifact, something with too much weight. But Daisy meant Matthijs, the incurable Dutchman, the man who wandered through a different city every autumn until some child across the Channel remembered who he was.

Florence twisted the pepper mill closed. In her head, she searched for the right packaging. Not too much drama, not too much air.

"Next month is autumn break," she said, casually. "Maybe you can stay over."

Stay over—a phrase of modest promise and low stakes. It tasted like plastic forks and liquid pudding. Daisy's eyes refused to rise above the table.

"Is he ever coming back?" she asked—no question mark this time, only the soft descent of her voice.

Florence thought of the last time she'd spoken to Matthijs—how his voice always evaporated into ironic plans and salad talk, how his attention doubled everywhere except toward his daughter. She hesitated, uncertain whether honesty belonged here. Maybe Daisy needed the myth: the faraway father, a man with jobs and important things to do—instead of the truth, the man who had forgotten how fatherhood worked, reducing himself to a role in a poorly staged play.

"He's not coming back to live here," Florence said slowly. "But you can always call."

She tried a smile, hoping her voice carried enough courage. "And it's never forbidden to know where you come from. He hasn't disappeared—just stayed apart."

Daisy seemed to accept that. Her fork made small circles again, and she took a bite without another word. Florence felt in her gut the open wound of her own failure—the inability to keep families intact, or to keep her children safe from everything that quietly broke apart. She thought of the Tate installation, of mirrors that reflected without judgment, of water that could convince you of anything if you only kept looking at it from the right angle.

The rest of the evening unfolded like most—filled with leftover sounds and the released sigh of endless scrolling. Florence checked her inbox fifty times, as if a message from Matthijs might suddenly make everything less awkward. It stayed silent. The children sat on opposite ends of the couch, Daisy playing a game, Samuel lost in TikToks flashing by at light speed. Florence wiped the table clean, picked up the plastic knife she always used for bread, and felt the same hollowness that followed a bad review: everything built up, nothing left behind.

Later, in bed, she pulled the blanket over her head. Tried not to think about the awkward conversation, not about Daisy's eyes when she asked about her father. It always came down to this: no matter how long you brooded, there were never enough words to make things whole. She thought of the awkward, yawning silences of her own childhood— how the quiet between her and her mother stretched just as wide as the one in this house. Florence tried to imagine a version of Daisy where sadness wasn't the dominant note— or rather, where sadness had a place, beside books and tea and the cutting of her hair. You had to learn to carry something, secretly.

Her thoughts drifted along the ceiling, tracing cracks in the plaster; to her surprise, it brought calm. In the dark, she heard Samuel fumbling softly in the kitchen—probably milk or water. He was barely older than Daisy but moved like someone twice his actual age. Florence wondered whether she had given him that heaviness herself.

Later, they all lay under their own blankets, three small islands in the same apartment. Florence rested her hand on the bedroom wall, feeling the cold concrete, and suddenly understood why people once placed hands on walls—to keep from getting lost in the dark. It gave you something to hold on to.

In the morning, Daisy was already beside her bed before she was fully awake.

"I dreamed I was standing on the lake and you saw me," she said.

Florence thought for a moment, tried to hold the image. "You stood on the water?"

Daisy nodded, hair wild from the night, eyes fixed on the curtain swaying in the morning draft.

Florence cleared her throat, tried to sound steady.

"Maybe in autumn you can take Dad to the canal," she said. "Show him that water doesn't always have to be cold."

Daisy shrugged but reached under the table for her mother's hand. It was something.

That day, Florence tried to lighten her expectations.

She emailed the Tate curator with a revised text ("the breaking point of reflection is that it always rebounds").

Cooked a meal that even Samuel ate without comment.

Got a voice message from Matthijs—three false starts before he was satisfied:

"Hey, little one. I'm still saving for the trip, but I'll call soon. Big kiss."

Florence let the phone glow in her hand for a full minute, unsure whether his message was good news or proof of the opposite. She played it for Daisy, who listened with her head tilted, her lips forming a faint expression that was neither hope nor relief.

The days grew shorter, and mornings lingered in cold mist. Florence pushed through the project plan, deleted and rewrote, and gave the installation the title Invisible Current, despite doubting it would ever truly mean something. She answered school and gallery emails with polite precision, stalled in conversations with Daisy about science facts ("Did you know water never really stops moving?"), and dreamed more and more often of being in a leaking boat with her children and all the things she'd forgotten to bring.

Sometimes, Samuel stayed awake deep into the night, shuffling through the hallway or sitting with his back against the bathroom door. When Florence found him like that, she tried not to make too many words out of his silence. Occasionally, she made pancakes at three in the morning, as her mother once did with her, in quiet conspiracy against time. Samuel always ate, never commented on the absurdity. In their halting ways, they resembled each other more than Florence dared admit.

Autumn battered the house. One Thursday, Florence stood before the bathroom mirror and saw that her face was roughly drawn, with lines extending toward her temples. Yet she found herself beautiful too—a disheveled kind of pride. She thought of Daisy, who loved to imitate her and sometimes ran through the house with scarves and tissues on her head like a shaman from a forgotten tribe. Maybe,

Florence thought, her daughter would one day remember that being different didn't mean doing everything right.

She decided to arrange Daisy's visit with Matthijs herself. Bought plane tickets for a week in Amsterdam and emailed her mother: "If you don't mind making up an extra bed for a night," she added, deliberately light. Then she booked the cheapest Ryanair flight and forced the thought out of her mind that Matthijs might mess something up.

The days leading up to departure padded softly through the house, like wet socks. Daisy counted the crosses in her planner and gathered all the questions she wanted to ask her father—" maybe I'll write them down," she said —and Florence found it tragic but also beautiful. Samuel grew suddenly quiet again, stopped peeking into her studio, ate only late at night, and left YouTube videos playing at full volume during odd hours. At first, Florence thought he was jealous—or that his fear of being left behind had gone into overdrive—but with him, nothing was ever one-to-one. Between it all, she painted furiously, as if the Tate project could drive every trace of doubt from her body. Sometimes she startled at her own intensity—the way she pressed her palm into the coarse canvas, her craving for everything to be messy and real.

A week before the trip, Daisy couldn't sleep and crawled into Florence's bed. Her body against Florence's shoulder was warmer than she remembered from when the kids were small, and so different from Samuel's sharp-edged presence when he curled up like a cat.

"When I see Dad," Daisy whispered, "do you want me to ask him something for you?"

Florence laughed into the pillow—the question was so careless, so full of care without clumsiness. She thought of a hundred things: why did you leave, why do you call so little, was I ever enough—but they all became useless when said aloud.

She said, "Ask if he still remembers what stroopwafels taste like."

Daisy giggled and squeezed her hand.

Florence realized how small her desires had become— and found she liked it that way.

On the day of departure, hail battered London, and the taxi had to dodge flooded streets, but none of it unsettled Daisy. The girl grew calmer as things became more intense. After check-in, she sat with her knees tucked under her chin, drawing on a napkin, absentmindedly chewing her pen.

Florence pretended to read but watched her every move from the corner of her eye. Airports always sounded the same—everyone was deaf to everyone else. She found it comforting: you didn't need to be more than a speck in the crowd.

The flight passed without disaster, and afterward, Florence couldn't fathom how a machine could lift so many people above themselves while the world below simply kept turning. She looked at Daisy's hands—the child had her father's fingers, long and elegant—and thought of the innocent luck of things that simply get passed on.

She found a cheap hotel near the station and mapped a route along the canal. The boys at Daisy's school would mark off the autumn break on their calendars; Florence ticked off the days in her mind. She had no expectations, except this: that Daisy would see her father, and afterward come home—not whole, but no longer broken.

The journey itself unraveled unevenly, with the usual bruises of travel: delayed trains, bad weather, wet coats—

The rest of the visit unfolded like a simple pattern: groceries, cooking together, wandering through the narrow streets. Matthijs tried—she could see that. A little gift for Daisy, a walk along the murals, and ice cream from the "best" stall (which, according to him, still didn't compare to a real Italian one). He was good at keeping things light; as long as they didn't touch too deeply, everything stayed pleasantly thin.

In the evening, they ate fries from a paper cone on a damp bench beside a bridge, where the streetlights were already announcing the night. Daisy wiped a streak of mayonnaise from her cheek, glanced at her parents—Florence on the left, Matthijs on the right—and laughed that unexpectedly restrained laugh of her father's, while the wind blew her hair over the fries.

Florence watched and thought: this is half the victory—fighting becomes easier as long as moments like this continue to exist. Maybe she only now began to understand her own mother; that you don't have to fix everything, that sometimes it's enough just to sit together in a draft and keep the food warm.

That night in the hotel, Daisy didn't dream—or maybe she preferred to keep her dreams to herself. In the morning, she wrote on a napkin what she wanted to ask Matthijs that day: "Have you ever regretted it?" Florence didn't read it, but she could feel the trembling energy of the letters through her whole body. Maybe that was the essence: not to spare your child from drama, but also not to let them drown in it.

On their last afternoon in the Netherlands, with their suitcases zipped shut and the remains of breakfast still between their teeth, they went together to the park by the river. Florence let Daisy and Matthijs walk ahead; she followed a few paces behind, her mouth still dull from a bad cappuccino and her head full of sentences that refused to finish. She watched as father and daughter strolled side by side—not exactly in step, but in the same rhythm—a physical proof of their kinship, at once new and ancient.

Matthijs pointed to a grey duck preening between the reeds; Daisy, hands deep in her coat pockets, nodded as if following an instinctive rule of politeness. Florence clung to the sight. A strange kind of grief passed through her—the awareness that generations had momentarily collapsed into this single second, somewhere between a pile of wet leaves and a rusted trash bin.

On the way back, Daisy tapped Florence's arm. "Can we get that cookie we always used to have?" she asked. It sounded less like a wish than like a small tactical gesture— a way of collecting memories instead of being ambushed by them. Florence nodded, felt the tightness in her neck ease slightly, and thought that everything became more bearable when it could be about a cookie.

The shopping street was busier than she remembered, people clustering around sandwich shops and vintage stores. Florence's body remembered how she had once belonged here—a central thread in a fabric that had seemed to move on its own. You walked as if you couldn't help but stumble toward the next coincidence. She watched as Matthijs effortlessly greeted old acquaintances, hand on shoulder, tossing off teasing remarks about their hair or their shoes. Even after all this time, he was still a magnet for contact, even when it meant nothing. Sometimes Florence thought she missed that kind of superficiality—that living constantly on the edge of meaning had exhausted her; the small jokes, the idle chatter, were gentler than any deep conversation.

At the bakery, Daisy ordered three stroopkoeken, paid with a coin she'd found on the mantelpiece at home, and handed one to Florence with the grace of a sommelier. It felt like old times, being offered something freely, with nothing expected in return. They sat on a bench, the smell of sugar and yeast caught in their collars, watching a single rowboat glide past on the water.

Matthijs broke his cookie in half, looked at Daisy with mock seriousness, and said he'd always thought water was only fun in summer—that in winter it was mostly a physicist's joke.

"You're one of those physicists too," he added, "because you love to dive into everything."

Florence laughed. Daisy pulled up her collar and grinned, showing her teeth. This was enough—Florence didn't need to see it to know it. She didn't know if she could say goodbye gracefully, but the sense of togetherness lingered like a stain on an old tablecloth—impossible to remove, inseparable from the pattern itself.

The hours in the city stretched out. By late afternoon, they were on the train to Schiphol, a plastic bag full of torn pastries and a book for Daisy. She read silently, sipping from a can of cassis, while the city rolled past faster than Florence had hoped. Rain streaked the window; she thought of all the words left unsaid—how maybe those took up the most space of all. She wondered if Daisy would one day drink these memories like milk or like wine—whether a hint of sweetness would cling to their sour aftertaste.

Just before landing, Daisy's head fell onto her shoulder. Florence let it rest there, her chin pressing into the child's haircut she'd trimmed herself only a week ago. She wanted to stretch time, but felt in her bones that everything was stiffening again—in the air, on the English pavements, in the return to their flat with its musty boiler and toothbrushes in a glass.

Back home in London, the apartment felt different than before the trip; it smelled of earth, of everything you only miss when it's gone for a while. Samuel sat on the couch, legs tucked up, headphones crooked over one ear. Florence kicked off her shoes, felt the damp edges on her heels, and walked silently to the kitchen. She poured three glasses of water and placed them side by side on the table. The circle was complete again.

"So?" Samuel said then, without looking up, the question pared down to its minimum.

"He's got a new coat," Daisy said, "and he still remembers what stroopwafels taste like." Florence grinned and thought: if there was only ever one possible outcome, then perhaps this was the best one.

That evening, when the lights were off and the curtains drawn, Florence felt a bare kind of satisfaction prick through her. Nothing had changed; fathers would always be half-present, and children would keep tugging at their missing pieces. But there was air now, a small opening in the window of their house that had so long refused to budge.

She lay in bed, fingers folded on the rough sheet, and thought of tomorrow, of coffee stains she'd make again, of lines she'd draw across the white of paper and canvas. Maybe she'd help Daisy with her school talk on water—build the experiment together, step into the grey water with bow and arrow, see what reflected back.

And in that shimmering surface

Florence saw their three faces: blurry at first, then slowly sharpening, as if the water carried a memory that longed to relive every variation.

She drank too. With every sip, she felt the sediment of fear thinning, how even in remnants, everything somehow still fit. Maybe a life wasn't meant to be held together, but refilled again and again, so the glasses would never have to be empty. She wiped her lower lip with her sleeve and refilled her glass. At the table, Daisy was already charging toward her next question, hungry for tomorrow, while Samuel sank a little deeper into his chair with a quiet smile.

It was evening by the river. Florence thought of mirrors, of water, of invisible currents between generations. The children didn't know it yet, but they were already their own stream. She laughed—awkwardly, unexpectedly—and decided to preserve the moment the way her mother used to make jam: syrupy, but with just enough sour.

Later, when life would tear another hole, she'd do what she did now: draw the circle again.

Sit at the table.

Breath.

Water.

And for a moment, miss nothing at all.

She caught her reflection in the windowpane—a smudged line beneath her eyes, as if the city's fog had moved indoors. Florence hooked her pinky around the mug's handle. Sunlight kaleidoscoped through the glass, stringing together the remains of old breakfasts in a curtain of drizzle and dust. In her head, she counted the hours until Daisy's presentation. She felt a giddy kind of anticipation—not because her daughter would struggle, but because Florence had promised herself she wouldn't break when Monday came.

Daisy had prepared her water experiment like a TED talk—complete with videos of flooded gardens and years marked in neon highlighter. She'd been nervous that morning; Florence had seen it in the way she sliced her bread and rearranged her toppings. But now, her children were watching a British quiz on TV, and if Florence was honest— or maybe just too cowardly to hide behind deadlines any longer—she felt a strange peace in that collective silence.

The day evaporated in the house. Samuel plugged in his headphones and blacked out in his room. Daisy withdrew behind her poster-collaged desk with a stack of leaflets. Florence moved between tasks like a cat in a room of mirrors—borrowing an academy book from the online library, washing just enough socks to survive the week, texting the neighbours about the damp stain on the ceiling. In between, she read about liquid dynamics and surface tension, trying to link it all back to her project at Tate. Sometimes, very briefly, her work felt meaningful; more often, it dissolved into a race between time and disappointment.

That evening, Daisy stood in the doorway of the studio, her silhouette just a little too tender for the hint of spring that lingered there.

That night, when the lights were off and the curtains drawn, Florence felt a bare kind of contentment prickle. Nothing had changed—the fathers would always remain half-present, the children would keep tugging at their own missing pieces. But there was air now, a small opening in the window of their house that had otherwise stayed sealed shut.

She lay in bed, fingers folded on the rough duvet, thinking of tomorrow. How she would spill coffee again, draw lines across the white of canvas and paper. Maybe she'd help Daisy with her presentation on water—build the experiment together, shoot arrows into the gray water, and see what reflected. And in that shimmering surface

Florence saw their three faces, blurry at first, then slowly sharpening, as if the water had a memory that wanted to relive every variation.

She drank, too. With each sip, she felt the lime-scale of fear thin out, how even the leftovers somehow fit again. Maybe a life wasn't meant to be held together, but constantly refilled—until the glasses never had to be empty. She wiped her sleeve across her lip, poured more. At the table, Daisy was already steering toward her next question, hungry for tomorrow, while Samuel sank deeper into his chair with a small smile.

It was evening by the river. Florence thought of mirrors, of water, of the invisible motion between generations. The children didn't know it yet, but they were already their own current. She laughed—awkwardly, unexpectedly—and decided to preserve the moment the way her mother once made jam: syrupy, but with just enough tartness.

Later, when life tore open another gap, she'd do what she did now: draw the circle again. Sit at a table. Breathe. Water. For a moment, miss nothing.

She caught her reflection in the windowpane—a smudged line beneath her eyes, as if the city mist had moved inside. Florence hooked her pinkie around the handle of her mug. Sunlight kaleidoscoped through the glass, stringing together the crusts of old breakfasts into a curtain of drizzle and dust. In her head, she counted the hours until Daisy's presentation. She felt a giddy kind of anticipation—not because her daughter would struggle, but because Florence had promised herself not to break when Monday came.

Daisy had prepared her water experiment like a TED Talk, complete with videos of flooded gardens and fluorescent-marked timelines. That morning, she'd been nervous—Florence could tell by the way she sliced her bread and rearranged the toppings. But now the kids were watching a British quiz show together, and if Florence was honest— or just too tired to keep hiding behind deadlines—she felt a strange kind of peace in that shared silence.

CHAPTER 5
GEERTRUIDA DE VRIES

Mother of son Matthijs. Single woman. Worried, because her son lives with her again after having travelled half the world. His fuck-around-the-world tour had left him with seven children.

The first morning that he sat on her couch again, there was coffee for both of them. Silent, that was true. Outside, the wind blew, a wind from the North Sea, the smell of wet grass and mud all the way into the kitchen. Matthijs made his phone disappear as soon as he saw her. As if he thought she didn't understand what one got up to on a screen. She had seen enough of his biology to fill in the rest. The morning sun shone oval on his crown, the hair thinner than she remembered.

"You can just sit in the kitchen, you know," she said, while she observed his face. The skin was adorned with wrinkles he hadn't had in Brazil, which she knew for sure. She had seen that photo, a group picture at a beach bar. His arm around that girl, no idea anymore what her name was, but she had worn Gucci sunglasses and laughed exuberantly with her full mouth. That mouth had caused the most commotion in the family app. She could remember it all perfectly well.

"I prefer sitting here," he answered. The couch still had that ink-blue stain in the left corner after all those years; the color had faded to something like a depressed sea creature. He let one leg hang over the armrest, his whole body a question mark.

"They'd rather you didn't smoke on the balcony," she added. "Lots of people die of COPD these days. Not that you ever listen to me."

He grinned. His teeth were battered, yellowish, and irregular. "Maybe you want me to die before the neighbours do."

The joke didn't land, but she poured again out of habit.

In the afternoon, she fetched tulips, because the house felt like an empty bowl without flowers. On the way, she thought that her son was the only one who brought something of spring into the house, if only through the thick, floating smell of his aftershave. When she returned, she found him in her room. He stood before the old chest of drawers, the wooden one she had taken from her marriage. The pinnacle of what could once be called "family property."

"What are you looking for?"

"Nothing," he said.

She stayed at the door, her bunch of keys still cold in her hand. He turned to her now, wearing a brown turtleneck of her deceased ex. That had to be deliberate, provocative perhaps, but probably careless.

"Your father was cremated in that sweater," she said.

Matthijs pulled the fabric around his shoulders. "Apparently not completely."

She tried to ignore her son, there in the sitting room, but he had made tea again. A ritual: he never asked what she wanted. Every time Earl Grey with too much milk, lukewarm, as if he wanted to train her tongue away from bitterness.

"Mum," he said, the cup in her field of vision, "there's nothing on TV."

She held her magazine right before her face, making him wait with that stupid cup in his hand.

"I thought you'd try the gym today," she said, without looking up.

"Was closed."

"On Sunday?"

"Sunday," he said as if that explained everything.

She lowered the magazine. "In England, gyms never closed on the day of the Lord. In Jakarta, they even train during the Sugar Feast."

"This is Holland," said Matthijs.

He held his chin just a bit too confidently up. Out of the corner of her eye, she remembered his father's head: rusted neck vertebrae, jaw like a screw clamp. She put the magazine beside her, folded her hands.

"Don't you just want to do something with me for once?" he asked.

She had to try hard not to laugh. Or cry. It had become too tiring to feel the difference.

"I have a bridge club this afternoon," she said.

"Bridge club," he repeated, tongue on the irritation, eyes a fraction too bright.

"You can come observe, if you like. But I don't think you have the discipline for our conventions."

"Oh mum."

A silence unfolded between them. She inspected his hands: no longer brown from the sun, nails short but not cared for, scars on the knuckles from too many doors and too little love.

"Did you send that email yet?" she asked.

"Which one?"

"The one to Norway."

"Why should I?"

She shook her head. "I'm only trying to help you, Matthijs."

"You're trying to manage me."

"Manage?"

"Control is also a kind of love," he said.

She felt her jaws tighten, the unspoken name of his father in her mouth, sour as milk recalled.

"Go do something," she said. "Walk the dog. Go cycling. At least go dating."

"Am I allowed again?"

"By me? It's your right."

He turned the mug in his hands. The tea had drawn circles in the porcelain, like contours of an old map.

"Maybe I'll write Norway after all. Still have contacts there."

"Good."

She wanted to say that he shouldn't expect her to check up on him. That he was an adult and that she knew what that felt like: waiting for someone who once left you to write back finally. But she stayed silent. She placed her own cup on the table, her hands folded as if she could hold on to something better than a conversation with Matthijs. In her coat pocket, she felt the supermarket receipt prick. Don't forget to return it; the cashier had scanned too little, and honesty didn't necessarily pay, but it was the only thing you could hope for salvation with.

She heard downstairs the front door swing open, followed by shuffling footsteps on the hallway tiles. Matthijs didn't even bother to take off his shoes. She felt the sigh of mud and air mix with his departure. There also drifted a subtle sound through the room, a woman's laughter, short and not misplaced, meant for him, not for her.

She slid the tulips into a water glass with the logo of her old employer. It felt like a small revenge that she left the most beautiful vase unused. For a moment, she thought of the cat, which she had had put down earlier that year and which had always immediately knocked over the flowers. There was no one left to sabotage this comfort.

"Mum?" came the voice from downstairs. "I have a date later."

She didn't go to her son. She looked at the tulips, so straight and without shame, their streaks of yellow like snot and sun in one above her stack of books.

"Fine," she called tonelessly, "don't forget to brush your teeth."

Instead of waiting for the next dialogue, she locked herself in her room. She let herself sink onto the bed, looked at the ceiling with the fine cracks that branched like a faint relief of another world. She heard herself mothering in a way that slowly died out, until even her voice became unnecessary.

Awaiting news from Norway, or from the rest of the world, she dozed off. Through half a dream, she saw her son, older than now, a face that reached her with a softness she could not acknowledge in herself. And the tulips, always the tulips; every year again, but never the same.

Days passed in which everything dragged on with the grace of a wet rag. Outside, spring turned quickly; in the garden, hyacinths burst open, like blisters after a blunder, and birds crowed themselves hoarse with moisture. The silence in the house was not a luxury but a pretentious guest, for even when Matthijs was physically there, he remained a vague signal in the periphery. She heard him at set hours fiddling with the coffee machine, or saw him at the dining table, half hidden behind his laptop, always looking for Wi-Fi or an escape.

On Monday, she had treated herself to a bunch of fresh coriander from the Turkish shop. The scent was convincingly present — citrus with sweat, sharp as memories you thought had been digested. She cut the stems and thought about how few people in her life had retained their sense of taste. She adjusted her tulips in the glass, now faded to an intimate sadness of beige, and decided it was time for a walk. Where to? To the post office, because discipline was her way not to get lost.

The coat hung ready, keys in the pocket as reassurance. Her husband had always forgotten something: his wallet, his appointments, sometimes even her name when she called him at work. Matthijs was no better. As soon as she stood outside, she noticed he followed her. "Mum!" He called after her, gangly, as only men who never did homework could, and turned along her shoulder.

"You know you can do groceries online, right?" His face showed that jokester grin, but his eyebrows trembled as if he was worried.

"If you learn to cook, I'll do everything online," she bounced back. She increased her pace; he quickly caught up, dragging shoes, open jacket.

"Do you think Norway is really waiting for me?" He spoke it without sound; only in the movement of his lips did she read it.

"You have an education. You have experience. And nothing is as attractive in a person as keeping promises."

"Nothing?" He looked at her now, eyes blue, teeth visible in a half (fixed) smile. "Not humor, or looks, or, say, guts?"

She sniffed, warm in her scarf. "That depends on age."

They crossed a street where horse chestnuts began their bloom; the air smelled of diesel, but with an undertone of sugary spring. Now that they walked side by side, it felt a bit like before, when he still babbled unhindered by himself about everything he encountered. Even then, he had the tendency to greet strangers or to kick trash bins in thoughtless ways.

"What's wrong, Matthijs?" She stopped walking because time could be complicated enough without walking like a standing tram. "You have that look," she said, "of someone who just pulled a cookie from the vending machine and now regrets it."

Matthijs pursed his lips, then switched back to half power in his old role. "Last night, that date was here. Well, not here here, but… you know."

She nodded. Of course. She wasn't born at the end of an optical cable, but you did age faster when everything took place in your house.

"She talked about children," he continued. "About later and together and so on." He looked at her now with the gaze of a man who breathed on the seabed. "As if it were an Excel sheet you only had to fill in with names and birthdates."

Geertruida felt her jaws fall back into the old fold. She wished it would affect her less: the youthful drama that always came at the expense of later, exposing and addictive at the same time. She especially didn't want to answer what she thought, that her own life too had been composed of hasty tables and coincidentally filled cells.

She bought stamps, six for abroad and another sheet with cats for birthday cards. In the supermarket, Matthijs kept himself quiet between the pre-retirees and the baklava men. He scanned the shelves with a look that reminded her of searching for an exit, and she wondered for a moment if he would ever be able to stop. Maybe even that was a form of love: to make an offering, to seduce yourself into a life you didn't quite believe in.

At home, Matthijs poured milk into a glass, as if even that was a performance. She secretly let him do his thing, convinced that men ultimately all cried for milk when no one saw. She had resolved not to correct him anymore on his posture or his future, or the fact that he left his laundry lying around far too often.

"Mum—"

She turned to him, hands on the counter so her shoulder blades wouldn't betray that she was tired.

"I texted Norway," he said. "They want me to call on Monday."

She nodded. She felt her skin grow two degrees warmer. Bad things could always wait, she thought, but good news had to be taken in liquid form while it lasted.

"Only," he said, "they're looking for a couple."

She giggled, not out of mockery but as a reflex. He shrugged — typical, that slow-motion defeat.

"Imagine," he said, "me with a stranger, drumming on an Arctic farm."

She thought about how people attached themselves in times of need, sometimes for a while, sometimes out of pure exile. She thought of her own marriage, entered into out of necessity because in those days you couldn't just be loose and drink expensive wine with friends on the weekends. It had been all or nothing, and afterward, in retrospect, it all seemed so logical — you chose, and you bore the consequence.

Matthijs scrolled through his phone, fingers quick and searching, like a twelve-year-old in a candy store. He showed her the profile of a woman: black hair, laughing with her whole face.

"She might want it," he said.

She took her reading glasses and looked at the screen. Two degrees prettier than he was used to, she estimated, but also something determined in the jawline — such a character face that knew exactly what it came for.

"She has a child."

"Yes, from a previous man." He frowned, as if that required more explanation.

She waved her hand. "Children are friendlier than adults. They don't pry everything open and expect nothing back."

A silence, just too long. In her head passed old images of her own child, small and clumsy, with bruises on his shins because he never looked around him.

"Maybe I should just try it," said Matthijs.

"Maybe you should," she agreed, without softness.

He left the kitchen. She heard him rummaging upstairs, as if even there he couldn't choose between staying and leaving. On the sink lay the receipt for the stamps; naturally, she hadn't filed it. With two fingers, she smoothed it flat and placed it by the flowers, under the glass.

The next morning, she woke up early, before the alarm. The house had the stillness of something recently abandoned. The air was colder, thinner, as if the walls had forgotten their task. She made coffee, poured it into two cups out of habit, then poured one back into the pot.

On the table lay a note, written on the back of an old envelope. Thanks, I'll call when I land. No signature, just that one sentence. She read it several times, until the ink seemed to fade from repetition.

Outside, the sky had that indecisive color between blue and white. The tulips had drooped during the night; their stems bent like tired wrists. She straightened one, though it wouldn't stand.

In the kitchen sink, a single spoon floated in lukewarm water. She turned off the tap, dried her hands, and stood there without purpose. A plane passed overhead — faint, distant, indifferent.

For a moment, she imagined that she could follow it with her eyes all the way north, until it disappeared beyond the cloud line. But the window glass held her reflection, and she saw only herself: a woman holding a mug, standing in a house that had resumed its original size.

She took a sip. The coffee had gone cold, but she drank it anyway.

In the days that followed, she kept the routine. Coffee at eight, walk at ten, bridge on Thursdays. The tulips she replaced with carnations — sturdier, less dramatic.

Sometimes she thought she heard his voice from the hallway, or the sound of his shoes on the stairs, but it was always the mailman, or the wind pressing against the door.

She folded his laundry, though he hadn't left any. She checked her phone for messages that weren't there.

At night, she sat by the window, the curtain slightly open, the television murmuring in the background. The news spoke of storms, of ice breaking off in the north. She imagined him there, somewhere between sky and sea, a man among other men, trying to remember what home had felt like.

When she finally went to bed, she left the lamp on, just in case.

Coriander, as proof that things always came back.

The next day, the house was empty. She knew her son would not return for at least three hours. She made coffee, double-checked everything — windows closed, lights off, emptied the mailbox. Her routine was like a raincoat she couldn't take off. In the living room, it smelled musty, as if all the nights of her life had piled up in the carpet.

She chose to open the door to the balcony. Enough air today, the tulips bent under their own weight, the color now anemic but decorative. On her phone, there was a message from Matthijs: "To promise isn't the same as to do, but I'm going to call that woman later." She had to smile at his semi-poetic flabbiness. Everything in him was constructed to secure the possibility of failure already.

At a quarter past four, she came back from walking. At the dining table, he was already waiting, laptop open, gaze stuck on an online form.

"Can you fill this in?" he asked, as if he were ten again and the parent-teacher night started too early.

She came to stand behind him, let her hand rest on his shoulder — a thin, narrowly carried line, the smell of emerging armpits that moved her involuntarily. Together they filled in the letters with Norway, his name spelled as it should be — ij instead of y — his date of birth, the numbers of passport and citizen service number, and whatever else you had to fill in to get by as a modern farm laborer. His handwriting was terrible; even on the screen, it looked as if he typed with his foot. She didn't make a fuss, clicked the required boxes, and let the privacy declaration pass unseen. Everything had to be given away at some point anyway.

For half a minute, they lingered silently above the screen. The warmth of his shoulder seeped softly into her arm, not as discomfort but as confirmation that he really sat there. She knew few things more reassuring than the awareness that someone depended on you, even if it had taken you thirty years to recognize that out loud.

"That's it then," she said. "You can send it."

"Do I need a motivation letter?"

"Can't hurt."

He shyly searched for a Word document, typed with two fingers a whole piece that made no sense — about discipline, perseverance, love for the northern nature. She didn't need to read it to know it was a lie; the only trees he had ever clung to were the grimy poplars in their backyard. Still, it was a kind of achievement. You didn't get to know someone by what he said, but by what he left unsaid.

When everything was done, he closed the screen. It clicked loudly, as if he had definitively closed something.

"Now wait?" he tried.

"Now wait," she said.

She left him sitting, walked to the kitchen, and turned on a kettle. The device trembled softly, old lime-like teeth that had forgotten to rinse. There were still cookies in a tin her mother had left behind — hard bastogne, the kind you thought no one ever finished, until one of them always started again.

She gave him a cookie, no longer as an act of upbringing but as a kind of pact: we, the two of us, against the rest of everything.

"When you leave," she said, "at least don't let the milk go bad."

He grinned, a mouth full of crumbs.

"Maybe I'll take the milk with me. In case you miss me."

"You, with that lactose armor," she muttered.

It was a beautiful day. Sunspots hopped across the floor, again, a scent of tulips and coriander drifted through the window. She was sure that the white coat the plant wore — yeasts of mold, edges of disappointment — would in three days turn into a brown lump. She hoped he'd be home to see it.

At the end of the afternoon, they cleaned the counter together. She noticed that for the first time, he sorted the cutlery without asking where it went. That's how it goes, she thought: habit eventually becomes a second nature, and even men like Matthijs couldn't escape it.

The days crawled further toward an undefined departure. Matthijs sometimes disappeared for hours to the attic with his phone, probably to Skype with Norway, or with that dark woman from the app. Geertruida heard his voice echo through the stairs, never loud but always streaking against the silence, and she sometimes felt like an unseen extra in his half-preparation. She tried not to hinder him. In the garden, she weeded, ground coffee beans to fine grit, hung sheets outside so the house would smell of a lost season. When she looked up, she saw him through the window, his silhouette languid like a boy who couldn't bind himself to his place.

One morning, the rain beating hard against the glass, she found him in the kitchen with two coffee mugs ready. He had combed his hair back wet, his shirt tucked tightly into his pants, and she guessed he had tried in vain to wake up on time. It was a pose she recognized from her own father, who always prepared himself for unimportant days.

"Today's the interview," said Matthijs. He drew circles in the coffee foam with his finger. "Do you want me to do it downstairs?"

She shrugged. "I'm not deaf. There's no shame in trying."

He nodded, without looking at her. She heard him later upstairs, a monologue in halting English, as if he had to ventilate all he'd stored up over the years at once. She didn't wait for him to finish. She put on her coat, sat down on the couch, and let her thoughts drift through the room. Things rarely went as you hoped; better to fuss about the details than about the big failure.

In the evening, he sat at the dining table. His face was glowing purple, eyes without shine.

"They'll call back tomorrow," he said. "They found my experience interesting, but I first need to… fix a partner."

"Write her that email," she suggested. She had never had trouble calling things by their name.

He grinned, not cheerfully, but grateful for the directness. He quickly typed a message, determined, maybe even relieved that there was a next step.

A week passed. In that week, spring suddenly entered the house. The sky stood bright blue, and everywhere flowers burst open. The tulips turned white beyond their shelf life, but Geertruida couldn't bring herself to throw them away. Matthijs was home less often. He came, ate hastily, and told only what was strictly necessary. Sometimes he lay on his bed deep into the night dreaming, the smartphone a glowing egg on his stomach.

When the doorbell rang, she expected the parcel delivery man or a collector, but it turned out to be a woman with black hair, jeans, and a child next to her on the doorstep. The child's coat was too light for the cold, but children had their own thermostat.

Matthijs stood next to her, so still that he seemed to be waiting for permission. He pointed to the woman, said, "This is Priya." The woman looked at her with a kind of curiosity, a mild glance, as if she were collecting data. Then she introduced the child as "Amal, five" — all quick, measured, clearly not for the first time.

Geertruida left the door open longer than necessary. Eventually, the three of them stepped inside. The child immediately moved toward the litter box, as if it followed the same route in every house. Priya looked at her briefly, mouth in a half-smile, chin up. She spoke good Dutch, but with something in the tone that suggested she habitually scraped her tongue along an invisible border.

"This is my mother," said Matthijs.

She greeted her with a handshake, light, almost pro forma. Amal had already picked a plastic block from the shelf and examined it with penetrating purposefulness.

"Coffee?" It came out less warmly than intended, but Priya accepted it as an invitation to find balance.

They sat the four of them at the table, the air heavy with newness. Priya talked more easily than her son; at her own pace, about her work, her divorce, the advantages of a hybrid existence ("everyone works remote now, even the children"). Geertruida discovered a natural competence: Priya knew exactly how much to share without giving away a gram too much. She knew the type — women who make their own plans and only later disappoint when that plan ever falls away.

Matthijs held back at first, laughed too conspicuously at the jokes Priya made. Occasionally, he checked if Geertruida was listening, like a suspicious student going through his test with questionable enthusiasm. Amal climbed onto her lap after twenty minutes, playing with the zipper of her cardigan, and Geertruida remembered again how simple it once was — the days with a child at the edge of your vision, trying to annex every room.

After the conversation, Priya opened her bag, took out two forms. "This is from the employment office. They want proof that we're a team. Or something like that."

Geertruida looked at the sheets, felt how the dark blue of her pen barely slid over the paper. A team. She could still imagine that. She took a cookie for Amal, set down the coffee, and felt something like understanding for this new constellation, as if she, with her years of experience, was suddenly hired as the external consultant of a startup that had to invent itself.

She thought of how her signature always tickled under everything, never cramped. What days ago had seemed bizarre now felt almost like an office joke — one of those company parties where you don't know half the people but are forced together anyway. A team. She could picture it: a group of people, all too smart or too broken to fit anywhere else, doomed to cooperate on a slope. Maybe that was the whole joke of family; that it wasn't so much about love, but about the ability to turn protocol and expectation into functional chaos.

Priya asked if her son could borrow a charger. The boy walked small circles around the table, head down, his jacket much too thin; he clung to his mother's buttons as if those were the only fixed points in the room. There was something sharp in her questions, thought Geertruida, as if she were stirring the soup carefully with a wooden spoon before serving it. No man had ever truly been her boss.

Before the afternoon was over, all signatures sat in the right places. Priya noted her number, briefly explained when she was reachable ("don't call during swimming lessons, it's hell there"), and folded everything so tightly that it fit into the small pocket inside her bag. Amal wanted one more cookie but didn't dare ask. Geertruida gave him one anyway, nodded without a word.

When they said goodbye, it was stately and awkward. In her own hallway, it wasn't customary to embrace strangers, but Priya gave a light, warm nod — a lease agreement between people who didn't want to waste time. Matthijs walked a bit with them, then ducked back at the garden gate as if he were already used to the prospect of being on the road, maybe even together with this woman.

The door fell shut behind him. She stood in the kitchen, fingers greasy from the cookie, and let the conversation pass through her head once more. The silence was finally hers. Even the tulips looked neutral. She washed her cup, closed the dishwasher, and looked once more at the form that now lay on the counter, recklessly scribbled with names in ink. "A team," she muttered. "Good."

That night, she dreamed of a house without attics, without hidden places where sorrow could degenerate. Everything plastered white, the rooms smelling of young coffee and air. She slept as deeply as she hadn't in months.

Three days later, it was arranged. The email came early in the morning, with a logo that looked Scandinavian enough to trust. Matthijs read it out loud as if it were a verdict.

"They're taking me. I can start in May."

She nodded, as if she had been waiting for that line all week. "Good," she said, "then we know where we stand."

He grinned awkwardly, rubbed his neck. "It's only for six months."

"Half a year is still half a year," she said. "A decent length for a life."

He didn't answer. His hands went restless over the table, looking for something to do. She had the feeling that he wanted to say more — or maybe less — but couldn't find the exact angle.

"You'll need clothes," she said finally. "And a decent jacket. And that laptop bag that doesn't smell like beer."

He laughed, a sound that immediately dissolved again.

They went shopping that same afternoon. In the city center, between the shop windows and the drizzle, he walked like someone who temporarily borrows the world. He didn't like to choose. She picked out a winter coat for him, blue, waterproof, pockets big enough for hands and doubt. At the register, he made a half-hearted attempt to pay himself; she ignored it.

"You can transfer it later," she said, though she knew he wouldn't.

Back home, she spread the clothes over the couch — shirts, socks, things you didn't miss until you needed them. The suitcase stood open, gaping like a new chapter.

In the evening, they ate together, pasta with too much garlic. He had opened a bottle of wine, poured her a full glass, though she rarely drank anymore.

"To Norway," he said.

"To common sense," she answered.

They clinked glasses. The sound was thin, but not unfriendly.

That night, she couldn't sleep. The thought of departure lingered in her chest like static. She heard him walking upstairs, pacing. Once the floor creaked, she thought he might come down, but he didn't. She turned to the wall and let the darkness fill with all the versions of her son she had ever known — the toddler with jam hands, the teenager with the slammed doors, the man who came home with seven children he didn't raise. And now this one, somewhere between leaving and arriving.

In the morning, he was already downstairs, dressed, suitcase zipped. The tulips had finally collapsed; only stems stood like failed promises.

"Don't forget your passport," she said.

He patted his jacket pocket. "Got it."

They didn't hug immediately. The moment didn't ask for that. He put the suitcase upright, looked around the room as if it were a museum of himself.

"You'll water the coriander?"

"If it survives you," she said.

He smiled. "Maybe it'll grow better without me."

At the door, he finally reached for her, one arm, brief but real. He smelled of soap and nerves. Then he stepped outside, suitcase clattering over the tiles.

She watched him go until he turned the corner. Only then did she close the door, slow, careful not to make a sound.

The silence that followed was clean.

In the kitchen, she saw his mug still on the counter, a thin film of coffee on the surface. She didn't wash it. Not yet.

She went to the balcony, where the coriander had indeed started to wilt. She pinched a leaf between her fingers and smelled it — sharp, green, stubborn. Proof that things always came back, even if you didn't ask them to.

The noise of the pipes and the soft blowing of the wind. No idea what she should do with herself now that the silent fight was actually over. The phone lay limp on the little table; no news, no pings, only the echo of the previous conversation. She thought about what it must be like to really be alone, whether she would ever get used to it. In the bedroom, the bed seemed to have spatially shrunk into a cramped cell that didn't understand why the other half wasn't being filled.

Outside, the rain spun itself along the windows, like a streaming service that could never run empty. She thought of the voice of her son, who in Norway was already slowly slowing down; of the unknown air, new routines he might be making his own. Also, the fact that, in time, there would be no one to tell him not to let the milk boil over, or that his sweater really needed to be drier before putting it on. A reassurance, but also a loss — but she kept it small, like a leaking carton of yogurt that you just peel the cardboard off at some point.

The night after, she dreamed again of houses. They were always flawless, concrete spaces, with windows so large you felt you lived in an aquarium. In that dream, she sat at a glass table, someone poured her coffee, and for a moment, she thought it was her husband's voice. But when she looked up, it was a child, sweet and perfect, with a face that reminded her of nothing. Maybe she was even searching in dreams for alternatives, each night a new team to belong to somewhere.

The week flowed by without fuss. Morning coffee tasted different — more bitter, but not necessarily worse. Between groceries and the Bridge News, she kept a slightly closer eye on Instagram. Sometimes she found photos from Norway: a sparkling lake, a child in a raincoat, a pan of brown bean soup, with a thumbs-up at the bottom or a caption that always began with "Getting used to it...". Sometimes they didn't post anything; then she had to deduce from the silence that it was probably fine. At the end of the first week, she received a postcard — retro, with a solitary church on a poor-looking plain. His handwriting filled the back; Priya's child had added half a letter too. She read it three times. Then she kept it — not under the coriander, but between the old insurance papers, where it truly belonged.

In the second week, the usual rhythm returned: coffee, the newspaper, the awkwardness typical of meaningless days. Geertruida washed her hands until the skin split. She hardly noticed, not even when the soapy water stung the small cuts between her knuckles. To her surprise, on Wednesday morning, she got a phone call from Priya. No WhatsApp, no line of text, but old-fashioned calling.

It took three rings before she picked up.

"Hello?"

On the other side, a moment of silence. Then: "Hello. This is Priya." Voice flat, almost formal, as if confirming a dentist appointment.

"Hello Priya." She heard herself sounding too polite.

"This may be strange, but I wanted to ask… how do you do it? Being alone."

Outside, a bus rattled by. Geertruida wrung out the dishcloth, turned her face toward the window. The rain didn't seem to plan on stopping.

"You mean: surviving?"

"I think so." It sounded softer now. "Matthijs says you always knew how to keep yourself busy. I can barely stand ten minutes of silence."

"Matthijs exaggerates," she said. "Mostly, I just put on some music. Or I start a book and don't finish it." There was little point in pretending she had it all figured out. She still felt like a beginner at being alone every day.

Priya laughed, but it didn't get further than a sort of breath. "You know, Amal asked today if we could call you because it always smells like soup here. He misses the smell of flowers."

"I could send some tulips," suggested Geertruida, quicker than planned. "Takes some getting used to, because they don't survive a day without water."

"Everything takes getting used to," said Priya softly. "Even Matthijs."

The conversation after that was about practical things — packages, whether Amal might like to video call sometime. But in the background, Geertruida heard something brittle, a kind of homesickness without a name. She recognized the false feeling of displacement, the discomfort of teams that hadn't yet learned to work smoothly.

That afternoon, she walked to the florist, bought three bunches at once. At home, she put half in an old beer glass, and the other half she trimmed and packed with extra wet cloths. She had to laugh at her own train of thought: as if flowers ever meant more than a temporary, tasteless decoration. Yet she persisted — maybe stubbornness was also a form of love.

She emailed Priya that the tulips were on their way. Matthijs later that evening sent a selfie: him with a ladle, Priya with a grimace, the child crooked behind them. In the middle of the beer glass, with three tulips, fresh and barely open. The agreement seemed to be: one photo back every day, until the flowers were gone.

On Friday, the postman came with the flowers in wet newspapers and a box of cookies besides, as if everyone now knew about their diet. She had first doubted the address — the house number was wrong, typo, typical Matthijs — but the mail always found its way to places no one else wanted to go. Priya had unpacked the package immediately; within the hour came the thank-you email, with no more than three words, and a photo of Amal with a tulip as a paddle in both hands. The pink spot on his cheek betrayed that the house was still cold.

For Geertruida, life became a sum of habits. She followed her son's progress online, kept up with the local news, and wrote down the meter readings every month so there could never be confusion about usage. People sometimes said emptiness was a challenge, but she found silence as fillable as Christmas stockings: you just had to feel like it. She had quit the bridge club without much noise. Even the swans along the canal began to recognize her voice, though she pretended they didn't. On Thursdays, she cleared out the pantry — always a reassuring task, because somewhere in the back of her mind played the fear that someday it could be 1944 again.

Matthijs called more often than she had expected. Sometimes briefly, sometimes with more reason. There was always a reason: the oven had exploded ("I swear, within a day the whole house smelled like burnt rubber"), or Amal had split his lip at daycare. He never asked about her. But he also never hung up first, and that was enough. She listened, asked questions he didn't always answer, and learned to take long silences as compliments.

In the third week, Priya didn't send photos, but she did send an email. "We're a team now, I think. But I miss my mother." That's how it stood, plain, without a question attached. Geertruida didn't write back; she just left the message sitting in her inbox. You shouldn't respond too quickly, she thought; some things needed time to ripen.

That night she stayed up late, legs over the coffee table, coffee black and bitter as motor oil. She looked through the window at the blind streets and imagined how things must be in Norway: lots of wood, few words, drinking until you no longer think about leaving or returning. She remembered how little her own mother had ever shared, and how peace had only come when no one kept asking anymore.

On a Saturday, Matthijs came back unexpectedly. No announcement, only a banging sound on the window and his face, older still, behind the dirty glass. She opened the door, smelled his breath and the old shaving soap, and something sharp from outside. It was spring, but he wore gloves.

"We were in the neighborhood," he said, face pale from the maddening cold front that had blown in with him. In the hallway stood Priya, a scarf around her head, and a child nervously shuffling in rubber boots. They carried their travel stories like layers of plaster on their clothes: Norway hadn't spared them, but marked them, and now they were suddenly on her doorstep, Amsterdam light in their eyes.

"Surprise," said Matthijs, with that old boyish attempt. He had a cardboard box with him, the top sealed with Norwegian tape, wildly covered with address stickers, and the corners already soggy and bent.

She just looked at them, at first, because the shock couldn't land right away. Eyes, hands, mouths — everything moved, nothing was where it belonged.

"Amal misses the flowers," said Priya, while the child held tightly to her leg. "And Matthijs wanted to bring it himself."

She nodded, made space, because what else could you do? Sometimes the past came back in boxes at once; you didn't have to decide about the contents yourself.

Inside, it smelled of soup and dishes. The box was opened on the kitchen table, between the smudged cards and the remnants of a dandelion bouquet from the park. There was nothing in it she hadn't expected: a coarsely knitted scarf (bird's nest of white fluff and bread crumbs), a handful of postcards for the child, and a postcard stuck with lumps of frozen jam.

"You didn't have to bring flowers. I've got them here in boxes too," said Geertruida, and it came out more annoyed than planned.

Priya smiled, a little sad but firm. "It felt like a ritual."

"Everything is a ritual," she heard herself say, and there was little room left between the words.

Matthijs stayed standing at the counter, as if afraid to make the house dirty again. His hair was shorter, his face drawn open by wind and loss of sleep. In the kitchen light, wrinkles turned into grooves. She wanted to get the milk for him, but the child was ahead of her, climbing soundlessly via the chair onto the counter.

"I couldn't really leave there," said Matthijs, by way of explanation. "They don't do departures there. You stay until you no longer fit."

"Or until you have to go back," she said, not knowing who she meant.

Priya had taken off her scarf. Her hair fell thick and black over her shoulders, with the shine of a freshly oiled machine. It surprised her how naturally this woman moved in her house — as if she knew that whoever waited long enough would still end up in an alley of their own past.

They had to stay for dinner, of course. It became pasta, since the baguette was gone sooner than expected, the table full of sheets of cheese and butter, the wine in a carafe to make it seem like it wasn't just a temporary event. The child sat between the adults, first fidgeting with his legs, later with his hands, until he had taken all the pens from the kitchen pot and decorated the table with a graph of crossing lines. They talked about work, about airlines, and the differences between Scandinavian and Dutch childcare. Priya told how in Norway you never opened the door for strangers, unless they came to fetch something you wanted to get rid of. Geertruida barely listened; the tapping of the knife on the plate was a distraction enough. Everything was marked by temporality — even the conversation, even the way Priya spoke about her week.

After dinner, Amal used a napkin rolled into a tube to wipe the table. Geertruida didn't bother to help him; the pace suited her fine, and it was only fair that children also sweated after a meal. In the living room, Matthijs dropped himself onto the couch, rolled his shoulders, and spoke aloud to the ceiling. "Now that's sitting," he said, and for once she wasn't even bothered by how little he'd changed. Maybe no one in her family ever really leaped: always those small repetitions, always the same joke in a different wrapping.

She and Priya cleared the table together, without many words. The silence between women was no discomfort — it was rather a ritual in itself, the way you only truly bonded when there wasn't a man around trying to be charming. As the dishwasher filled, Geertruida asked about the house in Norway, whether it was really as cold as it looked on TV.

"It's not the cold that makes it hard," answered Priya. "It's the light. You never know when it stops. Or when it begins."

She nodded. In her head played the memory of her husband, who at every sudden shower had to wipe the window and swore he couldn't function without light. By now, she had taught herself to do everything in the dark, if necessary, with a baguette and cold tea.

"Matthijs says you gave up bridge."

"There was nothing left to win. Too many old acquaintances who had given up beforehand. Bridge is only fun if you still think you can surprise people."

"Is everything like that?" asked Priya, softly. "Even with family?"

She thought of the woman standing across from her — of the sweetness of her voice and the sharpness within it, of the hands that gripped everything but never held on. Maybe that was the whole trick: that family, just like bridge, a game of pulling and letting go.

'No,' she answered. She wanted to add something, but the words were full of air. It was the way it was now.

During coffee, Matthijs came back to himself. He wiped his hands on his pants, looked around as if he didn't know where to start. He hadn't touched the glass of wine; instead, he pressed his thumb into the edge of the tabletop, always in the same spot, until there must have been a light groove in his skin.

Priya had made herself comfortable again, backpack as backrest, legs stretched out under the coffee table. Amal sat between them, head on her leg, fingers cramping around a toy car that smelled just a bit too much like plastic.

'You don't have to stay, you know,' she said.

'It's raining,' said Matthijs. 'Norway in the rain is no joke.'

Geertruida sank into the chair by the window, her hands around the napkin she had secretly taken from the table while clearing up. On the threshold of the room lay the hem of her ex's sweater, as always, dozing on the edge of spreading out.

She wondered whether Matthijs wore the sweater on purpose, as proof of something, or if it was simply his way of reusing parts of the past.

She listened to the child: Amal made soft vrrrrr-sounds, pushed the little car over the V-shaped lines between the floorboards. The woman he called mother had, in Norway, immediately claimed the right to the name. Amal took no account of expectation; he fitted himself effortlessly into the opening between the adults. In that, he was not much different from Matthijs back then.

'We don't have to stay,' said Priya, as if it were an old knot that now finally loosened.

'It's late,' said Geertruida, her voice on the vague border of motherhood.

She looked through the window. Rain like a curtain of glass before the light from outside. The windows fogged, with small drops arranging themselves like constellations on her side. She felt the old reflex: reshaping herself into a hostess, even if she was only a bystander now, a signpost for people who had already chosen their own destination.

She poured more wine, asked no questions. Priya told about the house in Norway, about how the walls creaked at night, and it always smelled of mothballs and wood. She said it dryly, without drama, but Geertruida knew instinctively that she had called her not only out of politeness, but out of necessity. Everyone, eventually, called their mother.

Matthijs sat there, less uncomfortable than before. On the couch, he was a burden to no one. He waited – not for permission, but for the moment when enough had been everything.

Amal fell asleep on his mother's leg, the cheeks red, breath heavy. Priya briefly stroked through the child's hair, letting her hand rest. She didn't look up when she said to Geertruida: 'That's how it goes.'

At half past ten, only she and the woman remained by the window, the coffee cold, their voices an echo of the first conversation they had ever had. Matthijs had gone with the child to the bedroom to improvise a bed out of blankets and old pillowcases – exactly what a house was supposed to be: a way station where everyone with their spare stuff built a temporary nest.

Priya sipped her coffee. Her fingers were thin and tense above the earthenware, as if she might drop the cup at any moment. The silence that fell between them was not harsh, but rather lived-in and softly padded. Heavy rain on the glass, the sound rhythmic and nowhere intrusive. In her whole life, Geertruida had never had a conversation that didn't somehow end with rain. She wondered whether that was different for other people.

'You don't have any other children?' Priya didn't look up as she asked.

'One was enough.' She chuckled briefly. 'If I'd do it over again, maybe three. Like with tulip bulbs: they grow better when they're planted in clusters.'

The woman laughed, shrill and open, almost like a test. 'And you, would you start over now?'

'With children, or in general?'

'Both, maybe.'

She had to think. The conversation had no hurry. Behind her lay a decade of answers, all to be weighed again.

'I think most things grow naturally where the light allows it,' said Geertruida. She wondered if it was supposed to sound poetic, but it was simply true: everything grew where no one could break it. If the light was your enemy, then you rooted in the dark – that went for plant, animal, and human.

Priya rolled her mouth into a thin, content line. 'It's strange, but I can't imagine Amal having to live alone someday. As if every time a kind of umbilical cord grows back.'

'He'll manage.' She said it dryly, without hesitation, but her hands went cold in her lap. 'Children are a mirror for a while. Then they turn into a sort of mirage: you see them, but you never really touch them again.'

They both looked at the window, where dusk clung in reflection. In the glass, their faces spanned across: an old profile and a new one, barely attached. She wondered why it was always women who, in the deepest night, took stock.

No further questions came. Priya pushed her chair back, grabbed her backpack, and walked barefoot – the woollen socks like carpet from home around her ankles – to the room where the child lay. Geertruida caught the smell of something sour, maybe yoghurt, maybe just the quiet remainder of another life that had briefly fallen sideways into her house.

She wiped the coffee stain from the table, put away the cutlery. Nowhere in the house did the idea still hang that—

There was an adder hidden in those kinds of questions, always. 'I'm too old, Priya. Aren't you?'

'I have Amal.' Now they did look at each other, a moment without faint contours. In the rain, the face opposite her seemed cut from another layer of time: black hair, bare temples; a beauty born precisely from what was missing.

'Sometimes I think it's actually easier to start over when you already know how it ends,' said Priya.

She had no answer to that. Her hands lay loosely folded in her lap. In the past, she'd had the tendency to give strange women the benefit of the doubt. Later, there came the stories of her son, each time another woman, but always the same riddle. Even now, she saw in this woman the dreams and the scrapes, but no mask.

The night slowly drew the colors from the room. The lamp above the counter gave everything a yellowish glow that could turn any house in the world into a memory. On the counter, a piece of cheese slowly dripped out its fat; under the table lay a knot of rope, probably left behind by the child. The house had, without her noticing, adjusted itself to unexpected visitors. Even the sound of rain sounded different with another heartbeat rhythm in the room.

'We should really drive back. But it's too late,' said Priya. She didn't sound surprised, not relieved. Just done with making decisions.

Geertruida nodded. She thought of the guest room, of the small bed with the outdated down blanket, the cover she had once dyed herself because no one could paint tulips yellow enough. She thought of the house's noisiness, the wind that made a duet with every draft. And of what her son would dream tonight, now that the past didn't have to endure itself alone.

'It's fine. You'll stay here tonight.'

'Thank you,' said Priya softly.

A little later, when she really left the table, she looked at the woman who had fallen for her son as if by coincidence, as if love indeed was something as irrational as a place that always smelled of soup and where you simply stayed inside for the first best rain shower. Maybe her son had succeeded after all, if he could draw the right people toward him when it really mattered.

She closed the curtains, quietly cleared the cups, decided to let go of the fact that there was still bread on the counter, and that tomorrow nothing would be like today. At the end of the hallway, she heard the child softly singing in his sleep, a song without melody, but with the certainty of a house that was no longer empty.

She stayed awake for a long time, turned with effort in bed, thought of old times and of the joke that always arrived too late. But when she finally fell asleep, it was deep, almost triumphant: the feeling that with nothing to expect, you could still receive things, and that the rain on the window sounded far less lonely than usual.

Saturday morning. She was awakened by the rumble of children's feet in the hallway, the bleating of cartoons on TV, and the smell of stale bread and apricot jam. In the kitchen, trios waited for coffee and milk. Her son had his back to her, enclosed by the woman with the black hair who, it seemed, managed the morning ritual with a shrug. No whispering, no skittishness anymore, only the sober buildup of a collective breakfast. It could have been in a brochure: domestic happiness for advanced practitioners.

She greeted no one upon entering. She made coffee, cut bread, and poured milk from the half-liter that was left. It felt excessively ordinary, a bit too much of the existing to make it special – maybe that was exactly the irony of family that you fit best together when you weren't trying to be original.

The morning emptied into routine. The child had found a new hobby within ten minutes: counting all the curtains, opening and closing them one by one until it made sense in his head. His mother read on her phone, alternating with the staccato of typing messages and glances at the breakfast that grew ever slower. Geertruida washed cups, polished the sink, and folded towels, while in the back of her head she worked through a list of things that didn't need doing today.

Matthijs sat on the edge of the couch, his breakfast clutched in both hands. She noticed in everything that this was his best version: just awake, not yet fled into words, the morning mood that for once kept him in time. There was no urge to go outside, no impulse to be somewhere. Only the temporary balance of a house that demanded nothing.

Only later, when the household had thinned by half, Priya had left the key lying somewhere on the table, the child hung lazily in his sweater by the open kitchen door – he joined her for coffee. She poured, looked over her shoulder.

'You chose her yourself,' she said.

'She was available,' he admitted. No shame, only the laconic awareness that enough was always half of what you wished.

'It works?'

'Maybe you should stop looking for proof,' he said softly. 'Things can just exist, too.'

She nodded; not conceding, not fighting back, only registering that simple truth that had echoed in the house for years. She looked at his face, the way it had aged, lines like unpleasant growth rings around the eyes and nose. But he was there. Truly. There was no distance between them, no hesitation.

The day didn't stretch further than the house itself, than its own walls; no one had an agenda, even time seemed to want to spread itself out for them. Geertruida wondered if that was what people meant by happiness. Otherwise, she'd have to learn the word anew.

After the second cup of coffee, a quarrel broke out in a tone she recognized from her own youth. Amal had spilled a glass of milk, and it pearled slowly over the counter. Priya sighed deeply, pulled the child by the shoulder, the movement staccato. The boy didn't cry—he just looked at the stain, grim, as if regret was a craft you had to learn early. For a moment, Priya let her voice echo, just a bit louder than necessary. She caught the tone of motherly irritation, but also of sleepless nights and everything that built up inside such a woman. Geertruida looked away; she knew the no-man's-land between losing and holding on. She walked to the window, wiped the condensation from the glass, and saw the rain still standing still in the air.

Matthijs had nothing to do with the conflict, but his shoulders rose slightly higher than usual. Head tilted back, hands folded. She heard him hold his breath until the scene was over, until Priya pretended again that the morning routine could go on completely unharmed. Geertruida wanted to put her hand on his shoulder, but found it too sentimental— they were too old for that now.

The day slowly shifted toward what became an afternoon. There was puzzling, drawing, and occasionally a sandwich eaten. Priya tried to arrange something for work with two phones at once, disappearing one seat further into the couch each time while the child busied itself with pencils on the floor. The calm she had felt yesterday was exchanged for something sultry. Not even conflict, rather a pressing expectation, like ozone right before a thunderstorm.

'Mom,' said Matthijs finally, while he passed her on the way to the balcony. 'Come along? Smoking is cozy at least.'

She followed him; her slippers slipped over the laminate. Outside, it was dry, the air sweet from rain and manure. There was a crunch of traffic from the main road, and somewhere in the distance, a train. Matthijs lit a cigarette and blinked against an unexpected speck of sun.

'What is it?' she asked.

He shrugged, let the smoke out like steam. 'It feels like I can never do anything right. Like everything I touch somehow doesn't quite fit anywhere.'

She looked at the regret in the corners of his mouth. She didn't want to reassure him; the urge to mother had once already been her undoing.

'You don't get that from strangers,' she said. She did her best to look at him, but her gaze belonged somewhere else.

Geertruida had a list ready – get dishwasher tablets, old shoes from the attic, maybe wash the windows – but nothing took priority over observing the people who now, in this house, repeated their refuge. She caught fragments: the mechanical clicking of Playmobil in the room, the heavy breathing of the sleeping cat behind the radiator, the murmur of voices leaking through the open door into the hallway. Sometimes, very rarely, she thought back to how it had been with her ex, the man who had left the house in silence and gathered half-lives in other places. She never felt remorse, only a light tingle of pity. Or maybe she imagined that. Maybe it was simply the sensation of a park once again full of children after years of emptiness.

Somewhere halfway through the morning, while the house sighed like an old farmhouse after a night frost, the conversation returned to the kitchen table. The milk was now lukewarm, the coffee cold, and the bread had decayed in a plastic bag. Yet everyone stayed seated, as if leaving were only permitted after a tight conclusion. Priya leaned lazily against the counter, her hair tight in a ponytail. The child had barricaded itself with a laptop in the corner by the window, fingers flying over the keys as if it were directing local traffic.

Geertruida tapped her nail rhythmically against the mug. The word-cover of the day was thin; she felt that discussion hung in the air, a kind of crease between generations you only saw when the light hit it sideways.

Matthijs crossed over first.

'You know what's strange,' he said without looking, 'that you just leave things behind, and then think no one sees them. But everything just stays where it was.'

She thought for a moment he was talking about the house, maybe about life. But he was now looking outside, where the sky pressed grey into the locks, and the rain on the planter boxes tapped out memories of earlier springs.

'You mean things, or people?' she asked.

'Both.'

Priya stayed leaning. A tremor passed through her arm, or maybe it was an invisible thud from outside. She pretended not to take part – typical, thought Geertruida – but her eyes flicked briefly toward the child, who had already for hours avoided the conversation.

'Sometimes I think you just have to forget those things,' said Geertruida, while inspecting the inside of her wrist. 'Or that it's a luxury if you can.'

'Luxury?' Priya's voice sharpened on the edge of the word.

'Not everyone can afford to let go, I mean.'

'I had to leave behind everything that was mine,' said Priya, her voice in the kitchen cold as dishwater.

Matthijs laughed sharply, a sound that wanted to soften nothing. Geertruida looked at his face and saw nothing that surprised her: she may have molded this boy herself, but the air between his words had always been filled with echoes she couldn't control.

'Maybe some things are prettier if you forget them,' he said.

Geertruida felt the pull in her jaws again, like in the past, when her son had let something go wrong, and she had to glue it back together. She thought of awkward secondhand toys, rusty bikes, and a broken bracelet somewhere on a beach in Italy. Always the fixing, never the having.

'Maybe so,' she said. She looked at the woman by the counter, at how she held her coffee like a compass. In those hands, there was a certainty Geertruida herself had never owned. It struck her that Priya didn't have the impulse to divide herself into pieces for others. That despite everything, she could be completely present in a room, without apologizing for who she was.

A pause hung, full of movement. She suddenly became painfully aware of the space around her, the crumbs in the white of the table, the child in the corner, almost invisibly playing its games. That was perhaps it: you could be born for emptiness, but it only became yours when no one else bothered to come closer.

Matthijs got up, shuffled a circle through the room, picked up a sheet from the floor, and put it with the old paper. The curve of his sweater's back bent like a fist one had taught oneself. She knew he always grew nervous in these conversations—not because of the subject, but because of the inability to bend people to his will.

'What are you going to do today?' she asked the child, without forcing her tone.

Amal looked up, a flash of shock in his eyes, then a half-shrug as if it were the question of the day. 'Maybe outside. Or drawing. Is that allowed?'

She nodded, surprised at her own softness.

'Do you have plans, Priya?'

'Work,' said the woman. Then, with a gulp of air

The house held its breath.

Light from the kitchen window stretched long and pale across the floor, trembling slightly with the movement of rain outside. Priya leaned against the doorway, her voice low, her smile quiet and unreadable. When she turned toward Matthijs, something in the air shifted — a spark, small but unmistakable.

He said something Geertruida couldn't catch. Then the sound of footsteps on the stairs, slow at first, then fading upward. The walls carried their whispers like heat.

Geertruida stood alone in the kitchen. The clock ticked louder than it should have. She touched the edge of the counter, steadying herself, and for a moment she saw her son as a boy again — running barefoot through hallways, the same quick pulse of energy that now followed another rhythm entirely.

Upstairs, the light changed. Curtains breathed with the wind. What happened beyond those walls was unseen, but its presence rippled through the house — a quiet storm of movement, a collision of longing and recognition, the kind that leaves a trace even after silence returns.

Downstairs, Geertruida wiped a clean cup, again and again. The rag left damp streaks across the counter, catching the light like veins of silver. She didn't want to imagine, but her body already knew. Her heartbeat had its own memory, echoing theirs.

When the floorboards above went still, the moment seemed to suspend — like the air after lightning, charged and waiting. Then came a soft laugh, the thud of a closing door, and only the hum of rain remained.

Geertruida looked up at the ceiling, her throat tightening. She didn't know if it was jealousy, sorrow, or something nameless in between — only that it was real, and that she, too, was caught inside it.

The child took off his coat, put it back on, and ran through the house looking for a pen he had lost yesterday. That tiny cycle of loss and starting over—she could envy that.

Geertruida stood up, smoothed her skirt, and plucked a loose thread from her sleeve.

Geertruida felt the thread tear away, a tiny protest against her fingertips, and she dropped it on the floor where it would disappear invisibly among the crumbs. In the kitchen, Priya was still leaning against the counter, her hip slightly forward, eyes half-closed as she looked at Matthijs with that slow, searching gaze that Geertruida recognized from women who knew what they were coming for. Priya's lips parted slightly, and she murmured something about the heat in the room, her hand sliding down her neck, fingers slowly stroking her skin, and Geertruida caught the way her son reacted, his posture slightly straighter, his breath catching as he stepped closer. It was no coincidence that sudden closeness; Priya's voice dropped lower, her body tilting as if inviting him, and Geertruida felt the air thicken, laden with that unspoken hunger she herself had not felt in so long. She turned around, walked to the window to wipe away the condensation. Still, out of the corner of her eye, she saw Priya's hand touch Matthijs' arm, a touch that lasted too long, too low on his elbow, and her son leaned toward her, his mouth near her ear, whispering something Geertruida couldn't understand but could guess from the redness creeping into Priya's cheeks.

She coughed lightly to break the silence, but no one looked up; the moment hung there, sultry and inevitable, and Geertruida's stomach clenched at the thought of what would follow if she left the room. Amal was still sitting in the corner, fingers flying over that laptop, oblivious to the shift, and Geertruida wondered if children always did that, ignoring the tension until it exploded. She grabbed a dishcloth, wiped the countertop pointlessly, the damp fabric sticking to her skin, while her thoughts wandered to Matthijs' past, all those women he had taken with him, their names faded like old stamps. Geertruida's cheeks burned at the memory, not out of disgust but out of a strange kind of jealousy for that freedom, that reckless pursuit that had always driven her son, and now she saw the same pattern in

Priya's eyes, that smoldering desire to claim him, to devour him, just like the others.

The door to the hallway creaked open, and Matthijs muttered something about going upstairs. Priya followed him with a nod, her steps soft but determined, and Geertruida was left behind with the pounding in her chest, the heat spreading like a stain on the tabletop. She heard their footsteps on the stairs, muffled laughter, and then the click of a door closing, and she stared at the empty mugs, their rims smeared with coffee grounds, her hands trembling as she picked them up. Amal finally looked up, his little face questioning, and Geertruida forced a smile, crouching down to watch his game, the pixels flashing on the screen, anything to avoid thinking about what was happening upstairs, those old rituals of skin and sweat that filled her house with secrets once again. She felt the fatigue in her legs, the heaviness of years of observing without intervening, but deep inside, a curiosity pricked her, sharp as a needle, wondering if this was finally the moment her son would stay, caught in that web of Priya sank further until her chin touched his lower abdomen, let her teeth graze him gently, tasted his skin, chalk and sweat mixed with the smell of coffee and aftershave. Her hand enclosed the base of his cock, kneading it as if she wanted to squeeze the tension out of his entire body. Matthijs clung to the countertop, his knuckles turning white on the blue edge of the Formica. He hadn't been prepared for this, not for her technique, not for the hunger in her gaze when she knelt—first a glance upward, almost warning, and only then her lips around him.

She worked him as if there was something to be won. It felt almost athletic, a duel with his own control. He squeezed his eyes shut, focused on the sound of her tongue, the wet movement, the slight gagging she did not attempt to hide. His knees trembled. That eagerness, that she—here, on the kitchen floor of the house where he was staying as a son again—wanted him so shamelessly, penetrated him more deeply than he wanted to admit.

He stroked the shine on her temple, felt the hairs along her jaw, and slid his hand over her shoulder. He didn't know her like this at all, really, but now he knew her mouth. Her voice came hoarsely from her throat. She was right. He wanted her; he couldn't place her anywhere else but here, on this floor, between the cabinets with their old-fashioned, crooked doors.

Without saying a word, Priya pulled her skirt up above her hips, pressed her body against the cupboard, and turned around, her hands flat on the counter. She quickly slid her thong aside. Matthijs didn't even think, at least not with the part of his brain his mother so often hoped he would use. He held her hips and pushed himself against her, feeling her wetness, which let him in effortlessly.

She stood with her legs apart in front of him, her head down, her hair like a curtain around her face. Her back arched slightly under his hands. There was no time for subtlety, no awareness of the hour or the neighbors with their windows facing the garden. All he could think about was the past—the girls in the bike shed, the quick skirmishes at the gymnasium. But back then, he had always been an outsider, always more of a spectator than a participant. Now he was right in the middle of it, inside her, in the moment.

His body did what it had to do. He pulled her closer, made hard circular movements with his lower body, and felt her muscles contract around him. She moaned, not loudly, but deeply, like a bubbling sound.

Priya's hand moved nervously over his thigh, her fingers like warm chess pieces on a wooden board, each touch so charged with expectation that Matthijs hardly dared to breathe. She knelt between his legs, the fabric of her dress pulled up until she felt her thighs tremble with tension. No words, just gasping for air: Matthijs' hands in her hair, a maneuver borrowed from a previous life, when he thought she was sensitive to it.

He wasn't prepared for how natural this felt, her mouth welcoming his erection with a greed that had nothing to do with hunger, everything to do with control. She sucked him deep, her rhythm steady and vain, as if she were following an internal song he didn't recognize. He caught her gaze—dark and mocking—and felt himself shrink, or rather dissolve into liquid desire; he could no longer tell the difference.

The room still smelled of crumbly speculaas, but now sweat dominated, a scent of old leather and impatience, his own childish shame. Priya paused, biting gently into his groin, letting her tongue slowly trace a circle. She looked at him with that gaze he knew only from art history — women who are not ashamed of themselves, women who know they are making history.

He lifted her chin. She let herself be pulled up easily, her lips shiny and open, her pupils dilated as if in the twilight of a night garden. She leaned forward and whispered something, her voice broken between English and her Indian accent, something about wanting, something about now.

She stood up, let her dress fall, her brown-beige skin a revelation against the dull Dutch light. The rest was awkward: buttons that got stuck, a sock that got stuck halfway down his ankle. They laughed nervously, like children who have broken something but don't yet know if they will be punished.

She pushed him back onto the guest bed, the springs squeaking under their weight. She slid on top of him, her knees on either side, her hands resting on his shoulders as confirmation of possession. She lowered herself slowly, feeling him search, the resistance, the surrender. At first, there were only small movements: a cautious sliding, an exploration of boundaries, her buttocks soft in his hands.

It felt like something old and new at the same time, something invented in the eighties to write about exactly their kind of desire. He heard himself say something—nonsensical English, sorry, god, so good—it sounded like a repeat of a poorly dubbed movie. But Priya laughed and threw her head back, her hair cascading over her shoulders, and in that moment, he knew there was no turning back.

It slowed down, then sped up again: she kept pace, holding him tightly in her pelvis, and when Matthijs threw his head back and could no longer hold back his spasm, she let him come deep inside her, her whole body tense and receptive, as if she were sucking herself empty of his lust. After the eruption, she lingered for a second, her hand massaging around his base, her cheeks full, and her gaze fixed on him. Only then did she slowly withdraw, swallow, and smile with a grin that was somewhere between triumph and relief.

Matthijs was disoriented for a minute, lying on the bed with his arms spread out, his chest trembling like a newborn animal. In his head, everything revolved around the present, the now, the sudden connection between two lives that had never really wanted to meet. Priya let herself fall next to him, her skin sticky and warm with sweat, her hand still loosely resting on his thigh. He smelled his own scent mixed with her perfume, a blend of salty and sweet that was impossible to resist.

"You're not a screamer, are you?" she whispered, her lips close to his ear.

He smiled. "I was afraid of bringing down the walls."

"Typical Dutch," she laughed softly. "Always afraid of noise."

He turned his head toward her and touched the tip of her nose. He could still taste her on his tongue, his body half limp, but beneath the languid fatigue simmered a new hunger, a desire that had not yet been sated.

Without warning, Priya rolled over him, her knees digging into his ribs, her hands firmly on either side of his face. She looked at him with her dark, sleepy eyes and licked his neck like a cat, her tongue slow and selective. Now it was his turn; he could feel it. He slid his hands down her spine, pushed her dress further up, baring her buttocks with his hands, and pulled her closer.

She pushed her crotch into his face; her scent was stronger than anything he remembered from his childhood— not peach or chemical women's perfume, but an earthy, dense aroma, like the smell of soil after rain. He licked her gently at first, searching, exploring, but Priya was not one for gentle build-up; she grabbed his hair, pushed her pelvis against his mouth, and moaned deeply, as if she had to search for her voice in the depths of her chest.

He felt her juices dripping down his chin, her thighs jerking against his cheeks. For a moment, he thought of the woman downstairs making coffee, the silence in which all this was taking place, the possibility that at any moment a child might appear at the door, or that his mother might peek around the corner. But Priya pulled those thoughts out of him with every movement, every moan from her tongue, until his brain drained into his body. There was no outside world. The room, the woman, their salty taste: everything was reduced to this fearful, all-consuming craving.

The first wave had almost swept him away, but now he wanted her too, not as a mother conqueror, not as a failed boomer, but as a machine, as a predator. He sank his teeth into her thigh, pulled her toward him until she squealed. Priya didn't pull away. She remained seated, his head clamped between her legs, her breath wheezing through her nose.

She came, quiet for a moment, then her whole body contracted, her arms hooked into the mattress. Afterwards, she lay on top of him like a spent boxer, the smell of pussy and ash in her hair. She stroked his head, rubbing the sweat from his eyebrows. When he looked at her, he saw that she was smiling—no sarcasm, no irony. A genuine smile. He wasn't sure if he had seen that before.

They lay there for a few minutes like wrecks in the surf. Outside, the rain rustled against the balcony. The clock ticked in the hallway, and occasionally a step creaked. He no longer cared if his mother heard anything; this woman wanted him, and it wasn't nonsense, it wasn't a pose. It made him feel stronger, as if he now had a chance to start over. Priya shouted something in Hindi, forced him to his feet, and kissed him with a sweet, languid mouth.

For the first time in years, Matthijs felt completely awake.

They did it again, this time on the bathroom floor, where it was colder and the smell of bleach cut between their bodies. She bit his shoulder, leaving red marks that he would only later recognize as marks of possession. He didn't know what it said about him that it only made him feel better.

After showering and drying off hastily, they returned to the dining table as if nothing had happened. The older woman sat drinking her coffee, motionless, a sudoku puzzle in front of her. Priya had her hair pulled back tightly in a ponytail again. She didn't say a word about what had happened upstairs. The only traitor was her son, who now sat upright, with the air of a man who knew he had won something for himself.

"We're going home soon," Priya said as she poured milk for the little one. "Otherwise, we'll get caught in the evening rush.

CHAPTER 6
PREGNANT IN CHAOS

That morning, she had received an email from the university asking if she wanted to participate in a panel discussion about performance pressure. Iris sat at the kitchen table with her laptop and felt the baby kick like a hasty tremor. She bounced her foot against the edge of the table, secretly desperate that Nellie would not come home before the Zoom meeting was over. The front door creaked, her heart pounding against her ribs. No footsteps, just wind creeping into the hallway through the empty draft hole.

Matthijs was downstairs in the basement, working up a sweat on the old exercise bike, which squeaked with every revolution. Sometimes he called up, half-sentences, half-jokes. The walls of the house filtered all the words into meaningless hums. Iris didn't mind. This rhythm—homework, dishes, her father-in-law's snoring, the muffled echo of her boyfriend in the basement—felt like an awkward but safe kind of normal.

She turned off her camera as her turn approached. The familiar panel consisted of boys in fleece vests and girls with shiny foundations. Someone talked about FOMO, someone else about burnout. Iris hardly listened. She would soon have to explain what it was like to bear responsibility for an unplanned pregnancy, without playing the victim or coming across as sentimental. That was her greatest fear: earning pity.

When her name was called, she lifted her head and took a deep breath, perhaps too audibly. "Yes, sorry," she said. "It is indeed busy." She didn't say: I have a husband who could be my father, and a mother in a nursing home whom I hardly ever visit. She said: "Sometimes it feels like a race against yourself, against your past, against expectations." An awkward silence followed. "I think what I miss most sometimes is being able to wake up in the morning without immediately thinking about failure. Or rather, what others consider to be failure."

It sounded softer than she wanted it to. She turned off her microphone.

A moment later, Matthijs came upstairs with a towel draped over his shoulders like a cape. He grabbed a banana and looked at her silently as she rewrote emails. His post-workout scent lingered as he walked to the shower. She thought about his skin, the lines around his eyes, how his hands always touched her more tenderly when she felt vulnerable—how she missed that touch when he withdrew into himself, chronically detached.

The baby kicked again, and she felt the skin of her belly stretch, like a balloon with too much air.

She looked at her inbox. No one had responded to her panel contribution. Maybe no one had listened. Or maybe that was for the best—being invisible until you suddenly are there, living proof of everything you were so fanatically supposed to keep quiet about.

She closed her laptop, hitting the edge of the screen just a little too hard with her fingertip. A dry coldness swept through the room, coming from under the crack in the kitchen door. No sign of Nellie yet—probably deep in the night shift rhythm, coming home later with a flat roll from the gas station and stories about motorcycle accidents. Iris pushed her chair back and leaned her hand on the table for a moment. It was painful how quickly her center of gravity had shifted, literally.

The hallway smelled heavily of dishwater and old carpet. Iris walked to the living room, her gaze lingering on the wall full of Matthijs's yellowed childhood portraits. A child's mouth full of large front teeth, gray-blue eyes increasingly sharp but never really mature, as if he had stopped growing halfway through. Now, more than thirty years had passed since that childhood, but the little boy inside had never been completely erased.

She heard water splashing in the bathroom, the sounds easy to guess: Matthijs running a hot shower over his skin, followed by that dry cough that always reminded Iris of a poorly maintained radiator being bled. His clothes lay in a disorderly strip from the stairs to the shower room, as if he had started to have second thoughts on his way to his own shower, but didn't have the strength to turn back.

Iris sat down in the brown leather chair, which you had to slump into because the seat was broken. She slid her hands over her belly, trying to feel if there was a character rustling around in there besides limbs. Silent. Or maybe stubborn. She wondered if you could already tell in her case—or if the people around you preprogrammed everything.

"What a day," Matthijs exclaimed from the bathroom. She heard him brush the hair from his face. "Is the lecture still on hold?"

"Panel discussion. They even asked me to say something live about performance pressure."

"And?"

"I said it's a race against my own past, and that failure can also be a kind of stopover."

"Wow." He laughed, but it quickly turned into sniffling. "Was your camera on?"

"No, I had a morning head."

Matthijs came into the living room looking torn, wearing an old soccer jersey he always wore on days when he had no plans. His skin was still steaming from the shower. He grabbed the remote control and searched through all the news flashes for Formula 1. This was his default, his escape route: using other people's voices as a barrier to his own thoughts.

"That baby already has more discipline than I ever had," he said to her, without really looking at her.

Iris thought: That's what you get when your parents always told you you were smart instead of handsome. Or when you came from a family of teachers, where competition was a kind of domestic discipline—doing the dishes on time, being the first to know the weekly schedule, sitting next to your mother as a child with a pen that always stained. Discipline is a default setting, and now there will be a few more generations who immediately feel guilty every time they miss a deadline.

She looked at the television, the overheated voices of the race commentators. Matthijs tried to shift his attention back to her between turns. His gaze kept wandering away, as if talking about the child was easier when it didn't involve direct eye contact.

"The baby will be named after my father. Whether he likes it or not," he said suddenly.

"You said that yesterday, too," Iris said, trying to keep a straight face, but it sounded like a half-smile.

Matthijs stretched his legs over the stool. "I mean it from the first to the last letter. We'll call him Simon. No bullshit about matryoshka-like name ideas, just Simon."

"Simon de Jong de Vries. Wow, the clerk at city hall is already laughing his head off."

"Let them laugh. Simon sounds like someone who doesn't bow to pressure to perform; that's the whole idea." But he looked down at his feet, bare toes curled over the edge of the carpet.

Iris folded her hands around her belly and imagined her child walking through school corridors, with a name that was both old and unapproachable. She thought about how children are, how they absorb everything that is not yet finished, fluid like watercolor paint, and how she herself remained fluid in some ways as long as she continued to learn, always becoming.

"If it's a girl?" she asked, out of nowhere, the question tasting of apple syrup and old library dust.

"Then we'll name her after you."

That was typical Matthijs: deciding as if you were tossing a coin, even though you knew the result frightened him as much as it did you. A baby as a tabula rasa was a kind of illusion, because everyone who held her would leave something of themselves behind.

She wanted him to sit next to her; this was one of those afternoons when you had to share everything in silence because words became too heavy. But he remained lounging on the couch, pensively working on a crumpled sudoku puzzle from the Saturday edition.

She wondered who would be the first to turn "the baby" into a name. Maybe Nellie, who would soon come rushing in, still wearing her dentist's coat, and immediately set the tone with her heels: "Shall we show them who the real heir is?" Something in the vein of her own voice: prickly but also endearing, as if everything you initially found uncomfortable was then simply accepted into the family.

She heard a shrill bicycle bell outside, then the harmonica of the mailbox. Mail. Probably another catalog of baby packages, some congratulatory envelope with manufactured pink feet stuck on it. Even algorithms didn't like nuance; everything immediately became a mother candidate as soon as an online store got wind of a pregnancy.

She got up, a little clumsily, rubbed the back of her groin as if something was hanging loose there, and waddled to the door as if she were already eight months along. There were three envelopes on the doormat: a bill, a blue card from the midwife, and an anonymous brochure about online therapy. The card listed the first ultrasound appointment, in blue ballpoint pen: "Wednesday 7:30. Please come sober." As if that were possible, staying sober with what was going through your head.

Matthijs glanced at the pile of mail in her hand, but said nothing. She had thought he might make a joke about being "fasting," something boyish, but his attention was already back on the screen. This was the Matthijs her friends always warned her about: a man who put only himself on stage, everything else in the wings. With him, you always had to fight for attention, and sometimes she preferred to be an audience member rather than the star.

She sat down again, one knee pulled up, unfolded the blue card, and read the instructions a few times. What if you just didn't go? What if you skipped the first ultrasound and let the baby exist only in your head, secretly, until there was no other option? The thought tickled her rib cage, a secret sensation of space, until the baby kicked again and everything was back to square one.

"Is Wednesday okay?" she asked.

Matthijs nodded. "If you want to go."

"Do you want to come?"

"Sure." His gaze darted to her belly for a moment, and that was it—no sweet whispers, no hand on her hand, none of those things that always happened naturally in movies. Just that slight frown on his forehead, as if, besides the ultrasound, he was worried about parking costs or early morning traffic.

She thought of the mornings in her childhood home, how her mother always whispered that the city was only soft on Wednesdays, unfiltered light on the kitchen table, and fresh rolls in a paper bag. Maybe every Wednesday immediately became softer when you had an appointment somewhere together, even if it was about sound waves and spots on an ultrasound screen.

The rest of the afternoon passed in fragments of Formula 1 and lost WhatsApp conversations. Sometimes Iris van Matthijs looked at the display cabinet, where a little more blue tableware with gold rims gleamed in a wooden cabinet—family heirlooms of the de Vriesen family, who even saw glassware as a kind of DNA chip. The air pressure in the house changed as the hours passed; she secretly wondered if people could ever tell how long ago you had made coffee, based on the sour smell that lingered after pouring. Or maybe they could smell it if you had a secret, somewhere between the perfume and the breadcrumbs.

For a moment, Iris considered pushing the blue card back into a drawer unread, adding a note to her future self: "Not everything has to be done today." But she had always been someone who read ahead. Before the lecture began, she already knew which chapter would be tested. The comfort lies not in surprise, but in control, even if that control is over an impending disaster.

When the sun reached the windowsill, and the city finally fell silent, she slowly let the panel's 'performance pressure' wash out of her mind. She thought of the baby—Simon? Iris Junior? Or perhaps something unspeakable—and of the inexorable rhythm to come: ultrasounds, blood tests, standard milestones. She thought about how Nellie would soon come in, loud, brimming with confidence. No chance of hiding behind displays of indifference then.

The first to say "Simon," as if it were the name of a pet, would surely be Matthijs, just before or just after the ultrasound. In her head, she already said it out loud, practiced the intonation, and tested the emotional value. It felt like wet cement: heavier and stiffer than expected, but once it dried, it left a lasting impression on everything you built.

In the bathroom, the washing machine vibrated loosely against the wall, as if even the house was trying to vent its heart. Iris remained seated in the chair for a moment, hands folded, imagining Simon walking around this house, or Iris, or whoever else might emerge from her uncertain future. Everything could be recorded in a diary, but never predicted.

Perhaps that was their little tradition: always thinking they were ahead of fate, only to be surprised every Wednesday by whatever came their way.

She decided to go to bed early that night to reset her mind for the ultrasound. In her room, the laundry still smelled a little fresh, the sheets clinging to her legs. As she lay in the dark, she heard the stairs creak: Matthijs, in his socks, always quiet when he moved around her. His shadow lingered in the doorway. She pretended to be asleep, afraid he would ask how she was doing. Silently, he withdrew, his footsteps sinking into the carpet of their temporary life.

Her phone pulsed on the nightstand, a reminder of an online tutor group. She lit up the screen and glanced at it: messages about exam questions, memes of sleeping cats with titles like "Monday mood." She wanted to type that it wasn't so bad, that eventually you only felt responsible for the things growing inside your body, not for everything outside it. But she deleted her typing before the blue check marks would pop up. Tomorrow, she might understand. Or else Wednesday.

The night dreamed soggily. Iris woke up with a wet spot under her head, her pillow soaked through from her sleep. She had dreamed that her belly had become transparent, like glass, and you could see the baby dancing like a bicycle light behind bone. In the morning light, pale and cool through the frosted glass on the garden side, her body immediately felt the presence of the other next to her own—the unborn child, who dictated her daily rhythm with kicks, jabs, and plaintive hunger.

She ate yogurt with fruit and listened to Nellie's muttering as she forced the day into action in the kitchen with strong filter coffee and the smell of cigarettes. Nellie had heard everything about the ultrasound appointment. She said nothing, but Iris felt her mother waiting for confirmation, a kind of shared plan. Iris wasn't sure if there was a plan. Or if they would make one together.

Matthijs came downstairs with a sports sock around his neck, as if he had lost track of today on the way. He settled down at the table, dirt under his fingernails. For a moment, he was not the master of indifference, but just a human being with dark circles under his eyes, freshly torn from a dream. Their breakfast was like a strategy meeting: Can we have milk? Do we need sugar? Are you going straight there, or are we taking a detour? No one talked about the ultrasound itself until the moment was almost upon them.

The hospital smelled of disinfectant and weekend people; mothers with restless twins, men picking up their wives with flowers from the gas station. Iris sat in her coat, her hands crossed over her lower ribs, counting patterns in the carpet and signing in at the desk, waiting by the water cooler. She had never known that waiting consumed so much energy—it was waiting for the craving for an answer that always remained just as distant. She tried to imagine what would change after the appointment, but her gaze did not reach beyond the edge of the waiting room, the watery fantasy of translucent babies.

She had to go in alone; the assistant pointed with her lip to the treatment room. Matthijs lingered in the hallway, almost tripped over a stroller, and got back up with a grin that betrayed his anxiety.

The room was smaller than Iris had expected. Blue laminate flooring, prints of sea anemones on the wall, a computer humming softly. The gynecologist—much younger than Iris had imagined, with a ponytail and glasses that lifted her eyes into large saucers—pointed to the bed. Iris lay down, the paper beneath her creaking. For a moment, she felt like a school project, about to be assessed for growth, shape, volume.

The cold gel stung her belly. She thought of everything that did not yet exist, and at the same time was already complete. Of that small, unwilling heart, hidden somewhere deep inside the ultrasound equipment. The doctor tapped her screen awake, turned on the sound, and something irregular drummed from the speaker. Tick tick tick, as if someone were tapping a dice with matchsticks. Iris forced herself to focus on the image, the shadow where a human being should be, the unclear little ball of the future.

The doctor wrote down her numbers and didn't explain anything. Iris didn't ask either. She just nodded and asked, "Is it true that you sometimes feel it in your back, like a kind of nerve current?"

The doctor smiled, not frivolously, and said, "That's the nerve. You can... take it with you if you want." She meant the photo, a black-and-white print on glossy paper. Iris took it, looking at it as if she were looking at a map of an unfamiliar city.

Outside, Matthijs was fiddling with his phone. He looked up just as she pushed open the door and took a step toward her. For a moment, she thought he was going to touch her, but it was just a hand on her shoulder, a light pressure, a reminder that they were one.

"Everything okay?" he asked.

"Yes. It's... It's haunted in there," Iris said, holding up the printout.

They walked back outside, their steps not naturally in sync. They took the tram, not out of necessity but because it was the only place where you could look straight ahead in silence. The city flashed by, all the windows reflecting her belly, her hands, the image of the baby like a shadow in the background.

When they got home, Nellie was lying in the living room, still wearing her coat, her feet up on the coffee table. She looked at the print with amusement, her head tilted. "You can keep your eyes closed, it's not going to grow away," she said. Something in her manner of speaking, exaggeratedly matter-of-fact, shifted the weight in the room. Iris handed the printout to her mother, who looked at it as if you could spot a mistake in it, like a test paper full of unexpected signals.

"Looks healthy," Nellie said. She pushed the printout back a little, between the crumbs and the coffee cups. "Now you can tell the rest of them. Not that anyone will be shocked."

That last part was perhaps the worst: that no one was shocked by anything anymore, not by pregnancies, not by being young in an old city, not by a love that began as a secret and grew into a constant presence. Iris thought about how everything presented itself: you could dance around it until it became too heavy to lift, then the world would drag it in on its own.

The afternoon flowed on in the wall of sound of their house, with the occasional sound of a passing scooter, the wind singing through the broken drainpipe, the static whisper of the television. Matthijs disappeared upstairs, where he searched between the drying rack and the unopened moving boxes for something to put on bread. Iris still had the printout in her fingers; it felt smooth, fragile, just like everything you were responsible for.

She called Bram, her college friend and aspiring psychologist, who never answered when you needed him, and then called back out of the blue within three minutes. His voice always sounded just a little too cheerful for the time of day. Iris couldn't remember the last time he had shared anything about himself, except for facts about bizarre sleep disorders in the animal kingdom.

"It feels like there's an alien inside me," Iris said.

"That's because there is. A parasitic dichotomy, a masterstroke in evolutionary terms," Bram said. "Do you feel like a mother yet? Or still just yourself?"

She couldn't choose. Neither mother nor herself. Something in between, a kind of guardian of temporality.

"At least there's proof," Iris said, "and soon there will be a name."

Bram laughed. "If it's a boy, you really shouldn't call him Bram, because that will only make him lazy as a child."

"Maybe it will be Simon."

"Simon is good. He wins or loses in the end, but always based on talent, never by cheating."

She put her phone down next to her, her fingers still cold from the screen. Upstairs, she heard the tapping of a tea bag against a mug and the dull thud of a drawer slamming shut. Slowly, the house contracted back into the backdrop it always was: hallways, lamps, chairs, glowing stains on the carpet, the all-absorbing cochlea you always returned to.

At the end of the day, Nellie and Iris stood in the garden in the twilight. Nellie tied back the rose bushes with a frayed, thick rope, asking Iris with her back to her if she had spoken to Bram yet. "He called, yes," said Iris, "and he immediately started talking about parasites."

That was Bram through and through: always the biological mechanism, never the obligatory cliché. Nellie nodded as if she could guess the comment and pulled the knot on the roses extra tight. Something was reassuring about putting things in order, Iris thought. Even when the rope turned out to be too short, her mother simply doubled the strips around the thorny stems until they obeyed their new line.

Iris stood somewhat awkwardly in the pebbles. A piece of gravel pricked her heel, but instead of brushing it off, she stood still, feeling the little stone slowly become part of her weight. She wondered if children remembered that later: the discomfort that you didn't immediately remove, but simply let dissolve into you. Perhaps that was the inglorious core of parenting.

A moment later, Nellie came to stand beside her, her hands dirty. She bowed her head toward the ridges of Iris's sweater and said, almost casually, "I used to think I was doing everything wrong. Now I know that no one was ever watching." She smelled of earth, of rain that never quite dried. "You're doing fine, you know."

It was the kind of sentence where you didn't know whether you should feel reassured or whether it was actually meant for Nellie herself. Iris smiled and said nothing, looking at the brick wall at the back of the garden, the faint spots where she had written her name in sidewalk chalk as a child. In mild summers, the chalk didn't disappear until weeks later, each rainstorm making it a little fainter until only the suggestion of a letter remained.

They walked back inside. In the kitchen, Matthijs had taken charge of dinner in campaign-like fashion: oven pizza from the cellophane, finished off with extra slices of cheese for the occasion. Iris took off her sweater, ran her hands briefly under the tap, and watched the dirt wash away in syrupy strands. Perhaps the biggest transitions were always simple, abrupt, banal, like supermarket food on a Wednesday evening.

Words were scarce at the table. A dull mood, as if everyone was present at the meeting via their cell phones. Iris mentally retrieved the ultrasound photo from her bag; she held it under the table, thumb over the shiny edge, without actually looking at the print. She wondered how long it would take for this other life to really become part of her, not only in her body but also in her head.

Nellie cut her pizza with cutlery, one of those bourgeois habits that had seemed embarrassing in the past but now made sense. Without looking up, she said, "The baby will have fine hair, mark my words. And it will soon be eating more bread with chocolate sprinkles than is healthy for a human child."

Matthijs hummed somewhere between the upper and lower registers of his voice. Iris heard his fork tap the plate, saw how, even now, he was picking the cheese off his pizza in thin strands, as if you could go out to dinner with a DNA model. She looked at her reflection in the kitchen window, blurred by condensation and the reflections of the interior light, and tried to predict what face would be looking back at her in ten years' time.

"Have you actually thought about parenting?" she asked, in short, without hesitation.

Matthijs shrugged his shoulders, blew air over a bite that was too hot. "That will come naturally. Nobody takes an exam before they start."

"Did you do that when you first learned to ride a bike?" Iris asked. She immediately thought: why this metaphor, as if she couldn't just ask a normal question.

"No," Matthijs said, "but I did spend months restoring a children's bike. Not because I had to, but because it was nice and organized—every screw in its place, nothing just disappearing."

"And then you were ready?"

"No, by then I was just tired of tinkering. But cycling is always a bit like falling in slow motion; you just have to learn how to break your fall."

Iris didn't know exactly what to make of that answer, except that it sounded sincere. She smelled the salt from the melted cheese, heard her mother next to her pouring sparkling wine into a glass with a rim of chips. It sounded like the beginning of a new kind of Thursday evening: the three of them at the table, instead of the usual duo with sporadic extras.

Everyone ate quickly, as if there were still things to do, even though there was no rush. After dinner, Iris remained seated, sweeping the crumbs into a pile with her fingers, thinking about the gravel in her heel and how much of it had remained inside her. She leaned back, waiting for someone to kick off a serious conversation, but nothing happened.

Nellie cleared the plates, thick under her thumbs, not a sound other than the ceramics touching each other for a moment. She put everything in the sink, turned around, and said, almost solemnly: "I have to work late tomorrow night. So take your chance if you want to discuss something or eat secretly."

Her gaze was so brief that Iris wondered if it was just a practical announcement or secretly also an invitation to get together—it remained suspended between the lines. Matthijs stood up and moved toward the room with the same suppleness as a cat that knows it is not being watched.

Iris followed later, after the routine of clearing the table and washing her hands. She stared for a while at the shadows of the lamp on the ceiling, which were plastered across the table like blotting paper, and tried to imagine that this would one day be her family: with names, habits, patterns that hurt faster than you could describe them.

At night, she had restless dreams, again of those transparent bellies, but now filled with marble marbles and small television screens, each showing a different scene from possible lives. In the dark, her thoughts were logical, everything fit together seamlessly: soon Simon, soon a family, soon a rhythm of getting up, feeding, dressing, crawling through the day until night fell again. She was in the middle, like a kind of transposable cell, around which the rest would form.

In the morning, it was all more porous again. Socks cold, room empty, only the plop of the mailbox just after eight. A leaflet from the drugstore, a white envelope with her name in block letters on it. Iris tore open the edge and read that she was invited to speak at a conference on "young parents and mental health." She wanted to laugh, but it felt too thin.

She made tea, looked out at the garden where the rope around the rose bush was shifting again in the wind. The program for the day buzzed in her head: prepare for the panel discussion, appointment with the midwife, maybe finally call her mother about that appointment. The ultrasound was a day old, but her head felt hollow like a freshly blown glass.

Outside, a group of cyclists glided by, all wearing the same bright raincoats, their voices echoing through the street like a reminder: normal life thundered on, day after day. Iris considered herself lucky that soon she would have nothing to do – no social studies, no sports afternoon, just her body, an empty living room, Netflix if necessary, until her eyes stung with fatigue.

She had stuck the ultrasound printout in her diary, on a page with empty dates. Every time she checked her appointments, she stared at it, the strange silhouette that had already taken hostage her future. She wondered if she would ever talk about this lightheartedly. If she were ever, like mothers in magazines, to look back on her current uncertainty with perspective.

She made a list of baby names—Simon, Max, Bart (the last one crossed out, because it was too closely associated with her least favorite cousin). For girls, she couldn't get beyond Mara or Iris II, because even in her own mind, it was difficult to imagine having a daughter. Not that it mattered; she would just as happily have adopted a plant if it reminded her of her body with its kicks and stabs.

Around noon, Bram dropped in unannounced, reeking of six lagoons of aftershave. He hadn't heard anything, but he had seen everything online, and whistled admiringly when she showed him the ultrasound. "Look at him go. From now on, you are officially responsible for dying Dutch top talent."

She laughed half-heartedly. He plopped down next to her on the couch, fishing a plastic chicken sandwich out of his backpack, and narrowly avoiding the glass on the coffee table. "So how did it feel?" he asked, hand wide open, as if you could sell a banal peristaltic phenomenon between your fingers.

"Nothing," she said. "And everything at once."

"Epic." He chewed. "There are people who can't even keep their basil plants alive for a week. And then you just have six hundred grams of future on offer."

She decided not to argue. There was no point in explaining that it felt more like a piece of marzipan inside you, that you occasionally forgot for hours that it existed, until it kicked again as if angry at the neglect.

Bram licked his fingers, still half in college mode with his phone screen on his lap. "Are you going to tell your mother yet?"

"She knows," Iris said. "She was in the kitchen herself when I came back from the ultrasound."

"And?" His face scrunched up a little at that question.

"She said I'm doing well."

Bram nodded, as if he already knew the answer, and she let the moment linger. It was strange how little drama remained in her life when he was around. She could summarize half a day in three sentences, and he would at most chuckle and suggest that at least she wouldn't have to show up at family dinners at Christmas in six months.

Through the garden, the sound of excavators rustled in the distance. Spring had begun with street excavations, new pipes left unfinished halfway down the block, like the open-slash-end tag of an HTML code that Bram had once explained to her. Iris wondered if the house would ever be nicely plastered over again, or if every new beginning always came with remnants of the old.

After his third beer, Bram announced that he had to leave; he had a date in the city, or rather, as he admitted after some hesitation, a Tinder date for what he hoped would be a non-conversation evening. She didn't ask any questions, but wished him a good time, and as he left, he squeezed her shoulder lightly, like you would slide a piece of paper along the edge of a table with your index finger.

An hour later, Iris was back in bed. She tried to imagine Matthijs upstairs, perhaps with a book or perhaps just staring at the ceiling. The idea that he wasn't thinking about her at all downstairs. Somehow, that reassured her: the certainty that you didn't always have to feel responsible, every second of the day. That you could exist as a pause, and that life just went on between the silences.

The next morning, Matthijs was already downstairs, in the gray light, as if he preferred that edge of the day to the semi-darkness of the bedroom. He scratched his hair, his eyes red from insomnia, and Iris noticed that without coffee, he wasn't even trying to put on his usual lightheartedness. She ate a banana next to him at the table, her body sluggish from sleep and lactic acid.

"Don't you have to study?" he asked, hoarse from saying nothing.

She pointed to her phone, which displayed her schedule. "Not until eleven. But I have to prepare for tomorrow's panel discussion."

He shrugged his shoulders, a half-hearted non-response, as if her schedule required no further discussion.

Slowly, the house warmed up, with the sounds of radiators and the smell of fresh bread from the neighbor's kitchen. Iris looked at her fingers, her fingernails torn from picking at hangnails. In the corner of her eye, she saw the brightness of the refrigerator magnet with the ultrasound photo underneath it. She hadn't put it there herself, so maybe her mother was a little more interested than she let on.

Outside, the street rustled with children on their way to school and a moped that was too loud for the morning. Iris thought of her own old elementary school, of how strikingly fearless she had been there. Yet now, with an invisible baby and two grown men under one roof, she couldn't possibly take the word "motherhood" seriously.

"When you heard... that you were going to be a father... did you also have doubts?" she asked, unexpectedly aloud, to the tabletop.

Matthijs blew the breath between his cheeks. "I mainly assumed it would take a while. That 'having a child' was something in the distant future, not suddenly now."

"So you never had a plan."

"Who does? Even people with lists don't remember what their plan was after a month."

She chewed her banana as slowly as possible, as if to fill in all the gaps in the conversation. In the cradle of their silence, the baby was quieter than usual, almost as if yesterday's ultrasound had lulled the unborn child to sleep.

Later, when Iris opened her books on the couch, she heard Matthijs engrossed in the crossword puzzle, pencil scribbling furiously on paper. It was nice, this domestic indifference, where no one expected you to surrender to the tragedy of parenthood every day. You could plan a life, but most of it got stuck on a blank page or was put on pause by the technology of the day.

In the afternoon, she visited the university. The bike racks were soggy and empty, the square barren and blue under the sky. Inside, it was warm but nowhere crowded: an echo of lockdown regimes, or just the sluggishness of second-year students. Iris recognized Bram from afar, his shoulders slumped in his hoodie, his legs stretched out on the windowsill. He waved without irony; in that movement lay a hint of their old freshman years, when everything still seemed fluid.

The hall smelled of wet coats and powdered sugar. She followed the map on the large wall, route 3B, everything in impersonal yellow. In her head, she made small stops in each hallway, mentally taking stock of her former life. Disappointing, as usual, until Bram surprised her with sandwiches from the cafeteria.

"Let me guess, you didn't have breakfast again?" he asked, over his shoulder.

"Three bites of yogurt count, right?" She took the sandwich, mustard immediately seeping through the plastic.

"You think in data, not in guts."

They sat down at a table by the window. Outside, a cleaner was sweeping salt across the square, each movement a compact repetition. Iris bit into the hard crust. She felt how the world's idling sometimes existed only by virtue of those small actions, eating sandwiches, drinking, stretching her legs. In between, she answered an email from a teacher: deadline extended, due to "medical reasons." Bram looked at her over the edge of his screen, not questioning, just present.

"I think it's quite something," he said finally, not mockingly, but seriously in that passively accepted kind of way. "Now that you've seen the printout, have you changed your mind about the baby?"

She did her best not to make his attention too heavy. "More like a job that's now mine. Someone has to do it, right?"

Bram nodded slowly but kept looking at her until she had to break the first glance.

They talked about the panel discussion topic, performance pressure, and Iris noticed that Bram was phrasing his questions as if they were doing a diagnostic test together—what are your triggers, how often do you worry, do you sleep through the night? With each question, Iris allowed herself no more than a half-answer. She felt no less for it.

By the time her lecture started, Iris had her curiosity back in check: she wanted to know what she had missed, whether her note-taking group was still intact, and whether she could skip an afternoon with a clear conscience. There were fewer students in the lecture hall than she had expected. She heard whispering in the back, someone softly humming the beginning of a children's song. She wondered if everything about her already showed that she was going to be a mother, if she was already unconsciously pushing her belly forward when she walked, if her face had slowly shifted to a seriousness that no longer suited her age.

During the break, Iris went to the ladies' room, where a girl with raspberry-colored hair was brushing her teeth at the sink. She asked where she could find the midwifery practice.

The girl stared at her, slurped foam from the corner of her mouth, and said it was in the hallway on the left. She stood there until Iris was gone; Iris could feel her gaze on her back.

In the small waiting room sat a boy from her class, wearing a bright blue hoodie and staring intently at his phone. Iris wanted to ignore him, but he beckoned her, or rather himself, and asked, "You too?" without looking directly at her belly.

She nodded. She felt her heart beating in a place where no echoes were made. The boy had a girlfriend with him, a girl in leggings, her paleness showing through behind her ears. They didn't exchange real glances, only those sneaky, brief, delaying smiles.

Iris thought of the first time she herself had sat in such a cramped room, the smell of alcohol wipes and solvent permanently lingering in her nose. Today's ultrasound photo sat like a postage stamp in her coat pocket. She had actually wanted to show it; now she kept it with her, as if becoming a mother with proof was only allowed when it became official.

She kicked off her sneaker and kept wiggling her bare toes. She was nervous, but not overwhelmingly so; it felt more like preparation for an endless series of identical appointments: listen, answer, sign, leave. She read the posters on the wall and smiled at the slogans ("life in every fiber," "be carefree while pregnant!"). A slogan was never made for someone with her excesses of analysis, Iris thought. Performance pressure existed here, too, but in centimeters, kilos, and perfect blood values.

After the conversation—superficial, lots of polite laughter, hardly anything to really remember—she walked outside. Her head felt clear from the cold; the sky above her was watery blue, just like the ultrasound without contrast. The corner of the print pricked her coat pocket: proof of existence, proof of everything she would carry with her from here on out.

She decided not to take the tram, but to walk home. She counted the sidewalk tiles, forcing herself not to think about deadlines or choices or the word "failure." That worked until about halfway there, when her phone announced itself with a message from her mother — not Nellie, but her real mother, the one in the nursing home.

"How are your studies going?" it said. No "how are you," no question about the baby, which Nellie had surely already called about. Iris felt a kind of cold relief; it gave her a reprieve from the real conversation.

She texted back: "Fine, just worrying a bit. Everything else is okay." That was enough. Her mother didn't respond immediately, and Iris was fine with that.

On the way, Iris thought about the day she and Matthijs had left the city for the first time. They had had coffee in a rainy pancake house on the Amstel, where the menus were soggy from the water. Everything felt timeless at the time—she couldn't believe that on a weekday afternoon, you could just sit somewhere, talking about things that had no consequences. Now everything was weighted, a kind of latent idea that every outing would be recorded in the baby diary years.

At the bridge on Heemstedestraat, she paused and looked at the traffic below. For the first time in weeks, she felt like she wasn't running away—the air was crystal clear, and the water below smelled of autumn and old gasoline. Across the bridge, a woman was walking with a stroller. She moved slowly, pushing with her whole body. It caught Iris's attention more than it should have: the woman was not much older than herself, but every movement was gentle, as if she had already worn in the pace of the child in the stroller.

It was a strange kind of reassurance. More people did this, squeezing themselves into life with less preparation than an exam, knowing that no one really explained to them beforehand what the intention was. Iris followed her for a while in the reflection on the shop window, until the woman turned into a side street and the baby was nowhere to be seen, except in her head.

When she got home, there was a note on the doormat, written in Nellie's handwriting: "At the hairdresser's, then shopping, custard in the fridge x." Matthijs had forgotten his coat, and Iris could see from the trail of mud in the hallway that he had gone into the garden, perhaps to smoke, perhaps to reset himself. She took off her shoes and planted her feet on the cold tiles. She was still buzzing from the walk.

The custard had been put in the fridge for her without her asking. Iris spooned it up in bursts, trying to remember if there had ever been a moment when she had trusted her body without reservation. Perhaps as a child, when everything came naturally: running, falling, getting up again without ever thinking about what your digestion was doing with your breakfast. She could almost recall it, the feeling of simply existing, of total innocence.

Her phone beeped. Bram again: "Still having existential doubts, or is everything under control?" She sighed and replied, "Shouldn't you be in therapy for your fixation on other people's crises?" It was their old code: vulnerability only in irony, everything that was really important in the subordinate clause.

She hung out on the couch until the news came on TV, then she turned off the TV and stared at the ceiling. The incandescent light cast vague shadows across the wall, as if the backdrop of her life were slowly collapsing. In the dark, it started raining again. Iris heard it tapping against the windows as she lay on her back, ankles stretched to the end of the bed. Above her fingers, a faint glow of dust particles danced in the light of the desk lamp—each particle floating, like a miniature version of the universe. She tried to imagine how much of her would end up there, whether there would be a point where she stopped spinning around her own axis and simply entered into orbit around the baby's life. She swung her legs out of bed, felt the cold prickling against the soles of her feet, and walked to the bathroom.

She looked at herself in the mirror for a long time. Her face was the same as always, as it had been for years; no expression left any traces. But there was something new in the profile of her body, a soft bulge that seemed to creep forward a fraction every day. She pulled her T-shirt tight over her belly, frowned for a moment, then danced lightly back and forth on her heels. So much movement for something so invisible, she thought. Or maybe she was the only one who saw it that way.

She brushed her teeth with a worn-out toothbrush. In the distance, doors slammed in the stairwell. Iris thought of panel discussions, deadlines, baby names, everything in a big jumble against the background of toothpaste buzzing. The lamp above the mirror was yellow and uninviting; it made her skin thinner, her cheeks a shade too pale. She looked at herself one more time, trying to see herself as her mother had once seen her. Penetrating, but with a layer of irony.

In the living room, Matthijs sat on the couch, feet on the edge of the table, eyes fixed on the faint blue glow of the television. He had a beer in his hand, but hardly drank; the bottle was mainly on standby, a backdrop to male discomfort. Iris sank next to him on the couch, leaning slightly so that her shoulder touched his arm with the slightest movement. She felt his breathing, slightly delayed, and wondered what was going on inside him. You couldn't just read the inside of a person, even though she had practiced it for years.

"Are you on break?" she asked. Her voice was thinner than she wanted it to be.

"No, the last class was canceled. So I thought I'd start doing nothing." The corners of his mouth turned up in a half-smile. "I'm good at doing nothing."

She let her head fall back against the seat and watched the images of a soccer game with him. Neither of them had ever had any interest in sports, but television could fill gaps where words got stuck. Iris tried to remember how their relationship had started. In the distance, water hit the window. Not drizzle, but real, heavy rain, as if someone on the third floor was emptying a bucket onto their balcony. It muffled the sound of the television, drawing Iris's attention outside, where the streetlights made the raindrops sparkle like crackling electricity in slow motion. Something in that rhythm drew her body to his; she slid her legs up onto the couch, her knee just below his thigh. He didn't miss it—his hand followed the line of her shin, casually, as if checking to see if her skin still existed, not melted under the weight of a whole new life.

"This is what I like best," she said softly. She didn't mean the rain. She meant the lazy, the watery, the air between their shoulders, and the fact that the baby was quiet under the noise. The childish reassurance of bad weather, being indoors, knowing that no one was expecting you until you felt like it again.

Matthijs looked at her for a moment, his eyes lighter than usual, and she felt his hand on her leg grow heavier. No expectations, no signals, just that small weight of knowing you were together. She thought of the city, of all the houses around them where people were now closing their windows, folding themselves against each other until the weather cleared. What was being together other than resisting, every storm a reason to crawl closer?

Her belly pushed between them like a blunt pillow. Matthijs leaned over it, letting his chin fall briefly on her knee, lingering in that half-movement where you never knew if words would come out.

"Imagine if it stayed like this forever," he said, his face still against her sweater. Not a question, not an exaggerated dream—just the expression of a possibility, something you could think when the world seemed to stop turning for a moment. She didn't answer right away, just felt the tingling in the soles of her feet, the welcoming warmth of their little homemade nest. Everything she needed right now was within arm's reach.

She slid her hand into his hair, the gray strand that always stuck out at the nape of his neck. "But it never stays that way," she said, not reproachfully, but rather as if that was the very essence of the promise. Always right now, never later.

The rain almost drowned out the sound of engines. Outside, it was getting darker, and inside the screen flickered like a campfire. They watched football together, the frantic pace of other people's lives, each with their own game, their own wet grass, their own sprint. Opposite them, their two bodies on the sofa, lemonade and sandwiches on the coffee table, their baby in the role of silent spectator.

Matthijs poked her in the side, a gentle nudge, and said, "I hope he doesn't get too noisy."

She chuckled, and there was a warmth that spread from her face to her belly, a softness that Iris had never encountered anywhere else in life. This was the only moment when the weight felt better than what you used to be able to endure with your body.

Matthijs nestled deeper beside her, and when the game went into halftime, he moved his hand up over her knee, the old route they had now appropriated together. First with fingertips, then wrist, and palm. In slow motion, like a test of how long you could wait until touch meant something on its own.

She let him do it, felt her muscles relax one by one—hamstring, groin, that strange rope in her lower abdomen that had always been tight since she was pregnant. She thought about how it used to be, without a baby, how every beginning of sex was a blitzkrieg of desire and stupid bravado, and how now it was almost solemn, almost wittily cautious.

He pulled her leg over his lap, a sweeping motion that contained no urgency. His hand slid up the inside of her thigh. She felt how her skin was warmer there, smooth beneath the fabric of her sweatpants. It was strange—now that everything was so fragile, every touch seemed firmer, as if he were rebuilding her in small pieces.

She pushed her face into his shoulder, smelling him: shampoo, beer, that typical trace of nicotine from his pores. His finger found the edge of her panties, slowing down as if it were an exam question where you weren't allowed to cheat.

She held her breath; outside, the rain rumbled as if the night were deliberately getting harder. Matthijs's hand moved, a shiver along her buttock, fingers pulling down the fabric and exploring what lay beneath. In her head, she counted the pulses of her heart, heard the commentator on TV shouting, a goal somewhere far away, but here in the room, everything was tailor-made for the two of them.

His fingers moved, cautiously at first. There was no rush, more exploration than hunger. She was startled, as always, by how quickly her body reacted now: everything sensitive, everything directly connected to her lungs, her eyes, the layer of sweat that gathered between her breasts. Her lower abdomen contracted, briefly and sharply, like a wave rushing over a sandbank.

She found herself caught between laughter and moans, a sound that was both irritating and reassuring. His fingers found their way, the technique familiar, but the body around them full of new territory. Iris thought of the baby—not who it would be, but the strange fact that there were now three of them, and yet exactly alone. She let her legs fall open a little further, felt the moisture on her thighs, the pounding in her chest.

He was still half in her sweatpants, the fabric pushed halfway down her thighs, his thigh cold from contact with the air. She lowered herself onto him, everything heavy and loose at the same time, as if she were loosening her bones one degree at a time, leaving only skin and heartbeat. He slid into her, cautiously at first, playfully testing the friction. Inside, her body contracted around him, feeling like a muscle stretching beyond its comfort zone.

A shiver shot across her shoulder, down her spine, everything flowing with his rhythm. She felt her belly over him, the baby just below her navel, tighter now, as if even inside something was looking up at what they were doing here. He held her knees—firm hands, cold on her skin, knuckles white from squeezing—and guided her pace without commands.

Iris couldn't hear herself above the hum of the TV. She moved in time with him, up and down, higher and higher, and then back again, the wave fed by the tension in her lower abdomen. In her head, it expanded into a universe, a crackling in every fiber of her body. Sometimes she sank through her arms and felt the creaking of his chest, his heartbeat pushing against her breastbone.

He looked at her sharply, eyes unblinking, sometimes with a half-smile when she pushed harder or lost her balance. She wrote herself over him, landing more and more boldly, feeling the sloshing of their bodies, the wet spots spreading along her thighs. There was no beginning or end, just trying the same thing over and over again, until it naturally became a climax.

She coughed once—a dry laugh, or a moan knocked out of her—and then she felt it, that threshold where everything was allowed to let go for a moment. Her muscles contracted, her pelvic floor clenching around his entire body, and he grabbed her without mercy, holding her until she herself no longer knew whether she was above or below. For a moment, everything went black, a cramp in her neck, her stomach tense like a curved arrow.

She fell on top of him, not elegantly, more like a pile of wet clothes. He whispered nothing sweet, just his breath along her hairline, the smell of sex and shampoo, everything steeped in togetherness. She felt the baby push, a brief protest, then a languid kind of calm.

He let her lie there for a moment, her back sticky under his hand, his thighs restless under her butt. She thought of nothing, or maybe her head just stood still, like a race that only started again when you were allowed to start a new lap. Upstairs, she heard a tap from the heating pipes, the house regaining its balance after their storm.

She felt the wetness between her legs with a mixture of irritation and shame. She wanted to run straight to the bathroom, rinse herself off to the bone, but Matthijs's hand stopped her by the ankle. He didn't smile, looked at her seriously for a moment with those narrow blue eyes of his, as if he was saying that this moment didn't just have to disappear into the past.

Before Iris could express how uncomfortable it was— the smell, the possibility that Nellie would come in soon— Matthijs had already pulled her to his side. His hand found the back of her neck, soft but firm; his other hand pushed her head down slightly. She wanted to get up, her mouth open to ask if it wouldn't be wiser to wait until the half-time break was over, but his penis was already there, tapping against her lips, hard and warm and salty from her own moisture.

She hesitated for a moment, then felt the tip of his cock against her gums. She opened her mouth cautiously, allowing it in at first as a test, a reminder of how she used to do it, after going out, quickly and without paying too much attention to technique. Now it was different: he pushed himself gently but firmly into her mouth, his hand remaining on the back of her head, the light pressure not threatening but compelling, as if he were coaching her in the right direction.

Iris let her tongue circle his glans. The taste wasn't clean, but that was apparently part of it. She tried to relax her jaws, using as few teeth as humanly possible, but with each thrust, her jaw still clenched slightly. He was breathing differently; the depth of his chest, his breathing pushing away the nerves of the moment.

She was hyperaware of her pregnancy, her belly against the edge of the couch, the position that didn't feel elegant but simply worked. She thought about the biology of it all: sperm, egg, everything that from now on would seek reproduction through her body. She made a half-joke in her head: maybe this was the only part of parenting that everyone had a manual for but never talked about.

Matthijs didn't let go of her. He nudged her palate gently, then pulled back a little so that air could brush past her tongue. She heard the voice of the soccer commentator in the background, fragments of another world where people weren't stuck to their bodies, but could just shout without their jaws full.

She felt his hand pull her hair, a little too roughly, but that might have been part of the ritual. She squeezed her eyes shut and let herself be guided, her chin against his stomach, the stiff hairs along her cheeks, the small jerks of his thighs. There was no awkwardness, no regret, only the pure present.

It wasn't uncomfortable, more slightly absurd, that she was sitting there on her knees, manipulating his body almost mechanically in her mouth. Something in the corner of her eye caught the score of the game; she had never scored goals before, she joked in her head, but now she counted every movement as a lead for him.

And yet—the line in her head tightened, somewhere between the idea of woman and mother-to-be, a kind of double identity that coincided nowhere else as it did in this place. The smell of his skin, the salty edge of his pre-ejaculate, even the soft tremor of his hand around her neck; everything felt like a confirmation of existence, an admission ticket to the new role that awaited her.

She noticed from the faltering of his hips that the moment was approaching. His grip tightened, his breathing became staggered. She had resolved not to grimace, even though her jaw was now working against her. The thought that every bit of control now lay with her gave her a bizarre power: she could let him go, or pause. For a moment, she held herself still, toneless, his cock against her tongue without moving. The tension in his body. The flash in his eyes, like an overexposed camera.

Then it came down to it. He pulled away just in time, a reflex she didn't even have to ask for, and his hands guided his cock to the mound of her breasts—large now, swollen with pregnancy, the instinctively perfect canvas for his seed. He came with a short, restrained sound, not a word but a sound, and the warm, sticky fluid flew in two streams across her skin. It landed first on her collarbone, then slid in thick drops along the soft curve of her left breast. The rest spread like a kind of glaze over her skin, perfect for a second, then sticky and cold.

He let her go. There was a silence that was not filled by the television; even the commentary had fallen away, soundless. She folded her arms over her breasts, the semen sticky between her skin and her sweater, and looked up at Matthijs. For a moment, she was afraid he would find it embarrassing—that a woman, pregnant and all, would let herself be decorated by his orgasm—but his gaze had never been so sincere. No shame, just a reckless kind of recognition.

She grabbed the towel that was always on their couch (for snacks, not for this), dabbed the stuff off her chest, and felt the warmth of his gaze on her cheeks. "You never miss me," she said, a joke that could also count as a reproach, but there was little emotion in her voice. It was part of it, she realized. Everything became registering, groping, inventorying: where did her body end, where did his desire begin.

He gently pulled her up, slipped his hand under the edge of her sweater, wiped away what remained of her body and stickiness with his thumb. She felt her chest pain secretly echoing a laughing muscle under her skin, as if she could endure anything for a moment as long as there was someone to take it away from her.

They remained seated, pressed against each other like two soft pillows on a couch that remembered their shape. She longed for sleep like a deer longs for fresh water; her eyes closed, until the wet coldness of her skin held her back. "I'll take a shower later," she muttered. Her voice was strange, hoarse.

He chuckled. "Together?"

She pretended to find it a silly suggestion, but the thought of running water, hot drops washing the remnants of their bodies off each other, was almost more tempting than sex itself. "As long as I can pee first. Believe me, it's impossible not to when you're pregnant."

Matthijs bowed his head against her temple, his breath tickling her hair. "You can always go first." And it sounded so serious, almost sacred, that she didn't know if it was a real joke or some kind of vow.

The shower was more stuffy than usual, the steam immediately fogging up the glass. She was used to showering in silence, the routine of soaping up, rinsing off, forgetting what had once stuck to her skin. Now it was different: he stood behind her in the small cell of tile and glass, his body as physically present as ever, hands resting on her shoulders as the water splashed down their backs.

She let the warm water pulse on her face, then turned halfway around so she could look at him. For the first time, she noticed how much older he looked, now that the light accentuated the folds in his skin. The streak of gray in his eyebrow, the frayed edges of his fingertips. Yet it didn't feel like a man and a student, more like two people who had invented a different kind of unity.

She soaped her belly, carefully, as if dusting a terrarium with the tip of a feather. "You're soft," Matthijs said, half whispering so close to her ear. He caressed her somewhere between her shoulder blades, his fingers continuing to circle. She allowed it, even when his hand slipped toward her hip, his thumb resting just above her buttocks.

Everything that normally drove her away—the awkwardness, the idea that this wasn't right—was now on pause. She turned completely around, leaning her forehead against his chest. It wasn't resistance, more a kind of surrender to the gravity of their togetherness.

She remained standing with her face against his chest, the shower head warm on her neck, water zigzagging down her back to her thighs. Iris registered it—every splash, the unwilling scraping of his toenails against the shower drain. In her field of vision, the scar on his collarbone, left over from a fall long ago, that he had never explained in her presence. It was always interesting what kind of stories men saved, and what kind they left to oblivion.

Everything evaporated in the shower. There was little left of them, a set of bones, skin, softened hair. She washed herself with the precision of a lab technician: small circles of shampoo, then rotate, lather over the body, rinse, done. No more lingering hands, no cloud of steam to inhale. Matthijs grabbed the towel, shook his head like a dog, water splashing everywhere.

She pulled her own towel up to her hips, folded it tightly. When she looked in the mirror, now—face, body, hair wet on her shoulders, the white band around her belly— she was almost ready to face the idea of becoming a mother. Not sacred, more like tough; not a gram left of the image of pregnant women in glossy magazines, it didn't suit her. She imitated the bathroom wall; cool, steamy, keeping all moisture within its own boundaries.

"Are you done now?" Matthijs asked, not her, but their reflection in the glass.

She nodded, tied her hair into a wet bun, and stuck her chin out. It was time to pick up the normal day again: homework, dinner, and preparing for the panel discussion via WhatsApp. Maybe a text to Bram with a summary; chaos always ventilated best when she could capture it in text. The letter from the kitchen was still waiting, a call from the municipality. Now that she saw it that way, it suddenly seemed as if life had pushed her over the threshold, without a hand on the banister.

Outside the bathroom, the house felt stranger, as if the walls were nowhere colder than on these Thursdays. Nellie's voice blared from the living room; the smell of cigarettes greeted her, mixed with that specific kind of floor wax smell her mother used to clean everything that wasn't hers.

She knew exactly how it would go. Her mother, half a meter shorter in her tracksuit, with one eyebrow raised. An attempt at indifference, but always a fraction too much attention in her gaze, as if she were afraid of missing something. Iris went through her routines: bread out of the plastic, a slice of cheese in between, then lingering at the sink until Matthijs had tidied up his things from the bathroom.

In the kitchen lay the envelope with the bold blue municipal stamp, like a trigger no one could escape. She carefully tore open the top edge, holding the paper close to her eye. It was a notice for an information evening about young parents, organized at the community center, with beanbag chairs and lemonade, "open to anyone who feels involved in parenting." The latter made her laugh. She could already see Matthijs sitting there with one of those plastic cups, his legs too long for the IKEA folding chair, everything about him too cynical for the celebration of the average. But when she concentrated on the list of speakers, she was shocked to see her own name as an "experienced expert" from the university.

She dropped the note on the kitchen counter and clasped her hands together, her knuckles white. The very idea of an evening filled with the kind of people who would weigh everything she had done so far, like sugar cubes on a kitchen scale. She thought about tearing up the note right away, never telling anyone she had been invited—but something rang with pride in her chest, stubborn as a growth ring in an old oak tree.

She stifled the feeling and opened the refrigerator: yogurt, the rest of dinner, half a punnet of strawberries already turning brown around the edges. She closed the door, letting the vacuum suck at her eye for a moment. It took a moment before she realized she was standing in a puddle of water in her socks; her mother had apparently just mopped the floor. With wet toes, she walked to the living room, where Matthijs had curled up on the corner of the couch, a book open but his gaze fixed on the air above the cabinet.

She stood still, waiting for him to see her. When he looked up, there was no evasion in his eyes, only the slowness of someone who has nothing to hide. "What's wrong?" he asked, not with a list of assumptions or intentions, but as if everything always had to have a concrete reason.

She wanted to say something about the letter, about how she couldn't imagine herself for a second in a circle of mothers with burp cloths and fathers with strollers, while she herself was doing her best to understand if her life even resembled anything. But she settled for: "Did you know we've been invited as a model family?"

A smile tugged at his lips, as if he were trying hard not to grin. "Then we can show off our parenting skills as much as they want," he said. "Life is one big poster campaign."

Somewhere inside, she felt angry, but not really. That smooth indifference—a shield with which he rendered everything uncomfortable harmless. She wondered how on earth you could ever raise a child if nothing threw you off balance anymore. But maybe that was exactly the ingredient she had always missed from her own childhood: the ability to let everything roll up to the finish line of the very much wanted to avoid, her head burst into a migraine-like throb. As if it were really going to happen soon: Iris on a catwalk of insufficient self-confidence, put in the spotlight as an example. Her fellow students in the audience, WhatsApp memes at the ready, all smiling smugly in their coat pockets. All that collective waiting for a mistake.

She considered throwing the letter straight into the compost bin, but her fingers protested. She folded the form back up, slid it under her textbooks, unintentionally creating a sarcastic altar of to-dos that hung over her generation's heads. A sigh, not a big one, more like a leak of pressure.

In the living room, Matthijs was already lying on the couch, feet stretched out in white sports socks. The television was silent, the screen reflecting the underside of his chin and the blue of the outside air. She wanted to join him, head against his shoulder, but remained at the kitchen sink, sulking about her own scenarios. The baby's craving was back: a sucking, almost unreasonable hunger for everything that wasn't in the house.

On impulse, she grabbed her coat from the coat rack and walked outside. The air was chilly and cold after the rain. The sidewalk tiles seemed like a wet reflection of the sky, and every bicycle along the racks was still dripping. She had no plan, except perhaps the supermarket, a bag of chips, a chocolate bar, and a product that could easily serve as comfort for expectant mothers.

On the way, she caught herself in the rhythm of her walking: firm steps, each step a statement. She felt the lump in her groin, not unpleasant, almost familiar after weeks of practicing being pregnant. It helped that the city was virtually empty—a few older men sitting on a bench by the church, one woman walking her dog, nothing else. She could imagine that if things really got out of hand, she wouldn't be a bother to anyone. Absolutely no one.

In the supermarket, the music was more cheerful than the staff could bear. She walked past the aisle with baby products, pausing at a wall of jars, organic puree in more colors than the rest of her week combined. She read the labels as if they were exam questions, trying to extract the fun from them with her eye muscles. Baby food: Who came up with those descriptions? It always sounded like you were expecting a new pet and had to sign a contract for it. "Suitable for ages 4 to 6 months." Was there already pressure to perform in baby food?

She bought the chocolate and chips, plus a can of soup for Matthijs, because he always got cranky in the evening. At the checkout, she felt like she was being watched, but the cashier didn't keep her in her sights any longer than necessary, beep-beep, new customer, done. What a relief

that it could always be so smooth, Iris thought. Nothing to attach your subcutaneous stress to, no shared judgment, just the thumping of scanners and the rustling of bags and chip bags. She wished she could always keep it that way—the city a transit station, not an obstacle course.

On the way back, she was overcome by an impulse to take a detour, past the old elementary school that was now a community center. She didn't recognize it anymore, except for the smell of moss and wet concrete. A young woman was just walking out with a toddler by the hand, the toddler wobbling in a raincoat that was much too long. The image stuck in her mind, something between coincidence and the future. She calculated how many months it would take for her own life to take shape, and realized that it might never become so clear; rather, it would be a series of snapshots, each school vacation a new version of the same memory.

When she got home, she went straight to the bathroom. Her breath immediately fogged up the mirror. Her face had a lightness that didn't match her head, as if she wanted to give herself a six-hour head start on the storm that was coming. She washed her hands, ignored the stains on her sweater, and only then walked to the living room, where Matthijs had hidden himself in a nest of fleece and pillows.

He looked at her with something that resembled relief; perhaps she had missed him after all, or perhaps he was just glad that the soup didn't have to come from his own initiative. She kicked off her shoes, pushed the bag of groceries against his thigh, and plopped down next to him on the couch.

Outside, the light from a nearby thunderstorm crackled, and Iris felt the tension in her legs slowly dissolve into the soft fold of the sofa cushion. She rubbed her hands over her belly, stubborn as ever, and thought: this is it. This is what remains.

She had no idea now whether she would turn out to be a good mother. But the thought that it might not matter — that everything that happened tonight could still be erased by tomorrow, that even the worst panel debut or the most embarrassing echo would fade in the passage of time — gave her a sudden sense of calm. What failed now might soon right itself. Or not; then it would just remain in the margins, like a crooked school sweater that no one ever dared to exchange.

She took the chocolate out of her bag and cut open the paper with a knife. Matthijs watched silently as she broke off a whole bar between her thumb and forefinger and handed him the largest piece. It felt like a kind of sacrifice, a compromise between desire and logistics, between everything that was uncertain and everything that would soon melt on their tongues.

Life continued with an exasperating self-evidence until the day it had to break abruptly. She was standing at the sink, her T-shirt too short, her hands lost in a bag of chips, when suddenly moisture pricked between her legs—not a normal puddle, but a rush of warmth that immediately dripped into her slippers. The chips suddenly tasted like metal; she put the bag away in one motion, as if you were eating candy during a fire alarm. She looked at the trail across the tile floor, foolishly thinking for a moment that a water pipe had burst, until her stomach tightened like a sharp injection, a wave that came out of nowhere and put everything in her body on edge.

Matthijs only noticed when she kept leaning her hand on the counter, toe on the floor, sweater tight across her stomach. "Are you okay?" he asked. His voice had that strange, light tone, as if he didn't want her to notice he was worried.

"No," she said, without hesitation. "It's started or something."

He jumped up, fumbled between his shoes and car keys, and even forgot his phone. She had to instruct him herself—

grab her bag, lip balm, those strange sugar things Bram had once recommended for her blood pressure—which reassured her more than anything she had read during her pregnancy. On the back seat lay a folded baby blanket with a cheerful owl pattern. She rubbed her belly, unable to believe that after months of emptiness, everything was now coming together in these five minutes.

In the car, the seat suddenly felt too hard; every turn pulled at her kidneys. She tried to focus on the music coming from the dashboard, but her head kept bumping to the rhythm of the contractions. Matthijs drove slowly, overly cautiously, as if he were afraid that the baby would pop its head out at sixty kilometres per hour. At the first traffic light, he squeezed her hand, too tightly, as if she would otherwise fall out of her body. She said nothing, looked out the window, and tried to count how many times she held her breath per kilometre.

The maternity ward was less pastel than she had expected. Steel chairs, a sheet too thin to sit on, a wall with an advertisement for face masks. She folded her legs, rocked back and forth, waiting for someone to address her as an expert. It was bizarre that she suddenly felt like an amateur here, as if all the preparation in her head had now dissolved into adrenaline and a little fear. The midwife was a girl barely older than herself, with freckles and a name that Iris forgot as soon as it was spoken.

"Exciting?" the girl asked, without a trace of irony. When the IV was inserted, Iris almost crushed the edge of the mattress. Her legs felt strangely loose, as if they were a thread that could break at any moment. Time became strangely elastic: sometimes passing in seconds, then so long that she forgot where she was or who was standing next to her.

Matthijs talked to her as if she were a patient he had to take care of. A few times she scolded him, only to discover that he was still holding her hand, his fingers blue from the effort. This time, he had no breastfeeding joke at the ready, no tough talk, just his sweet panic that seemed to anchor his shoes to the ground.

Waiting was now not a choice but a modality. She sat on a bed in a room with an echo of her own wheezing breath. The contractions came in waves, sometimes with intervals in which she could organize a very short life: a scene before her eyes, how her mother used to rub tiger balm on her knees, how Bram once threw a bottle of water over her head in a drunken dare. In the minutes between the attacks, she looked at herself, a girl on a blue hospital bed wearing an oversized sweater and socks that had long since been soaked through with sweat. Did she feel like a mother now? No. She felt just as much like a child, or an animal, or just a piece of hardware trying to resist time.

It was bizarre how the body took over autonomously. She didn't have to think, just comply and follow what her muscles had been secretly preparing for months. The first few hours were like a live version of her textbook: dilation, pushing, guidance. The midwife kept pushing her on to the next step with a half-smile, as if it were a sporting event, a race that Iris really had to finish now. There was no time for lists or perfectionism, only for sweating, grunting, and occasionally the feeling that she was screaming the whole ward together.

After an indefinable amount of time—it could have been minutes or an entire school year—she felt the burning, the cliché of "your body breaking in two," which Bram had once delicately described as "unforgettable, but not necessarily in a good way." For a moment, she thought about destroying the entire room, smashing everything in sight, including Matthijs, who had once again placed his hand on her hair out of nowhere.

And then, without warning or direction, her body pushed a baby out. The air became thin for a moment, then filled with an unbearable scream that cut through her to the bone. It wasn't her own scream, but that of her child. She looked down, saw arms that didn't seem to be hers, saw how someone—another woman, not herself—placed a small body on her chest. She saw the head, the strange old person's face, heard the midwife say something about breathing and liveliness, saw how suddenly everything was no longer a plan but just an event.

Matthijs laughed, a hoarse smack in her ear, and immediately a second wave of panic rolled through her. She couldn't adjust, not to the sound, not to the body on her wet chest, not to the smell of blood that flooded everything. At the same time, she thought: It's a mistake, this can't be, someone has to put it back. But then the panic receded somewhere in her hip. She breathed in, a whiff of pure air, and the little body lay soft as a cat on her rib cage, pounding with disgust and hunger.

Someone said, "Congratulations." It echoed, as if they were shouting at her from a floor below. She looked back and saw the nurse with her thumb up, and next to her the pale green face of Matthijs, a kind of hero who was now almost aligned with the mattress, white up to his hairline. He grinned, but something jerked in his neck: she felt it almost like a vibration. The baby screamed, mouth open like a fish gasping for air. "He's here," Matthijs said, barely audible, as if he couldn't believe the ultrasound.

At first, Iris didn't dare touch the little body. She had expected that everything would immediately fall apart, break like Christmas bauble glass. Yet she picked up the child, finger by finger, feeling how warm and syrupy the skin was, how the little body blindly clawed its way toward a breast. She wanted to smell the child. She did. It smelled of steel and something chemical, but through that, a clammy sweetness she would never be able to forget. She heard voices in the distance talking about umbilical cords, placentas, statistics of weight and urgency, but the only thing that stuck in her head was the feeling that her body was no longer empty, but overflowing: as if you could exist twice in one moment.

Someone put a hand on her shoulder, a little too hard. "He's doing well." And the voice was cheerful, perhaps relieved for her, but Iris only heard the way people always want to reassure you with someone else's happiness. Her mother came in, still wearing her raincoat, her hair a curtain of wetness. She looked briefly at the child, briefly at Iris, and then at the edge of the bed. "The worst is over?" she said, rubbing her hands together. Iris nodded, because anything else was too big to say.

The midwife asked if they had already decided on a name, as if it had only become urgent now that the body was separated from her. Iris looked at Matthijs, who was staring at the ceiling with a wild look in his eyes. "Simon," he said without hesitation, as if it had never been in question. Iris tasted the word, felt its echo in the room: a name that immediately belonged not on her tongue but on the little body in her arms. Simon was not big, not imposing, more of a problem child who had to fight his way through the first few days. But his eyes, when he finally opened them, were dark and all-encompassing, like the depths of an ocean politely awaiting its first real storm.

After the pushing, the stitching, the bandages, and the soothing scents of pine from the aftercare, it became quieter than Iris had ever thought a hospital could be. In the hallway light, she counted the seconds between cries. The baby was placed in a plastic crib, under an instant hat that didn't fit his face. Nellie had immediately claimed the child, letting him make the rounds among those present. Everyone felt the little hand, everyone commented on the jaw, the neck, or the wrinkle on the forehead. She had to laugh, despite the burning between her legs. So you're never alone as a mother; everything is collectively inspected, scrutinized, and measured from all angles.

Matthijs had white knuckles and remained sitting on the edge of her bed. He gave her a smile, but at that moment, he had nothing to say. Perhaps he needed to process the event, store it in his own archive, before he could say a word about it. This was exactly how they had always been together, Iris thought. First the spectacle, then the silence, only then the meaningful naming, if it was necessary at all.

She lay alone with the baby for a moment, skin-to-skin, the drizzle of his breath, his head perfectly nestled in the crook of her arm, his eyes closed as if the outside world could wait for now. She stroked his back, no plans in her head except for now, these minutes, this fur under her fingers.

Outside, it was getting dark early. In the hospital room, there was a rustling from the radiators, sometimes a crack as if the world had just straightened its spine after pushing. The night was a series of small alarms: monitors beeping like a graphic equalizer, nurses walking in like shadows, babies trying out a new siren every fifteen minutes. But Simon slept, or watched, at his own pace.

Iris did not sleep. The adrenaline still tingled through her skin. She leaned halfway upright, stared at the ceiling throughout the long night, trying to figure out how much of her own mother was now in her, how much of everything had led to this version of herself. She felt the throbbing knot in her lower abdomen, the residual pain like a second heartbeat, but she didn't care. So this is what all mothers mean when they say that after giving birth, you no longer know who you were, but all that matters is what you will leave behind.

Five years later, Iris had forgotten three jobs at once, but not a single day of her children. The apartment in Nieuw-West had exactly four corners where you could hide as a parent, but less than one minute of privacy per day. Ruby was only three, Simon six and a quarter if you counted the months of the pandemic as bonus years. Matthijs came and went with the clock of his freelance life, always somewhere between realistic hope and slightly sabotaged expectations.

When Iris walked past Ruby's bed in the morning, you could tell from the blanket which parent had been responsible for putting her to bed. Her own routines: tucked in tightly, pacifiers lined up, stuffed rabbit within arm's reach of the child. Matthijs: blanket like a pizza slice, night light on disco mode, Ruby usually sleeping crosswise, one leg sticking out of the crib window as if she were preparing to leap to freedom.

The days were a parade of voice memos from schoolyard mothers ("Did Ruby still have a fever after Friday?") and, in between, customers trying to dump their data stuff on Iris. Since she had been on the childcare board, her emails were answered with more exclamation marks than punctuation marks. She didn't mind.

Control freakery and modest drama kept her going, as long as she didn't have to play the leading role herself. Matthijs usually slept in, sometimes on the couch, usually with her—their bed a minefield of old-fashioned Sudoku puzzles, dog-eared children's books, and old laptops.

Iris used to loathe this bourgeois lifestyle, but now that she had it, she never wanted to lose it. She counted her treasures in decibels: Ruby's screams when she was allowed to watch TV, Simon's kicking of the cupboard, Matthijs' subsonic humming as he complained about his lack of sleep while doom-scrolling on his phone.

On Tuesday evenings, they carried each other through the week with wine and greasy fries, sometimes with sex, usually with Netflix. Iris knew exactly which series the children weren't allowed to watch, and exactly how to hide chocolate in a house full of hidden chocolate. On the evenings when Simon didn't want to sleep, she would crawl into bed with him, his smooth, boyish skin against her arm. He still smelled of wet earth, of that first morning after the birth.

She loved this time, but she never said so. She knew it was temporary, like the child's hand that would soon become an adolescent's hand and then no longer fit in her coat pocket. All the clichés from the panel discussions—letting go, being in the moment, gratitude—felt bizarrely real with two children on your lap.

Even the guilt about too much screen time quickly became old news. Matthijs had adopted his own ritual with the children. Every Saturday, he got them out of bed for the "quick break": get dressed in one minute, then off to the basketball court, even in the rain.

The children climbed over the fence in their pajamas, sweating as they ran laps between the wet tiles, while Matthijs timed their sprints with his phone like a real coach.

It didn't matter who won, as long as the time stayed under two minutes. Then home, breakfast, the smell of chocolate sprinkles on white bread. He thought there was no better start than sitting together in wet sweatpants and using the newspaper as a tablecloth.

Sometimes, Iris forgot that there was once a time without this routine. She looked at Ruby, who was seriously sticking her thumb in a sticky Nutella jar, and Simon, who kept playing fireman until he fell asleep next to his bowl of milk. It wasn't that she no longer knew herself, but rather that she had completely merged with the house: every stain on the wall, every morning that started with a wet floor. Even waiting for the elevator became predictable over time. Always the same smell of detergent, of the neighbors downstairs making curry, of life settling into your clothes without warning.

Iris was no longer in a hurry when she had to go to work. She drank her coffee in the strange half-hours between daycare and the tram, peered at the screens of other mothers in the waiting room, and tried to read from their faces whether they had all planned it this way too.

The answer was always no; no one had planned this, not the double child, not the double number of sleepless nights, not the feeling that you were becoming more of a manager of your own life than a participant. Bram was still there, but now as the referee of all playdates. He knew exactly which Wednesday afternoons the best playgrounds were empty.

Ruby's hand in his, as if she had spent her entire childhood preparing for that moment. Bram had a new girlfriend, twenty years younger, and told everyone that he was surprised himself. Iris liked her. She made no attempt to pretend to be a stepmother, but always made oatmeal for "the children," as if she immediately understood that the truth lay in the small gestures.

Matthijs hardly worked in the consensus environment of the university anymore. He was now self-employed, gave mindfulness training to companies, and every Friday gave a workshop on "Storytelling for Introverts" in a yoga studio with tacky curtains. He told Iris that he had finally found himself, but she mainly noticed that he went to the pub more often with his old college friends and sometimes came home nervously, smelling of menthol and gin.

Her mother, still sleeping in the same apartment on the other side of town, came by every Wednesday to "corrupt" the children: with candy, YouTube, and an unstoppable stream of inappropriate jokes. Simon loved it, but after two hours, Ruby was fed up with it, like a wristband around her nights: the realization that they were now a family, no longer a by-product of their parents' lives, but a colony of sleepless weeks and subcutaneous drift. Matthijs had taught Simon to negotiate screen time (the first lesson: start low, raise the stakes during the evening ritual) while Ruby bombarded the household with experiments for which the soap literally never finished on time. Their apartment did not become more spacious over the years, but the top layer of their lives grew into a type of busyness that even her mother would warn her about.

On Tuesdays, Iris worked from home; Ruby would invariably enter the bedroom alone at half past eight, wearing slippers, her face a half-moon crescent, and command herself onto the big bed. Matthijs had taken the family out in the morning; Simon would jump around him, brutally wet, begging for fifteen more minutes of slow motion in the playground. By ten o'clock, the house was quiet except for the small sounds: the refrigerator humming, the dishes mirroring her breathing, the prim tapping of Ruby's plastic toys in the hallway.

Then Iris hummed herself into a state of calm: the Zoom meeting as an anchor, the oven on a timer, the knowledge that Ruby would be busy with crafts or "storytelling," as the latest craze in childcare circles was called, until at least lunchtime. She sometimes looked at the girl, her body just too tight in her pajamas, her hairline wavy deep over her forehead, and wondered if children's characters could really be read from the patterns of their play. Ruby built houses out of bouquets, Simon demolished them, always holding the baton of the family story in his hands.

She saw her work history as a filing cabinet whose drawers sprang open spontaneously. Here was an email from a customer about an error in the algorithm, and there was a text message from Bram saying he was considering quitting his job ("never hated everything so much, maybe that's a good sign?"). Iris strung hours together through messages, deadlines, and schedules that she had sometimes made unnecessarily complicated for herself. Life increasingly resembled the clinic clowns her mother hated so much: whoever laughed the longest was the winner.

In the afternoon, when the children were at their most energetic, Iris let them loose in the park next to the apartment building. On good days, it was windless, a rectangle of sand surrounded by trimmed bushes and a fountain that didn't work. Simon tried to ride his old scooter up the hill while Ruby ran after a group of city pigeons with a backpack full of acorns. Other mothers stood with their backs to the wind, their phones like miniature mirrors between their fingers. Iris didn't recognize herself in their attitude. After half an hour, Ruby was back on the iPad. "Your mother is a hero," she invariably texted Bram on Wednesday afternoons, "but it doesn't make the children any faster." Her own mother was always kind to Ruby and Simon, but with every visit, Iris felt how she failed to show that her daughter had not exactly done what she had once dreamed of, or had succeeded in doing just that: a minimum of drama, a maximum of perseverance.

On Thursdays, Iris was usually home alone with the children because Matthijs had "a meeting" — the word so vaguely pronounced that it could just as well refer to extra groceries or a clandestine smoke break. She had learned not to ask questions about these evenings, although she could tell from the smell of his clothes and the delay in his gaze that the meetings were not always limited to mindfulness or rooms with burlap or tapestries.

She only noticed it that particular evening, not because of the time, but because of the chilly silence in the house after the children had finally fallen asleep. She remained seated at the kitchen table, in her sweatpants, while the weather outside pounded on her windows. The city had slowly emerged from early winter: you heard ambulances more often, and people shouted longer in the streets. She tapped her fingernail on the counter, thinking of nothing, or perhaps of everything that had played out like a movie under well-intentioned domesticity over the past year.

It was well after midnight when Matthijs came home. He immediately smoked a cigarette in the garden, clicking his lighter shut three times, a tic she had found endearing at first. Iris listened to the sound, trying to read from the duration of the rattling on the sidewalk tile whether he had been preparing for something. She didn't hear him close the door and noticed how his soles became sticky on the wet mat in the hallway.

He entered the room, finger in a box of pistachios, his hair wet from the rain or the bike. "Everything quiet?" he asked, just loud enough not to wake the children. She nodded, wanted to say that Ruby had gone to sleep without crying today, but he didn't let her finish. "I saw someone."

His voice was lighter than usual, as if there was a lump in his throat.

Iris was silent for half a second, finding it somehow exciting that he was speaking vaguely. "At your mindfulness club?"

"No. At the bar. I didn't go home right away—my mind was too busy. At De Reünie. You don't know her." He scratched his neck as if he were now playing a soap opera cliché.

She let it sink in, not for the drama, but for the focus it brought. "Who?"

He grabbed a handful of pistachios and shook his head. "Madelon. Utrechtsestraat, when I was still at the publishing house.

It wasn't the evening Iris had planned for herself: she was sitting in her nightshirt with half-melted chocolate under her fingernail, while Matthijs presented her with a name as if it were a record player at the thrift store. Madelon. The name had vaguely lingered in her subconscious somewhere during her student days, but never as a threatening phenomenon. She looked at his hands, how he restlessly struck the shell of the nut, and only after a fraction of a second did she slip into her role: "You say it as if I would even want to know her."

He grinned. "Nothing special. She was always opening bottles for everyone on Friday afternoon drinks, talking a lot about cats. It wasn't sexy at all," he added, with a vague gesture, as if anything that wasn't immediately dangerous wasn't worth mentioning.

Iris touched the counter, feeling in the trembling fluff of her reading that it was not an affair, not a bomb, at most a smoke grenade that lingered in their relationship for a week. But it continued to gnaw at her, the tone with which he said it, the ease with which everything could be made fluid, even after twelve years together in a flat that was too small.

She shrugged. "I saw Bram yesterday, for clarity. His new girlfriend does Ayurveda, she's inviting us to a 'ritual' at the Amstel. Bram says that couples who do that become truly faithful."

Matthijs laughed, but the sound was just too tight. "Those kinds of rituals always cost more than you'd like." He tapped her knuckles softly and waited for the little laugh they usually gave when the world around them became too ridiculous to take seriously. Tonight, the laugh didn't come.

The children slept restlessly in the room next to the kitchen. Since kindergarten, Ruby had developed a new habit: getting out of bed once a night for water, then haunting the apartment for at least half an hour with the face of a stranded ghost. Simon slept with his fists under his pillow, like a dog that could only be awakened with sugar or panic. Iris had not set out to be a much better mother than her own mother, but she wanted to do things differently at least: less drama, more of a fixed schedule, as all the books claimed a nervous child needed.

She heard the stairs creak, a sloppy shuffle of bare feet across the sticky PVC. Ruby, in pajamas down to her ankles, her hair pulled further and further up at night by static electricity. She appeared in the doorway like a squeaky mobile phone, her hand pressed against her face.

"I can't sleep. Simon says I'm breathing weird."

Iris got up from her chair, trying not to look at her husband, who was already preparing for his own night. She lifted Ruby up, feeling her rib cage like a stiff rag doll, a moving skull with the arm span of a dragonfly. Behind her, Iris heard Matthijs say very softly, "Come on," and for the first time in months, she felt that her family could become smaller and larger in one night. She rocked Ruby, her head against her collarbone, her body limp in her hand. Over her shoulder, she looked at Matthijs, his gaze briefly on her, and it seemed as if everything corrected itself as long as someone who knew you really looked at you.

Ruby fell asleep on her lap after three minutes, with a hot water bottle with teeth. She remained seated until her daughter's body became completely still, until her breathing trailed softly and evenly along her arm. She thought of her own mother, who talked just as little when things got complicated, and knew exactly when to remain silent to preserve the moment. She was a carbon copy, really: all good intentions, all just-not-quite-enough patience, but slightly softer around the edges because she never thought of herself as important than the child.

On the couch, they watched short videos together, videos about animals and TikToks of children burning their homework. Ruby kept poking her cheeks into her shoulder, the whiskey breath of a child who had just been crying. Time did not pass; it remained light in her head, a strange, sugar-rich fever like she used to have as a girl when you knew at seven o'clock that you could stay up longer. When Ruby finally nodded, her fingers loosening their grip on her mother's sweater, Iris carried her back to bed. She straightened the blanket, tucked the stuffed animal under her arm, and kissed her just above the hairline, right in the crease of her sleep.

As she left the room, she saw Simon light up for a moment—his eyes open, but he pretended to be asleep. She raised her hand, fingers straight, and he waved a mini-hello back. Everything came together in her heart at once—the guilt, the expectation, the addiction to the smell of your own child so close to your face. She didn't understand any of the books she had ever read about motherhood, because nowhere did it seem as simple as when you circled around your children at night in a dimly lit apartment building, hoping that every tremor or groan was just a sign of normal growth.

Downstairs, Matthijs had dimmed the lights, only a small charging cord casting a blue glow on the walls. The tokens of their lives were scattered across the floor: empty cups, a strip of paracetamol on the corner of the table, an open bottle of sunscreen for a postponed beach season. She walked past them, into the bedroom, trying to close the day behind her. Her husband was lying in bed, on his back, his eyes half closed. She slid under the blanket, her foot against his shin.

CHAPTER 7
VAGABOND HEART 2

It started as a joke. A profile switch with an inappropriate bio, "seeking two for the price of one, preferably with old-fashioned English humor and a veto against ketchup." He didn't expect such specific nonsense to be popular. But on a weekday Tuesday evening, between defrosting frozen lasagna and a series of pointless TikToks, they responded: Jasmine and Pippa. They came up with suggestions for a Shakespeare-worthy first meeting, until the conversation suddenly turned to their shared fascination with obscure cheeses and the Dutch tulip industry.

Matthijs went into the first date with no expectations. No one stuck to the literal agreements on dating apps. But when the duo walked in. Jasmine, with her dark blonde hair and bright orange lipstick, Pippa a lot smaller but with the look of someone who notes everything down for later use; he knew immediately that his own rules didn't apply. They were too real, too confident. They ordered cocktails under protest ("Dutch gin? Seriously?"), took control of the conversation, and took him to an obscure karaoke bar in the Pijp where they sang "Don't You Want Me" without hesitation. Each chorus meant a push, a pat on the back, a brief moment when they pulled him into their twin energy. No one took themselves seriously, except when someone had to.

The second date, this time without the noise of an audience, showed that their humor and bravado were rooted in years of practice. They laughed at everything, but less loudly at each other. They were used to observing people and immediately recognizing when they overestimated themselves. This became apparent when Pippa suddenly placed her hand on his thigh, just as Matthijs was trying to tell a story about a stolen bicycle. Jasmine followed suit, caught his eye, and said as casually as she could, "We share, if that's okay. It's kind of how we were raised." And everything in him said no, except his mouth, which mumbled yes and already planned how he would keep their names apart when he got home.

After a month, his neighbors discovered through the stairwell buzz that he had acquired two English daughters. "They walk down the street every morning with their sandwiches and jokes," said the neighbor with more pleasure than jealousy. Matthijs felt his mother's gaze on the back of his neck as he smuggled them in, three torsos in an ill-fitting

IKEA bed. But everything about this relationship felt light. As if every date was meant to be comical, every argument a metaphor for something all three of them could laugh about.

At night, Matthijs was usually the last one awake, with their English breath on his neck, the rhythm of two different hearts beating simultaneously under his arm. Sometimes the thought surfaced that he had been mistaken all along: he wasn't running away, he had simply underestimated his previous life. As if everything had become unnecessarily complicated by always trying the same thing, when it really wanted to be simple: eat, laugh, sleep, carry on. Jasmine's legs pushed him out of bed every morning with a kind of childlike efficiency, and Pippa sent him to pub quizzes and soft-launch events until his calendar filled up with plans he no longer even tried to avoid.

On Friday mornings, when they drank their coffee together on the balcony, Matthijs felt the silence there differently. No demands or mocking comments, just a few minutes of nothing. He got used to the whisper of their voices, the comments about the neighbors, and their borderline tragic longing for Dutch events. Liberation Day, King's Night, Museum Weekend. The sisters thought it was all excessive, but experienced it with a kind of relentless enthusiasm. It became their sport as foreigners to pretend they had more right to speak than the locals: "Matthijs, explain again why all Dutch snacks taste like a sponge soaked in mustard?"

They always laughed at him, but never at him. That difference affected him more than he wanted to admit. Even when Jasmine accidentally dropped her bag in the canal, and Pippa made him spend half a day looking for a new one, he only felt pleasure in their predictable chaos.

The rest of his life shrank a little more each day until the house consisted largely of their mornings together and the evenings when no one expected too much. Even his mother gave up and allowed the sisters into her home without complaint. By then, she had learned two English words: "puzzled" and "strange."

One evening, after one of those endless trivia nights and a bottle of cheap cava, Jasmine suggested formalizing things at the notary. Not a marriage, too ostentatious, but a cohabitation contract, "with an opt-out clause if someone freaks out about commitment." Pippa looked at him as she always did: not angry, not sentimental, just with an open gaze that wouldn't blink until he answered.

Matthijs laughed because it was so ridiculous, because he had never felt so little freaked out about a contract. He didn't have to try to come up with an alternative. "You have to sign it with red wine," he said, and Jasmine nodded, as if she had been waiting for that sentence.

That night, he was the last one awake again, between their sleepy bodies, trying to figure out why he had wasted years procrastinating. But nothing came. No explanation. No analysis. Just the feeling that some things only make sense when the people involved are crazy enough to call it normal.

And so it continued: life as a permanent sleepover, three breakfasts, three different types of toothpaste, and a laptop for each of them. On Monday, Jasmine threw a bowl of yogurt at her head, Pippa set up a virtual meeting, Matthijs took milk out of the fridge, and concluded that he had secretly grown to love their bizarrely slow morning rituals. He no longer read the newspaper; the news came to him automatically via their phone. Or via their mouths, which filtered everything until only juicy anecdotes remained. Matthijs had never thought his life would take this turn, but he was happy to go with the flow.

There was a permanent traffic jam in the bathroom. Driving instructions: whoever finished first with their bladder, whoever finished last with her eyeliner. Hair bands, face creams, and strange English nail files were scattered everywhere. Sometimes Matthijs wondered if he was living in an episode of a sitcom, or in one of those documentaries about alternative families where the voice-over waxed emotional about "new forms of cohabitation." But everything felt functional. No one cut anyone else off, no one was left out. Even when Pippa had a run-in with the downstairs neighbor (he thought the laughter was too loud, it was upsetting his pet), she solved it by inviting him over on Friday as a test audience for their secret karaoke basement. Matthijs thought that was incomprehensibly bold, but it worked: the neighbor sang falsetto and always stayed for cider afterwards.

Sometimes Matthijs noticed how their routine differed from that of their neighbors, his friends, and especially his mother. The latter had stopped sending WhatsApp messages about good doctors and cheap potatoes. Now she sent links to English gardening programs and questions about "how they manage to keep it up." If there was one thing Matthijs didn't want to explain, it was exactly that.

The contract was finally signed at a notary's office three streets away, with red wine in plastic cups. No one found it awkward. As they signed, Jasmine looked at him with that expression of hers that made everything seem ridiculous and yet was deadly serious at the same time. "Now you're stuck," she said. Her voice had the same kind of threat his mother used to use when he didn't make his bed, but it felt like a compliment.

After the notary, there was no party, just a walk along the IJ. It was raining in that thin, English way, barely worth mentioning, but wet to the bone. They came home soaked, put on each other's sweaters, and sank onto the couch as if the day was over. No one talked about the future. As if it were a product they could pull off the shelves when supplies ran out, and that wasn't going to happen anytime soon.

At night, Matthijs dreamed more and more often that he was being chased by a flock of swans, all opening their beaks to tear his life apart, but when he woke up, he only saw Jasmine, eyes open in the dark, or Pippa with the blankets pulled over her head. Sometimes he would lie there for an hour, staring into the darkness, their breathing the only proof that he hadn't accidentally become lonely again.

In the morning, the house was cold, and the heating was too lazy to kick in on time. He listened to the stuttering of the old radiator. This monotonous beat matched their morning rhythm: Pippa with a half-drunken gaze into the coffee maker, Jasmine with her feet on the kitchen table, the day always starting later than agreed. No one was in a hurry. Everything was prepared for delay, extension, the luxury of not having to go anywhere. On Thursdays, they ate fried eggs in their pajamas, watched English game shows, and pretended that reality had to adapt to their rhythm.

The house itself, the characterful rental property with damp in the windowsills, molded itself around their lives as if that was the way it was meant to be. No symmetrical Ikea nests here, but a cozy, semi-organized ecosystem of second-hand chairs and socks in impossible places. Even the plants on the windowsill seemed to bend to their pace: they grew slowly but suddenly shot up when they were neglected for a weekend. Matthijs noticed that he was watering plants more and more often without thinking about it, as if he were making his contribution unobtrusively.

It wasn't until breakfast on a Monday morning, when Jasmine spread her hair on his bread, that he felt the need to tell someone something important. But what? Was he happy? That he had finally found a place to call home? It sounded like something you would put in a moving card, not an announcement for a table full of crumbs and dirty coffee mugs.

The sisters had now isolated themselves in their own language. Sometimes they made jokes he couldn't join in with; a kind of whisper code that remained inviting at the same time. You were always welcome to listen in, as long as you didn't laugh at the wrong moment. He tried less and less to understand and more and more to just be, which became easier once Pippa had taught him how English marmite really works ("Don't spread it. Almost scrape it.")

On market days, the three of them cycled across town, Jasmine on a rickety gray city bike, Pippa on the back of Matthijs's bike because her own bike always had "something" wrong with it. They bought organic eggs, weird English tea, and everything that didn't exist in their supermarket routine. He enjoyed their competitive shopping: who would be the first to find the best blue cheese, who would be the last to spot a bargain on the shelf.

In the evening, they ate together at the small table. There was a lot of complaining about the day, but no one took the complaints seriously. Eating was not a chore, but rather a sport in which the rules could be adjusted with each meal. Sometimes it was Turkish food; other times, toast with hummus and whatever else the fridge had to offer. There were always leftovers and always discussion about how to use them up—a kind of shared thriftiness that Matthijs strangely recognized in himself. Sometimes he heard himself speaking with an English accent, especially when he imitated Jasmine ("I swear, darling, this is barely cheese, it's just vieux rubber"), and he found that less embarrassing than he used to. Their strange eating habits also rubbed off on him: cold beans from a can, toast with too much cream cheese, licorice in unexpected places around the house, his own little victories.

With each passing week, it became clear that he had adopted a new daily routine. For the first time, all his appointments were not dominated by work or deadlines, but by the movement between small and large favorites: the couch, the market, the balcony, the endless parade of shared breakfasts. Even his phone no longer asked him why he always "checked in" at the same place. Everything started in a fixed way, ended vaguely, and in between, enough happened to keep him from getting bored.

His tendency to procrastinate, always his strongest trait, got an upgrade. Now he shared it with two people who put everything into perspective ("it's only breakfast, Mat, not heart surgery"). They pulled him into their vortex of relativization until he realized that procrastination could actually be just another kind of planning. Everything felt lighter, with little reflection. Even the chaos in the house became normal: the dirty socks, the hallway full of low shoes, the pile of magazines that no one ever really read.

On one of those unplanned Wednesday afternoons, Matthijs received an email from his ex, a formality about overlapping tax credits. He read it on the couch, with Jasmine's feet on his lap and Pippa's laughter coming from somewhere in the bathroom. The tone was friendly, as if they hadn't argued in years. There was even an attachment: an old photo of himself on a beach in Scheveningen, beer can in hand, surrounded by people he now knew mainly from Facebook memories. He stared at the image while Jasmine casually wiggled her toes. It felt like a snapshot of a life that was still in circulation, but somewhere on a sidetrack.

He sent a polite reply, clicked away from the photo, and tried for a moment to pretend he was back in that time. It didn't really work. Even the smell of wet towels in the house, the sounds of two women thinking through absurd scenarios ("What if cheese were banned, would the Dutch economy collapse?"), pushed the past further and further away.

Everything that had once felt urgent or profound was now background noise. Jasmine's phone buzzed. She pulled it out from under the pillows, looked at it, and slid the screen toward him.

"We are invited," she said. A housewarming party for one of their vague Amsterdam acquaintances, with a dress code. He read the message, and it immediately struck him: dress code "colorful & extravagant." Nothing British, nothing Dutch, just show up as colorful as possible. He looked at the closet in the attic. It mainly contained shirts in which even the color blue seemed to be hiding. Jasmine raised her eyebrow, disapproved of his entire clothing history at a glance, and promptly pulled a jacket out of their shared drawers that they wore with the houseplant ("print is print, who cares about gender"). Pippa found a pair of glittery sunglasses, put them on immediately, posed in front of the mirror, and approved of herself. She was the only one who could pull off extravagance without winking.

Matthijs tried on the jacket, hesitating for a moment—his shoulders barely fit through, the fabric didn't give. Jasmine stuffed a bright red handkerchief into it ("that's called flair, Mat") and slipped him into the new version of himself. He hadn't known he could function in someone else's house style without it feeling like theater. On the street, people occasionally looked back, not mockingly; curious, perhaps. On the tram, it even went so far that a stranger complimented them on their "family feeling." No one corrected the assumption. Pippa just winked, Jasmine stubbornly held his hand, and Matthijs felt like some kind of mascot in a team he didn't know he wanted to be part of.

The housewarming turned out to be more of a concept than a party. The house itself was bare, except for a few strategically placed works of art. Groups of people dressed in colors you normally only saw on slot machines revived each other with such decibel levels that Matthijs kept himself in the background for an hour. He watched their hostess give a monologue about the influence of red wine on emoji use, but he hardly understood a word. Jasmine apparently connected immediately; Pippa pressed herself against a man with chalk-white hair and studied his ring fingers as if they were artifacts. Matthijs only realized how little he had to contribute when someone asked him, "What do you do these days?" and he hesitated three times before answering. "I'm home," he tried. A frown, followed by an approving nod, as if that had now become a mainstream answer. Great, he thought. He didn't have to explain himself any further.

After an hour, Matthijs drank a bottle of blackcurrant beer and let the noise around him close in like a thick curtain—conversations in Dutch, English, and something that tried to be both languages at once. Jasmine suddenly stood next to him, with a glass of orange wine and an unreadable look on her face. "Let's go," she said, with the familiar tone of someone who was behind the wheel. Pippa gathered him from the corner, tugged at his sleeve, and within five minutes, they were back outside. The air was strangely empty, the streets shiny with wet asphalt and hardly any people, not even taxis. They walked in silence, under an umbrella that was too small, which Jasmine held in the middle. Matthijs noticed that he was touching the girls' shoulders, sometimes at the same pace, sometimes not.

It wasn't until they reached the first bridge that their conversation picked up again. Pippa was the first to laugh, a kind of relief that Matthijs immediately shared. Jasmine said she thought all the people in the house were awful ("full of jokes, but no punchlines"), and Pippa nodded, trying to pry her heels off the wet sidewalk. Something in that shared disapproval felt comforting, even cozy. They quickened their pace, away from the light of the shopping streets, toward the dark part of the park where only dog owners could be found at this hour.

They walked non-stop to the late tram stop, three-quarters of an hour early for the end of the evening. The tram arrived immediately. They sat next to each other, Jasmine by the window, Pippa between him and the glass door. Their coats stuck coldly together, their hair smelled of rain and unfamiliar perfumes, a mixture that had already become natural.

He sat there and tried to recall something of his old routines, but it had all dissolved: only the realization that he would rather be nowhere else than in this tram, with their dry, cold hands on his left and right and the certainty that the rest of the night would fill itself. The tram shook, squeaked, made turns that seemed illogical, and for a moment, Matthijs wished he could hide in this compartment longer.

They got off one stop too early. True to form, Jasmine was the first outside, Pippa dangling from his sleeve until they crossed the wet square to get home. The rain had stopped, but it still smelled of untold stories. They stopped in the front yard. No one said anything; only the sounds of the city fell silent for a moment.

Jasmine squeezed his shoulder and pushed him up the stairs. Inside, it smelled of warm gingerbread, a scent he couldn't identify until they walked into the kitchen. There was a plate waiting for them: cake, not store-bought but homemade, something from the English island that was now definitively part of their household.

He suddenly remembered an old remark his mother had made, one of her classic predictions when his bike had been stolen: "You'll always need someone to call you home." He had laughed at the time, knowing full well that she was wrong. Now Matthijs thought that maybe it did work that way, that he only felt at home when someone opened the door for him.

They ate cake at the kitchen counter. Pippa spread butter on it. Jasmine pointed to his collar, pulling it askew so that the print showed better. The clock ticked aimlessly, and it only then became clear to him that he wanted nothing more that evening than to stay exactly where he was.

The next morning, hungover, full of vague remnants of sugar and butter. Matthijs woke up in an Ikea bed that was completely unsuitable for three bodies. He had underestimated this in the run-up: how impractical it actually was, the physical space of a threesome, the simple cardboard bed frame that creaked with every turn, the duvet too narrow, everything too warm. But from the moment Jasmine had thrown her arm over his chest, and Pippa had stubbornly found a spot against his side with her knee, he had known there was no way out.

They wore nothing but a T-shirt as a compromise, Jasmine his, Pippa a pale green one she must have found somewhere on the clothesline. It smelled of sweat, perfume, and something sweet. His hand was trapped between the shoulder blades of both girls, a kind of people clamp, and for the first time in weeks, he felt awake without that automatic urge to get out of bed immediately. They breathed slowly, in sync, as only young animals seemed able to do.

The strange thing about a threesome, he discovered, was not the traditional discomfort or the constant presence of someone else's skin. It was the lack of silence. Every time you thought the act was over, that everyone was finally exhausted and satisfied, another comment would come. A quip, a strange question, a comment that put everything into perspective. Even when Jasmine pressed her face against his cheek, half asleep, he heard her whisper, "You snore like a drowning walrus." Pippa giggled, put her arm around his shoulder, and countered, "That makes you the walrus wife, Jazz."

To be honest, he could never have imagined this. A few weeks ago, he had exactly zero intimate partners, let alone two. The fact that sharing a bed with two sisters now felt so natural surprised him every morning. They made it a sport to do everything as normally as possible: the same morning routine of searching for socks, toothbrushes, and breakfast, even coordinating their schedules, was effortless. There was no drama, just an endless series of brunches and minor household negotiations.

After breakfast, they wandered around the house together, each waking up at their own pace. Jasmine stuck herself to the radiator in the kitchen, and Pippa sat on the windowsill with a bag of chips. He watched her fingers grab the chips: quickly and without hesitation, as if she were signing a contract. At first, he constantly tried to decipher the unwritten rules, who would take the lead, and whether he was missing something in their glances or comments. By now, he knew that their dynamic didn't work that way. There was no master plan.

Matthijs felt the heat rise as Pippa's lips closed around him, warm and demanding, her tongue twisting in a rhythm that made him grab the sheet. He tasted salt and sweet at the same time, his breath catching as she sucked, slowly at first, then more urgently, her head moving up and down with a focus that made everything around him fade away. Jasmine's weight shifted above him, her thighs clamping around his ears, her warmth pressing down on his mouth, wet and demanding, her scent filling his nostrils like a wave of musk and desire. He licked instinctively, tongue pushing against her, feeling her rock, her moans vibrating through his skull. Everything revolved around that double sensation, Pippa's mouth enveloping him, Jasmine's movements covering him, their bodies in sync in a chaos that left him gasping, his hands grasping at hips and hair, not knowing where one ended and the other began. The room smelled of their sweat, the bed creaked beneath their shifting, and for a moment, he thought this was it, that simple surrender, no more talking, just this. Jasmine leaned forward, her fingers touching Pippa's shoulder, a whisper in English that he didn't catch, but it made her hips move faster, his tongue work harder to keep up. Pippa's sucking intensified, her hand squeezing at the base, and he felt the pressure building, his own hips pushing up, lost in the heat. When Jasmine came, she shuddered above him, fluid dripping down his chin, her nails digging into his chest, and that pushed him over the edge, wave after wave into Pippa's mouth, her swallowing palpable against him. They collapsed, panting, Jasmine sliding beside him, Pippa wiping her mouth with the back of her hand and crawling up, their bodies entwined in a clammy heap. He stared at the ceiling, heart pounding, the aftertaste of her on his lips, and for the first time, he felt no need to get up, just to stay here, in this tangle of limbs and breaths. Later, when the sun pierced through the curtains, Jasmine got up, naked and unabashed, and fetched water from the kitchen, her footsteps light on the floor. Pippa turned around, kissed his shoulder, muttered something about breakfast, and he nodded, knowing that the day would begin as usual, with coffee and jokes, but now with this memory attached to it, indelible.

He felt a tingle rising as Pippa's hand slid under the sheet, her fingers closing around him with that playful grip he now recognized as a precursor. She slid down, her breath warm against his skin, and took him into her mouth, sucking with a slow rhythm that made his hips jerk, each movement a wave of heat coursing through his body. Jasmine chuckled softly, climbed over him, her knees beside his ears, and lowered herself, her warmth pressing against his lips, wet and demanding, her taste filling his mouth as he moved his tongue, licking and tasting her, her moans muffled but vibrating through him. The bed creaked under their weight, his hands gripping her thighs, kneading, while Pippa's tongue swirled and sucked, the pressure building in his lower abdomen, a jumble of sensations that left him panting, not thinking, just feeling. Jasmine's fingers dug into his chest, her hips rotating faster, her breath catching, and he tasted her climax, warm and overflowing, pushing him to his own edge, pulsing in Pippa's mouth until she swallowed and released with a soft sigh. They slid off him, panting, their bodies sticky against his, and he lay there, staring at the ceiling, his heart pounding in his ears, the room filled with their scent and the faint light seeping through the cracks. Jasmine rolled onto her side, pressed a kiss to his jaw, her voice languid: "Another round, or breakfast?" Pippa laughed, nestling against his shoulder, her hand lazily caressing his chest, and he grinned, knowing that the day was already going off the rails in the best possible way. He pulled them closer, felt their warmth mingle with his, and thought that this was it, that strange perfection he no longer had to think about. Later, when they finally got up, he tripped over a stray sock on his way to the kitchen, the smell of coffee already in the air, Jasmine fiddling with the machine while Pippa sliced bread, their laughter echoing through the small space, and he felt lighter than ever, as if the morning stretched on forever. He poured glasses, tasted the bitter sip, and caught their eyes, that same playful gleam as before, a silent agreement that the day might just as well end back in bed.

Matthijs put down the glass, the coffee still hot against his tongue, and leaned against the counter, watching Jasmine wipe the bread crumbs from her fingers with a grin that looked straight at him. Her eyes had that sparkle, playful and challenging, as if she were already hatching another plan without words. Pippa cut an extra slice of bread, spread jam on it with slow, almost lazy movements, and slid the plate toward him, her foot hooking around his ankle under the table, warm and firm. He felt the tingling return, low in his stomach, as he took a bite, the sweet contrast to the bitter coffee making him swallow hard. The kitchen smelled of toast and their skin, still that musky aftermath from earlier, and he wondered how long it would take for one of them to suggest it, that return to bed, without saying it out loud. Jasmine stretched, her shirt—his shirt—creeping up, revealing a strip of pale skin, and she caught his gaze, sliding her tongue over her lips in a way that made him shift. Pippa laughed softly, took his hand and pressed a kiss to it, her lips sticky with jam, and he felt his pulse quicken, the heat building as if the morning had only just begun. He pulled her closer, tasting the jam on her mouth as he kissed her, slow and deep, while Jasmine watched with that half-smile, her hand sliding over his back, squeezing his neck softly. The day felt elastic, infinite, with their bodies so close that he no longer knew where the rush should come from, only this, their touches holding him, promising more. He broke the kiss, exhaled, and Jasmine whispered something in his ear, her breath warm, words that made him grin, knowing that breakfast could wait. Pippa got up, tugged at his shirt, led him back to the bedroom with a wink, and he followed, the door closing behind them, the bed waiting, creaking at the first touch.

A shrill squeak cut through the room, loud and persistent, like a siren flashing out of nowhere. Matthijs froze, his heart pounding in his throat as he jumped off the bed, throwing off the sheets in a reflex that gave him goosebumps. What the hell was that? The smell of their earlier sweat still hung heavy in the air, but now something sharp mingled with it, a faint burning smell he couldn't place. He fumbled for his boxer shorts on the floor, yanking them on as he searched for the door, the squeak pulsing in his ears, penetrating his bones. Jasmine was already up, her shirt half off her shoulder, eyes wide open in the dim light, and Pippa stumbled out of bed next to him, her hand grabbing his arm, nails digging into his flesh. "What the fuck," she muttered, her voice hoarse with fear, and he just nodded, pushed the door open, feet cold on the wooden floor as he stumbled into the hallway. The alarm was coming from the kitchen, it seemed, that constant, piercing wail that made his head throb, and he ran toward it, almost bumping into the doorframe, now smelling smoke more clearly, acrid and grey, curling out of the stove. Shit, the coffee, he thought, that damn machine Jasmine had turned on and forgotten, now hissing and smoking like a time bomb. He yanked the plug out, coughing as the smoke hit him in the face, hot and acrid, while Jasmine came after him, grabbed a towel, and threw it over the appliance to smother it. Pippa turned on the tap, filled a glass with water, and threw it over the machine, hissing and splattering, the alarm finally faltering, dying away in a final beep. Matthijs leaned against the sink, breathing heavily, feeling the adrenaline still tingling in his fingertips, looking at the two women who were now laughing, half hysterical, their hair tousled and their bodies still naked under the hastily thrown-on shirts. "That was close," he said, his voice hoarse, and Jasmine shook her head, wiping away a tear of laughter, her hand finding his waist, squeezing it with that familiar playfulness. The kitchen now smelled of burnt coffee and wet metal. Still, the tension ebbed away, giving way to that strange relief that made him grin, knowing that this would be another story, an anecdote for later. At the same time, Pippa cleaned up the mess, and he wondered if the day was really starting or if they could just crawl back into bed, the shock still echoing in his chest. He pulled them both close, felt their warmth against his skin, and thought that this was it, this unforeseen chaos that held their lives together, not perfection, but this, with the smell of smoke slowly fading and their laughter filling the silence.

Matthijs fumbled for his pants, which hung over the chair, the fabric rough against his fingers as he pulled them on, the adrenaline still reverberating in his chest like a forgotten vibration. Jasmine bent down to pick up a stray shirt on the floor, her laughter fading as she pulled it over her head, and Pippa wiped the counter with a cloth, the wet metal glistening under her movements, the smell of burnt coffee hanging heavy in his nose, pungent and sharp. He grabbed a sponge, wiped the splatters off the floor, felt the cold water splash against his toes, and muttered something about how that machine was always malfunctioning, but his voice sounded hollow, as if the shock had opened a door to thoughts he usually pushed away.

As he wrung out the cloth over the sink, the water dripping in a slow rhythm, he caught Jasmine's gaze, her eyes more serious now, without that playful gleam, and she said softly, "What if this is it, Mat? This chaos, us three, but what about later?" Her words hung there, heavy in the air, and he felt his stomach tighten, not from fear but from that familiar prick of something real, something he had avoided for years with jokes and distractions. Pippa stopped wiping, leaned against the stove, her arms crossed, and added, "Yeah, like, I've been thinking about kids someday, or maybe not, but it scares me, the idea of settling without knowing."

He dropped the sponge, it plopping wetly on the tiles, and stared at his hands, rough and stained from the water, as the words seeped in, his own dreams bubbling up like bubbles in a glass, unasked for but insistent. "I always thought I would travel," he said, his voice low, the words tasting bitter on his tongue, "away from here, new places, but now... now it feels like running away, and I'm afraid I'll keep doing that, that I'll lose you because I can't stay." The confession hung there, raw and exposed, and he felt his heart beat faster, waiting for their reaction, but instead of ridicule, he heard Jasmine sigh deeply and step closer, her hand finding his arm, warm and firm.

Pippa nodded, her fingers drumming softly on the countertop, a rhythm he recognized as nerves, and she whispered, "I'm scared of losing this, too, this weird family we've made, but I dream of a house somewhere quiet, maybe back in England, with a garden where we can just be." Her words touched him, made him see how their fears mirrored each other, how his own desire for stability coincided with their dreams of a shared life, not perfect but real. He felt a warmth rising in his chest, stronger than the earlier heat, a bond that pulled and strengthened, as if this conversation tied up the loose ends.

As they cleared away the last of the mess, threw the clothes into the laundry basket, and straightened them, that feeling grew, making the kitchen smaller, more intimate, and he pulled them over to the table, sat down with a sigh, the chair creaking under his weight. "Let's do it then," he said, the words rolling out before he thought about them, "make a plan, not too rigid, but something for the three of us, because this... I don't want to lose this." Jasmine smiled, genuinely now, leaning forward with her elbows on the table, and Pippa grabbed his hand, squeezing it, their fingers intertwined, warm and sticky from the morning. He felt the relief wash over him, like a wave washing away the fears, knowing that this was the beginning of something deeper, not just chaos but a future they could shape together.

The rest of the morning faded into that conversation, cups of coffee growing cold as they talked, about dreams of travels that suited their trio, fears of loneliness that they now shared, and he tasted the jam on his lips from earlier, but now mixed with this new taste of honesty, sharp and liberating. Outside, the city sounded like it was waking up, trams rattling in the distance, but in here, everything felt quiet, focused on their words, and he thought that maybe this was the best part, not the heat of their bodies but this, uncovering what was underneath, what kept them together. Pippa stood up, stretched, her shirt riding up, and suggested going for a walk, fresh air to finish it off, and he nodded, feeling his legs light as he got up, ready to step into the day with this new weight, lighter than he had expected.

He followed Pippa to the door, the wooden floor cool beneath his bare feet, and pulled his jacket over the crumpled shirt that still smelled of smoke. The fresh air outside hit him in the face as soon as they stepped over the threshold, sharp and biting like a sip of cold water, and he breathed in deeply, feeling it fill his lungs, blowing away the last remnants of the kitchen chaos. Jasmine walked beside him, her arm hooked loosely through his, her steps light and springy on the wet sidewalk, and he heard her humming, a vague tune he couldn't place, but it made him grin, that simple melody filling the silence without demanding words. Pippa walked ahead, her hair blowing in the wind, and she glanced over her shoulder, her eyes sparkling with that mix of relief and playfulness that always made him relax, as if she were inviting him to join in whatever was coming. The street was deserted, puddles reflecting the grey sky, and he deliberately stepped in one, feeling the water splash against his pant leg, cold and refreshing, a childish thrill that made him laugh. They strolled toward the park, the murmur of traffic in the distance a soft hum in his ears, and he thought about their earlier conversation, how the words still echoed in his head, not heavy but clear, like a map that had finally been opened. Jasmine squeezed his arm, her fingers warm through the fabric, and whispered something about a duck bobbing in the canal, her accent making it funny, and he leaned toward her, still smelling the jam on her breath, tasting the memory of their kiss. Pippa pointed to a bench further away, surrounded by bare trees, and he nodded, feeling his legs grow stronger with every step, the tingling from earlier now a soft glow deep in his stomach, not insistent but present, like a promise. They plopped down on the wood, damp from the night's rain, and he leaned back, staring at the clouds drifting slowly by, feeling Jasmine's head sink onto his shoulder, her hair tickling his cheek. Pippa sat on his other side, her knee pressed against his, and she stared ahead, her fingers fiddling with a loose thread on her jacket, but her silence felt comfortable, not charged. He closed his eyes for a moment, listening to their breathing mingling with the chirping of birds, and thought that this was the kind of moment he had always been looking for, without knowing it, three bodies together, sharing fears and dreams that were no longer his alone. The wind picked up, blowing a leaf against his leg, and he brushed it away, feeling the rough texture beneath his fingers, a small rough edge that brought him back to the present. Jasmine lifted her head, her lips curving into a half-smile, and she said softly, "Race you to that tree?" Before he could answer, she shot up, Pippa following with a giggle, and he stood up, his heart pounding with sudden energy, running after them down the path, the ground soggy under his shoes, laughing until his lungs burned. They reached the tree at the same time, panting and grinning, and he pulled them close, feeling their warmth seep through him, the heat building in his chest, not just from running but from that simple togetherness, knowing that the walk was far from over. Pippa's hand slipped into his, her palm clammy and firm, and they walked on, the paths winding through the greenery, his thoughts floating to the rhythm of their steps, light and free.

The sun pierced through the clouds, warming his face as he walked, the heat creeping under his collar, making his skin sticky. Pippa's grip tightened, her fingers squeezing his rhythmically, and he caught her sideways glance, that sparkle that always made him wonder what might come next, without him having to ask out loud. Jasmine's arm hung loosely in his, her steps matching theirs, and he heard her humming softly, that same tune from earlier, low and playful, as if she were sharing a secret with the wind. The path curved to the left, muddy and slippery from the rain, and he felt his shoes sink into it, a soggy sucking sound with every step that made him grin, reminding him of that time they had trudged through a meadow and ended up covered in splashes. His chest felt lighter now, those earlier words still echoing in his head, not as a burden but as something that made space, letting him breathe deeper, the air sharp with the scent of wet earth and distant blossoms. Pippa stopped suddenly, turned to him, her lips curving into a half-smile, and she pulled him closer, her mouth finding his in a kiss that tasted of jam and morning coffee, warm and slow, her tongue sliding over his with an urgency that quickened his pulse. Jasmine laughed softly, her hand sliding over his back, squeezing his hip, and he felt the heat building, low in his belly, that tingling returning, stronger now in the open air, with no one around except the birds and the rustling of leaves. He broke the kiss, exhaling against Pippa's cheek, smelling her shampoo mixed with the park scent, and Jasmine whispered in his ear, her breath hot: "Here, now, why not?" Her words made him swallow, hard, as he looked around, the path deserted, only trees surrounding them like walls, and he nodded, feeling his hands tremble as he ripped open Pippa's coat, the buttons popping, her skin exposed beneath his fingers, warm and soft. She pushed him against a trunk, rough bark pricking through his coat, and Jasmine sank to her knees, her fingers fumbling with his belt, ripping it off with a grin he felt more than saw, her mouth closing around him, warm and wet, sucking in a rhythm that made his knees buckle. Pippa's hands grabbed his shoulders, her kiss resumed, deeper now, her breasts pressing against his chest, and he tasted her moan in his mouth, felt the double sensation wash over him, Jasmine's tongue twisting, Pippa's hips pushing against his. His hands grabbed her hair, pulling gently, and he gasped, the heat building, pulsing through his body, the scent of moss and their sweat filling his nose, making everything more intense, as Jasmine went faster, her hand squeezing at the base, driving him to the edge. Pippa bit his lip, her nails digging into his neck, and he came, wave after wave into Jasmine's mouth, his legs trembling against the tree, the world momentarily vague and blurry. They stood up, panting. Jasmine wiped her lips with the back of her hand, her eyes glistening with that playful triumph, and Pippa laughed, pulling her coat closed, but letting her hand slide over his chest, promising more. He pulled them close, felt their hearts pounding against his, and the wind picked up. It blew through his hair, cooling the heat, but leaving the glow lingering, deep and satisfying, as they continued walking, the path ending at a bench, where he sat down, his legs heavy now, and thought that this was life, unplanned but perfect in its chaos, with their arms around him and the day stretching out before them.

Matthijs felt the words land in his chest, heavy and warm, like a blanket that had fallen over him too suddenly, his own breath catching for a moment as he looked at her, her eyes soft in the kitchen light, her drumming fingers now still on the counter. He opened his mouth to say something, but Jasmine stepped in between them, her hand sliding from his arm to his waist, pulling him closer with that familiar grip that always took away the tension, her lips curving into a half-smile. "Scared or not, we're in this," she murmured, her breath smelling of jam and coffee, and he nodded, feeling the heat of their bodies against his, the shock of the alarm fading to a faint aftertaste in his throat. Pippa's hand found his, squeezed it, her nails pressing lightly into his palm, and without words, she led him back to the bedroom, the bed still messy from earlier, sheets crumpled and warm. He let himself fall, felt their weight roll over him, skin against skin, their kisses slow and insistent, hands exploring without haste, and he surrendered to the rhythm, their breath mingling with his, the house silent around them as the morning stretched into something deeper, something that felt like a promise.

Five months later, he stared at the two pregnancy tests on the bathroom cabinet, the lines clear and unmistakable, his heart pounding in his ears as he heard the doorbell ring. Jasmine's voice calling from the hallway that she would open the door, but he couldn't move, feeling the cool tiles beneath his bare feet, the faint smell of toothpaste hanging in the air. Pippa leaned against the sink next to him, her hand resting on her belly, still flat but with that slight swelling he had noticed in recent weeks, her eyes meeting his in the mirror, a soft smile tugging at her lips, and he felt a wave of heat wash over his chest, not from panic but from something bigger, something that made him swallow. "Both positive," he whispered, his voice hoarse. She nodded, her fingers intertwining with his, warm and firm, as he thought of that night five months ago, the chaos in the kitchen that spilled over into bed, their bodies entwined without reservation, and now this, two lives growing, his, theirs. Jasmine's footsteps approached. She poked her head around the door, her hair in a messy bun, eyes wide when she saw the tests, and she laughed, that loud, infectious sound that filled the bathroom, her arms wrapping around them, pulling them both close, her belly touching his, already slightly rounded beneath her shirt. He felt the tremor in her embrace, smelled her shampoo mixed with the morning coffee. "We're doing this," she said, her voice breaking a little. He nodded, his hands sliding over their backs, feeling the warmth through the fabric, as reality sank in, no escape this time, just this house, these two women, and the babies on the way, his chest tightening at the thought of diapers and night feedings, but also at their laughter, mixed with his own.

The days that followed fell into a new rhythm. He noticed how Pippa's morning sickness came in waves, her face pale as she leaned over the sink, and he held her hair, rubbed her back in slow circles, felt the muscles tense under his palm. At the same time, Jasmine made tea in the kitchen, the clatter of cups sounding through the door, her voice calling something about ginger ale helping. He caught his own reflection in the window, saw the lines around his eyes seem deeper, but the corners of his mouth curled up, a strange calm settling in his stomach, no urge to pack and go, just this, the scent of mint from the tea drifting in, mingled with the salty tears on Pippa's cheeks. Jasmine brought in the mugs, sat on the edge of the bed, her hand sliding over her own belly, rubbing it gently. He felt a pang of tenderness, watched her sip, her eyes closing for a moment, and he thought of the ultrasound appointment next week, the black-and-white images he was trying to imagine, heartbeats that would beat in unison with theirs. In the evening, they lay on the couch, legs entwined, his hand resting on Jasmine's belly, feeling a slight kick, a tiny movement that made him stiffen, his breath catching as he waited for more, and she laughed softly, her fingers pushing his harder against the spot, "Feel that? Little rebel already." Pippa's head rested on his shoulder, her breath warm against his neck, and he nodded, feeling the bubbles in his chest bubble up, no words needed, just this moment, the TV murmuring in the background, an English sitcom they were half-watching, but his thoughts drifted to the nursery they had to decorate, the walls he would paint, light blue or yellow, something soft.

He woke up to Jasmine's sniffling next to him, her body turning restlessly, and he reached out, pulled her closer, felt the curve of her belly against his side, warm and firm, while Pippa murmured in her sleep on the other side, her hand instinctively finding his across the sheets. The moon shone through the curtains, casting streaks of light on the floor. He stared at them, feeling a wave of uncertainty wash over him, his stomach clenching at the thought of his mother calling, her voice full of questions about how he was going to handle this. Still, he pushed it away, focused on their breathing, synchronous and calm, and thought that this was his home now, not perfect, but real, with two babies on the way that would change everything, and for the first time, he felt no need to flee, only to stay, hands entwined in the dark.

His phone vibrated on the nightstand, a sharp buzz cutting through the silence and making him jump upright, heart pounding in his throat as he fumbled for it, the screen lighting up with "Mother" in bright letters. He swiped across the glass, pressed the thing to his ear, heard her voice come through immediately, sharp and familiar, "Matthijs, are you awake? I heard the news from the neighbors, two pregnant girls under one roof, what do you think you're doing?" The words landed like stones in his stomach, making him swallow hard as he stared at the moonbeams on the floor, Jasmine's belly still warm against his side, Pippa's hand now looser in her sleep. He mumbled something about it being late, but she rattled on, "Obligations, boy, responsibility, you can't just play father and think it will work itself out, who pays the bills, who takes care of those children when you run away again?" Each sentence stung deeper, made his chest tighten, thoughts swirled through his head, images of diapers and sleepless nights, of him trying to hold a crying child while he himself barely knew how to stay, not run away like always. He felt sweat beading on his forehead, tasted the bitter taste of coffee from earlier on his tongue, and whispered back, "Mom, it's different now, we're doing this together," but his voice faltered, doubt crept up like cold through his legs, making him unsure if he could really handle this, this role that pinned him down, offered no way out. She sighed heavily on the line, "Think about it, Matthijs, before it's too late," and hung up, leaving him with the beep in his ear, staring at the phone in his hand, the room suddenly colder. Jasmine turned over in her sleep, muttered something unintelligible, and he put the thing down, feeling his hands tremble, thoughts racing about how he was going to manage this, the babies growing, the responsibility that now truly gripped him, wouldn't let him go.

He slid back under the sheets, feeling the warmth of their bodies again, but his mind kept racing, images of his own father leaving, the empty chairs at the table, and now him, with two bellies he had helped fill, no idea how to fill them with more than jokes and mornings. The moon was shining brighter now, casting shadows across the bed, and he stared at them, feeling a knot in his stomach tighten, harder. At the same time, Pippa's hand instinctively reached for him, her fingers warm against his wrist. However, he couldn't relax, not with his mother's voice still echoing in his ears, forcing him to see what he had ignored, the real shit that came with being a father, paying bills, staying up nights, no longer living only for himself. He turned on his side, pressed his face against Jasmine's shoulder, smelled her skin, musky and familiar, tried to breathe away the panic, but it lingered, making him wonder if he could handle this, if he wouldn't just fail like he always did when it came to the real thing. The clock ticked softly in the hallway, seconds ticking away to a life full of responsibilities, and he squeezed his eyes shut, felt a bead of sweat slide down his back, cold and sticky, as he tried to sleep, but the uncertainty kept pounding, a rhythm in his chest that wouldn't stop.

At first light, he crawled out of bed, feet cold on the floor, crept to the kitchen where the smell of last night still lingered, burnt coffee and jam. He turned on the machine, heard it bubbling as he leaned against the counter, arms crossed, thoughts still full of that phone call, how it had shaken him awake, made him think about money, about a bigger house, about how on earth he was going to raise two babies without collapsing himself. Jasmine shuffled in, her belly protruding, rubbed her eyes, smiled sleepily at him, "Good morning, everything alright?" He nodded, forced a grin, but felt the lie stick in his throat, grabbed a mug, poured, felt the heat through the porcelain burn against his palm, and handed her one, watching her sip, her hand sliding over her belly, a movement that touched him deeply, made him realize that this was real, no longer a game, obligations that bound him to her, to Pippa, to what was growing. Pippa followed shortly after, her hair tousled, leaning against the doorframe, yawning, and he felt a pang, wanted to hold her. However, the confusion still swirled, silencing him as they talked about breakfast, their voices light, his head heavy from the night, from the responsibilities that now weighed on him, making him doubt whether he was strong enough for this fatherhood, whether it would break him.

They ate together, bread with jam that stuck to his fingers, sweet and sticky. He listened to their laughter, Jasmine's joke about the babies already fighting in their bellies, Pippa's hand finding his under the table, squeezing it, warm. Still, he couldn't laugh along, not really, his thoughts wandering to jobs, savings, to how he was going to prove to his mother that he wasn't running away, that he could handle this, the role of father that confused him, made him feel lost in what he had always avoided. He wiped his mouth, stood up, muttered something about showering, felt their eyes burning into his back, but said nothing, stepped under the stream, the water hot against his skin, let it flow over his face, tasted the salt of tears he didn't want to let fall, as he tried to untie the knot in his chest, to accept that this was his life now, full of responsibilities that frightened him, but also kept him here, with them.

He was still staring at those moon streaks on the floor, the uncertainty squeezing his stomach harder, when the phone next to the bed started to vibrate, a shrill buzz cutting through the silence like a knife through soft butter. His hand shot out, fingers clammy against the screen, and he saw it: Mother, the letters flashed up, her name that always made him swallow, now more than ever. Jasmine muttered something in her sleep, turned over, but he slipped out of bed, feet cold on the floorboards, and crept into the hallway, pressing the phone to his ear as he closed the door, his heart pounding like a drum in his chest.

"Matthijs?" Her voice sounded sharp, as always, with that undertone of judgment he recognized from childhood, the words heavy with the early morning, or was it evening where she was? He breathed in, tasting the night air in his lungs, bitter and dry, and walked to the kitchen, the tiles cold under his toes. "Yes, Mom, it's me." The words came out flat, but he felt the pressure building, that old urge to joke, to distract, to say something light about the weather or a silly anecdote, but not this time, this time there was too much at stake, with the babies, the bellies growing, the future stretching out like elastic that could snap.

She sighed, he heard it rustle through the line, and immediately started talking about the neighbors, her voice rattling on about trivialities, but he interrupted her, his own words tumbling out before he could stop them, raw and unpracticed. "Mom, wait, I have to tell you something. It's... It's not just Jasmine and Pippa. They're pregnant, both of them, and I... I'm scared." The confession burned in his throat. He leaned against the counter, felt the cool metal against his back, stared at the dark window, where his reflection, eyes wide, mouth half open, stared back vaguely. Afraid of what? Of failure, of repeating his father's mistakes, of the moment when responsibility would crush him as it had crushed her, years ago.

Silence on the other end, he heard her breathing, deep and slow, and then her voice, softer now, without the usual sting. "Afraid? Son, that's normal. I was terrified when you came, with your father who..." She stopped, he felt the pause like a weight in his chest, tasted the old pain in her words, that echo of abandonment he had always felt but never dared to touch. He swallowed, his fingers clenching the phone, and let more out, about the nights he lay awake, staring at the ceiling, wondering if he could be the man who stayed, who didn't run at the first kick of a baby's foot, about how the sisters held him. However, he still sometimes felt that urge to run away from the chaos that now filled their lives.

She listened, truly for the first time, her interruptions mild, and then she talked back, her voice breaking, telling him about her own fears, how she had stood alone, the loneliness that had hardened her, the regret that she had pushed him too hard for fear that he would break as she had. He felt tears sting, warm and unexpected, wiped them away with his knuckles, still smelled the faint scent of Jasmine's shampoo on his skin, and the conversation turned deeper, words like shards that fit, about forgiveness, about how home didn't have to be perfect, just real, just like what he was building now. "You're not like him," she finally said, her tone firm, and he almost believed it, felt a knot loosen in his chest, lighter now, as the first birds began to sing outside, the darkness slowly turning gray.

When he hung up, minutes later, he leaned there for a moment, phone warm in his hand, the kitchen filled with that new feeling, not relief exactly, but something more solid, an anchor. He heard footsteps in the hallway, Jasmine's sleepy shuffle, and turned, ready to share it, the words already on his tongue, as the day seeped in through the windows.

The door creaked open, a soft squeak cutting through the curtain of running water, and he heard footsteps on the tiles, light and hesitant, recognizing them immediately as Pippa's, her bare feet splashing in the puddles he had left dripping. Steam filled his nose, mingled with the soap scent he had just lathered, and he wiped water from his eyes, still tasting that salty trail on his lips, as her silhouette became faintly visible through the curtain, small and hunched, as if waiting for a sign. He turned the tap down a notch, felt the heat recede from his shoulders, and her voice came through, soft but firm, with that English accent that always sounded comforting: "Matthijs, whatever's eating you, I'm here, always, we both are—you don't have to carry it alone." The words hit him like a warm wave, loosening the knot in his chest for a moment. He stared at the wall tiles, water dripping from his chin, thinking about how she always did that, intuitively sensing when he was drifting away, without pushing but just being there, her presence an anchor that kept him from sinking. He mumbled something incoherent, feeling his voice tremble. She pulled the curtain aside a little, her face wet from the spray, eyes wide and concerned, but with that calm determination that always made him believe that everything would be all right, her hand reaching for his arm, fingers warm against his wet skin. He allowed her to touch him, felt the tingling sensation run through his body, not from desire this time but from relief, as if her words had dispelled the panic a little. She stepped closer, letting her shirt get wet without noticing. He pulled her under the stream, felt her body press against his, clammy and reassuring, as the water poured over them, washing away the tears. He breathed in her scent, shampoo and jam mixed, thinking that maybe, just maybe, he could do this, with her and Jasmine as his safety net, the babies not a burden but something that made them stronger, his hands sliding over her back, squeezing gently, and for the first time that morning, the fear felt lighter, a burden he could share. They didn't talk much, just whispers about little things, her lips against his ear. He nodded, feeling his pulse slow, the steam around them like a cocoon, while outside, in the kitchen, voices rang out, Jasmine calling to ask if everything was okay. He grinned weakly, knowing she would come in if he didn't respond; their trio always recovering, step by step.

When they finally turned off the tap, water dripping from their bodies, he grabbed a towel and rubbed her dry with slow movements, feeling her skin get goosebumps under his fingers. He thought of the day ahead, echoes and plans, but now with her words in his head, a reminder that running away was no longer an option, only forward, together, the uncertainty still there but less sharp, like a knife that had become blunt. They got dressed in the steamy bathroom, the mirror fogged up, and he caught her gaze in the reflection, that soft smile that made him believe in their strange family. He kissed her forehead, tasted salt and water, felt the glow in his chest expand, warm and solid, as they opened the door, back to Jasmine, back to the life that was growing, step by step, without running away.

Jasmine was already waiting in the kitchen, mug in her hands, steam curling up with that sharp coffee smell that tickled his nose. He smelled it before he saw her, that bitter scent mingled with the jam residue on the counter, and when he stepped inside, he caught her gaze, half sleepy, half questioning, her eyebrows raised in that way that always provoked more than words. Pippa followed him, towel still draped around her shoulders, water dripping onto the floor in small puddles that he felt under his feet, cold and slippery. He grabbed a mug, poured without asking, felt the heat burn through the porcelain against his palm, and took a sip, the bitter taste rolling over his tongue, waking him further as he leaned against the counter, legs heavy from the shower and the conversation still echoing in his head. Jasmine set her mug down with a soft tap, stepped closer, her belly lightly touching his, and he felt its warmth, that soft pressure that reminded him of what was growing, of the kicks he had felt last night, tiny but real. "Everything okay?" she asked, her voice soft, her accent rolling over the words, and he nodded, forcing a grin he didn't quite believe himself, still tasting the salt on his lips from Pippa's skin. Pippa brushed a strand of hair from her face, dropped the towel in a heap, and he heard the wet thud, smelled the soap scent coming from her, mixed with the coffee, as she stood next to Jasmine, their shoulders touching, a silent unity that always excluded him a little but at the same time invited him in. He put down the mug, felt the condensation under his fingers, and let it roll out, stammering at first, about the phone call with his mother, the fears he had expressed, how she had listened this time, really listened, without piling on judgment like she used to. Jasmine's hand found his waist, squeezed gently, her fingers warm through his shirt, and he felt the tingle, not of desire but of reassurance, while Pippa nodded, her eyes fixed on his, intense as always when she listened, her breathing calm, in sync with his. The kitchen felt smaller now, the walls closer, with the smell of bread still lingering from breakfast, crumbs on the table that he saw glistening in the morning light, crooked and bright. He talked on, about the knot that was looser now, how her words had touched him, that he wasn't like his father, didn't have to run away, and he heard his own voice grow stronger, tasted the relief like a sweet aftertaste behind the coffee. Jasmine laughed softly, that bubbly sound that always broke the tension, and leaned forward, kissed his cheek, her lips sticky from the jam she had eaten earlier, and he smelled it, sweet and fruity, felt her belly press against him again, a reminder that this was real, their trio expanding, step by step. Pippa grabbed his hand, intertwined their fingers, her skin still damp from the shower, and he felt the pressure, firm, as if she were holding him against the waves yet to come, while she whispered something about being proud of him, her voice low, her accent thicker now with emotion. He pulled them both close, arms around them, felt their warmth seep through, hearts beating against his chest, and thought of home, that word that used to feel like a trap, now something he was building, here in this kitchen with damp floors and coffee steam, not a perfect version but his own, with the babies that would come and the fears he now shared, lighter than solo. The clock ticked in the hallway, seconds that no longer threatened but simply passed, and he breathed in, smelled their mingled scents, felt a laugh bubble up in his throat, unexpected and real, as the day unfolded, coffee growing cold on the counter.

The clock ticked on, but he barely heard it anymore, his laughter catching in his throat as he felt Jasmine's belly again, now so round and heavy that she had to hold on to the counter to stay upright, eight months along, her breath coming in short puffs as she laughed at something Pippa said, her own belly momentarily bulging, equally insistent in how it pushed against the table. He stared at it, felt his hand instinctively reach out, palm flat against the tight skin under her shirt, a light kick vibrating through his fingers, sharp and unexpected, making him swallow as the heat in the kitchen seemed to rise, mingled with the smell of cold coffee and their sweat from the night. Pippa rubbed her lower back, grimacing slightly, her face pale in the morning light cutting through the window. He felt that twinge again, that mixture of warmth and pressure that had only grown in recent weeks, their every movement a reminder that the babies could come at any moment, his heart pounding harder at the thought of the bags already packed in the hallway, diapers and tiny clothes he had folded yesterday with trembling hands. Jasmine grabbed his wrist, squeezed it, her nails pressing lightly into his skin, and she whispered, her voice low and playful despite the fatigue in her eyes: "Feel that, Mat? Little soccer player in here, just like you with your restless legs at night." He grinned back, tasting the jam from breakfast still on his tongue. Still, his thoughts raced to yesterday's ultrasound, those tiny heartbeats he had heard, pounding in his ears like a drumbeat that wouldn't stop, making him wonder if he was ready for the moment when they would really be there, screaming and helpless, depending on him for everything. Pippa pulled up a chair, sinking into it with a sigh that made him look up, her hand sliding over the curve, rubbing circles he recognized as comfort. He felt the urge to step closer, to wrap his arms around them, but the kitchen felt too small now, too full of the smell of toast and the slight nausea that still came over them at odd moments. He poured another mug, the coffee gushing dark and hot, burning his fingers as he handed it to her, and as Pippa sipped, he caught her gaze, that soft glow that always calmed him, but now mixed with that tired shadow, made him feel guilty about how little he slept, lying awake with thoughts of bottles and rocking, of how his mother had called yesterday with advice he half heard, half pushed away. The sun climbed higher, casting stripes across the floor that danced to the rhythm of his breath, and he thought of the walk they would take later, slow and careful, their arms hooked into his to keep their balance, each step a small victory against the swelling in their feet, against the pressure he felt in his own chest, but also that strange excitement, like bubbles bubbling up at the thought of two pairs of eyes looking at him, expectant and new. Jasmine stood up, stretched with a groan, her shirt stretched tight, revealing her protruding navel, and he felt that tingling low in his stomach, not the old heat of desire but something tender, let him help her with her coat, the fabric rough under his fingers as he zipped it up, smelled her skin close, warm and slightly sweaty. They walked out the door, the fresh air hitting his face, sharp with the smell of wet pavement and distant flowers, and he kept pace with them, slow but steady, feeling Pippa's hand squeeze his with every bump, her weight leaning on him, while the city buzzed around them, trams rattling in the distance, but his world shrunk to this, to their bellies leading the way, to the kicks he sometimes felt through the fabric, a secret language telling him that everything was changing, and he had to be ready, or not, but he would stay, step by step through the morning.

The pavement felt harder under his shoes than usual, every step echoing in his bones as he carried their weight, Jasmine's arm clasped tightly in his, Pippa's hand warm and sweaty in his other fist. He smelled the sharp scent of the canal in his nose, that musty mixture of water and city, and tasted the morning coffee still sour on his tongue when Pippa suddenly stopped, her grip tightening until it hurt, a sharp groan escaping her lips that made him stiffen. What was that? He turned to her, saw her face contort, pale and glistening with sweat that didn't come from the walk, her free hand clutching her stomach, squeezing it as if trying to hold something in, and he felt his own stomach contract, heat shooting through his chest like a silent alarm going off. "Mat... It's coming now," she murmured, her voice low and breathless, and he nodded stupidly, trying to swallow, but his throat was closed, thoughts racing through his head about bags and taxis, about how to fix this without freaking out. Jasmine laughed at first, probably thinking it was a joke, but then she grabbed her side herself, a shock running through her body that he felt through their entwined arms, her knees buckling for a moment, and he smelled the sudden sharpness of sweat on her skin, heard her curse softly in English, "Oh shit, me too, this can't be..." Panic pricked his fingertips, cold and tingling, as he looked back at the empty street, no one in sight, only the murmur of traffic in the distance that sounded useless now, and he fumbled for his phone in his pocket, his fingers trembling so hard that he missed twice before dialing the number, the voice on the line sounding distant, instructions about breathing and coming to the hospital that he half-heard through the pounding in his ears. He supported them both, feeling their weight grow heavier with every second, Jasmine's breath catching against his shoulder, warm and moist, Pippa's nails digging into his palm like anchors that hurt but kept him awake, and he muttered nonsense, "Hang in there, we'll fix this," as he dragged them to the curb, hailed a taxi that thankfully stopped with screeching brakes, the door jerking open with a metallic grind that cut through his skull. Inside, it smelled of stale cigarettes and leather. He helped them get in, squeezed himself between them, felt their bellies pressing against his thighs, hard and tense, and the driver raced away after his garbled instructions, tires screeching on asphalt that he tasted like dust in his mouth. At the hospital, nurses rushed in, stretcher wheels rattled loudly on the tiles, he smelled disinfectant sharp in his nose, tasted metal on his tongue as he ran to keep up, hands grabbed his arms, voices shouted about contractions and timing he didn't understand, but he just nodded, felt sweat running down his back, clammy and cold. Hours melted together in a haze of cries and machine beeps, he held Jasmine's hand until his knuckles turned white, smelled her sweat mixed with something metallic, heard her grunt through clenched teeth, and then a cry, shrill and wet, that made him freeze, a bundle pressed into his arms, warm and wriggling, eyes blinking at him in a way that tore his chest open. Pippa followed shortly after, her cries echoing in the adjoining room where he sprinted, legs heavy as lead, and he caught her gaze, exhausted but sparkling, as a second cry filled the air, that same wriggling miracle in his arms, skin sticky and red, the scent of new life making him dizzy. He stood there, between the beds, feeling the fatigue sink into his bones, but also that strange lightness, like bubbles rising in his stomach, as he looked at them, the babies nestled against their mothers, Jasmine's fingers reaching for his across the space, Pippa's smile weak but real, and he thought that this was it, not the escape but the staying, with four hearts now beating in sync with his, the room filled with their smells and sounds holding him, no way out, just this, step by step into a new kind of morning. He sank into a chair, felt the hard plastic against his back, stared at the little fists grasping at nothing, smelled milk and soap from the nurse walking by, and for the first time, the responsibility didn't feel like a cage, but like something growing, just like them, warm and unexpected in his grasp.

The key turned in the lock with a click that sounded too loud in the quiet hallway, and he pushed the door open, feeling the familiar draft brush against his arms, cold after the hospital warmth. Home, finally, with those two bundles in their carriers, one strapped to Jasmine's chest, the other to Pippa's, their breathing soft and squeaky, like mice nesting in his ears. He stepped inside, smelled the musty scent of the house that had been waiting for a day, yesterday's coffee still on the counter, and his legs felt heavy, as if the exhaustion was only now really sinking in, deep into his muscles. Jasmine shuffled behind him, her footsteps slow, muttering something about the couch calling, and he heard Pippa sigh, that long, tired exhalation he recognized as relief, mixed with the pain that still lingered in her body. The babies, his babies, made little smacking noises, and he tasted the salty aftertaste of tears on his lips, from the moment in the car on the way back, when everything still felt hazy from the births, those hours that had stretched into an eternity of screaming and blood and then finally silence, broken by their first cries. He dropped the bags with a dull thud, felt the floor vibrate beneath his feet, and thought about how this house now smelled different, of milk powder and disinfectant soap that clung to their clothes, no longer just the three of them, but this new thing that held him with invisible threads. Jasmine plopped down on the couch, the leather creaking, and he watched her unfasten the baby carrier, carefully, her fingers still trembling from the effort, and the bundle—their boy, with that tuft of dark hair—nestled into her arms, eyes half-open, staring at nothing in particular. He felt a twinge in his chest, warm and sharp, as if his heart was stretching to take it all in, and walked over to Pippa, took the baby girl from her, felt the weight light yet heavy at the same time, her cheek soft against his shirt, warm and sticky from the journey. No more running, he thought, as he sat down, the sofa springing under him, and he breathed in their scent, milk and baby sweat, mixed with Jasmine's perfume that still lingered faintly. Pippa sank down next to him, her shoulder pushing against his, warm and firm, and he heard her whisper something about sleeping when the babies slept, but his thoughts wandered to the night ahead, the feedings and the crying he could already sense coming, a rhythm that would test him, but he squeezed his hand around the tiny fist, felt the little nails prick his palm, and knew that this was it, this messy beginning, with the sun shining through the windows and dust particles dancing in the light. The boy made a gurgling sound, and he laughed softly, tasting the fatigue in his throat, dry and hoarse, as Jasmine's foot touched his under the coffee table, a silent connection that grounded him. Hours later, or maybe minutes, he got up to get water, felt his legs protest, stiff from sitting, and in the kitchen he smelled the old coffee again, emptied the pot with a splash into the sink, thought about how everything now revolved around this, sterilizing bottles and changing diapers, no more jokes to laugh it off, but real actions he had to learn, step by step. Back in the living room, he saw them there, Jasmine with the boy at her breast, Pippa with the baby girl in her arms, their eyes heavy with sleep, and he felt that bubble in his stomach again, not of panic but of something growing, like the plants on the windowsill that he forgot to water but which survived anyway. He put down the glasses, sat down between them, felt their warmth on either side, and stared at the little ones, their eyes now closed, breathing calmly, and thought that this was home, not perfect, but full, with sounds he still had to learn to love, and fears he would carry, but not alone. The afternoon sun slowly sank, casting long shadows across the floor, and he leaned back, felt his eyelids grow heavy, let the fatigue wash over him, knowing that the night would come with its challenges, but for now, this was enough, this moment of silence with the four of them, entwined in everyday wonder.